The nameplate on the door read Fran Cordaro.

Alex knocked softly. This was his first opportunity to visit the firefighter who'd saved his life. He wanted to see that the guy was okay. And thank him, of course.

There was no answer. Maybe he was asleep. Edging open the door, Alex blinked to adjust to the dim light of the hospital room. A figure lay motionless in the narrow bed.

Alex crossed to the bed. The guy was facing away from him. In the filtered light, Alex saw the graceful slope of a back and the rounded curve of a hip; damp, dark brown hair came almost to the neckline of the hospital gown. Most firemen he'd seen sported military cuts.

The figure shifted. A skein of silky hair fell over the patient's face. A long-fingered hand rested on the pillow. And full breasts stretched the cotton of the gown enticingly. Her eyes opened and she blinked.

He'd got the wrong room. 'I'm sorry to disturb you,' he said. 'I was looking for the firefighter who saved my life last night. You're not him,' he added lamely.

'No.' There was amusement in her voice. 'I'm her.'

Available in November 2003 from Silhouette Superromance

Charlotte Moore
by Judith Bowen
(Girlfriends)

Feel the Heat
by Kathryn Shay
(City Heat)

Winter Baby
by Kathleen O'Brien
(Four Seasons in Firefly Glen)

Operation: Mistletoe
by Roxanne Rustand
(The Special Agents)

Feel the Heat

KATHRYN SHAY

SILHOUETTE®
SUPERROMANCE™

To Carol Backus, a wonderful friend whom I treasure
dearly, and to her alter ego, Suzanne Barclay, whose
mentoring was instrumental in this book and every
other one I've written.

*First published in Great Britain 2003
Silhouette Books, Eton House, 18-24 Paradise Road,
Richmond, Surrey TW9 1SR*

© Mary Catherine Schaefer 1999

ISBN 0 373 70871 8

38-1103

*Printed and bound in Spain
by Litografía Rosés S.A., Barcelona*

Dear Reader,

What made me want to write about firefighters? First, of course, it's an exciting profession. The strong, silent, heroic type of guy has always appealed to me, so I thought—wow, perfect heroes. And female firefighters intrigue me, because I admire their desire to break into this traditionally male job.

With that in mind, I entered the world of fire fighting. I set off on a two-year odyssey to learn about it and the people who do it. CITY HEAT is the result.

Feel the Heat was born out of one question. What would it be like to love a firefighter? He walks into potentially fatal situations every time he leaves home. That was how Diana and Ben's story—the sub-plot of this book—evolved. Then I turned it around. Women have been sending men off to war and hazardous professions for centuries. But could a man do it? Along came the hero, Alex Templeton, who is saved by the heroine, firefighter Francey Cordaro, and spends the rest of the book trying to adjust to her lifestyle.

I think this trilogy is an accurate portrayal of a fire department in New York. The books are, of course, fiction—but I hope I stayed true to the character of these men and women who are truly the very bravest. They are utterly courageous, often funny, always interesting, kind, sensitive, daring, adventurous and, yes, even romantic people. I hope you find that the characters in my books are all these things, too.

Please write and let me know what you think. I answer all reader mail. Send letters to Kathryn Shay, PO Box 24288, Rochester, New York, 14624-0288, USA or e-mail me at Kshay1@AOL.com. Also visit my websites at http://home.eznet.net/~kshay/ and at http://www.superauthors.com

Sincerely,

Kathryn Shay

ACKNOWLEDGEMENT

There are many people to thank for their help with my CITY HEAT series.

The first group is the Gates Fire Department, particularly their chief and officers, who invited me to the firehouses and shared their experiences with me. I also want to thank the many Gates line firefighters who let me wear their gear, taught me how to hold a hose, put out a fire with an extinguisher and observe several of their drills, including live burns.

Next, I had the privilege of working with the 542-person Rochester, New York, fire department. My appreciation goes to many specific fire stations for allowing me to visit. With meals, tours of their firehouses and the recounting of many of their experiences, the men and women at Engine 16, Engine 17, Quint/Midi 5 and Quint/Midi 9 gave me my first feel for the professional life of a city firefighter. Specifically, I want to extend my deep gratitude to firefighter Lisa Beth White for sharing her insights into the life of a female in this predominantly male department.

The Rochester Fire Academy personnel could not have been more welcoming. Battalion Chief Russ Valone, in charge of training, allowed me access to classes, training sessions and practicals, and he let me observe recruits simulating life in a firehouse and putting out fires. I want to convey special appreciation to the 1997 Fall Recruit Class and their trainers.

My warmest gratitude and affection go to the Quint/Midi 8 firefighters. They were all gracious in letting me ride along on the rigs, wear old gear and eat several meals with them. These guys spent many afternoons and evenings sharing their experiences, answering my questions, giving advice on my story lines and suggesting possible improvements. From that group, firefighter and paramedic Joe Giorgione was the best 'consultant' an author could ask for.

Any 'real feel' these books have is due to all these brave men and women who told me their stories.
Any errors are completely mine.

CHAPTER ONE

THE SIREN WAILED and the horn blared as Quint Twelve, one of Rockford Fire Department's state-of-the-art trucks, tore into the Templeton warehouse parking lot. Francey Cordaro felt a jolt of adrenaline when they hit the fire ground, and her heartbeat quickened at the sight of the thick black smoke billowing from the side of the warehouse. The truck squealed to a halt, and the crew catapulted out of the cab.

Captain Ed Knight sprinted to Incident Command for instructions from the battalion chief. Adam Genier, driver of the Quint, rounded the front of the rig while Francey, veteran Dylan O'Roarke and rookie Robbie Roncowsky yanked hoses out of the back. Dominic "Duke" Russo, driver of the Midi, the second, smaller truck, twisted the heavy steel valves to open its water tanks.

"Hell of a way to start your thirtieth birthday, France," Robbie said as they hefted a hose out of the bed.

"You got that right," she replied, jerking hard on the line.

Captain Knight strode back to them like a general ready to mobilize his troops. His radio pulsed as much static as orders from the chief. "Engine Sixteen's ventilating the roof on the east side. They got two hoses in the front door. They figured the place was empty this time of night, but just after they went in, somebody told the battalion chief there might be someone in there. Seems his car wasn't spotted till just now. We're going in the west side. There's a wrought-iron staircase on the outside wall leading up to the office level."

He faced Francey. "Cordaro, make a forced entry there.

Office is to the left about twenty feet—we'll look for the guy in there first.'' He flicked a glance at Dylan and Robbie. ''O'Roarke, take a hose in with her. Roncowsky and I will follow with a second.'' Genier and Russo knew to stay with the rigs and oversee water delivery.

Francey grabbed the pry tools, raced to the warehouse and bolted up the wrought-iron stairs, the men hauling the lines behind her. She reached the entrance in seconds and sprang the lock on the heavy steel door in less than a minute. Captain Knight barked their position into the radio, then all four firefighters donned their breathing masks and switched on their air flow. Francey shoved the axlike halligan into her pocket in case it was needed inside and took her place on the tip of the hose. With Dylan behind her and Robbie in front of the captain on the other side, they entered the burning building.

A thick blanket of black smoke enveloped them. It was like being blindfolded. Crouching low, they inched along the west wall. Francey's hand groped the floor in front of her. She and Dylan dragged the charged hose down the wide hallway while the rookie and the captain mirrored their actions on the other side. She heard the sound of water below them. Engine Sixteen must have found the seat of the fire.

About twenty feet into the warehouse, sweat trickling down her shirt, Francey felt the outline of a closed door on her left. She handed the hose to Dylan, stood, threw off her glove and tested the door with the back of her hand. Not too hot. She twisted the knob. It opened, but only partway.

A figure was slumped on the floor just inside the smoke-filled room, partly blocking the door. Dropping to her knees, Francey squinted to make out his form. She pulled him upright and dug her hands under his armpits. God, he was heavy. Over two hundred, she guessed. She dragged him into the hall. The smoke still a thick curtain, she and the others retraced their steps to the outside staircase, Dylan leading the way with the hose. When they reached the exit, Francey stepped onto the landing backward and edged around to take the stairs.

Still unconscious, the man jerked spasmodically. The movement threw Francey off balance. *Let go of him!* she thought wildly. *You're going down.* She did, and momentum took her down the steps. Her left arm banged on the railing, and pain splintered through her. Then her head connected with something hard—and the world went black.

EVERY MUSCLE in her body hurt—much like it did after a gruelling session with weights. Francey willed the pain away and tried to open her eyes. Heavy-lidded, they stayed shut. She shifted slightly and moaned.

"She's awake, Ben," a familiar voice called from beside her. The captain.

Then a hand stroked her hair, just as it had through measles and mumps and her first injury in the fire department. "Francey, honey, it's me. Dad."

Finally she was able to lift her lids. Her father, Ben Cordaro, hovered over her, his face etched with concern. His dark, just-graying hair was mussed, and his brown eyes were troubled.

"Hi," she murmured.

"Hi."

She shifted and moaned again. "What happened?"

Coming up beside Ben, Dylan grinned. "You fell down the steps, klutz. Did you know that fifty thousand people are hospitalized every year because of fire-related injuries?" Though he was considered quite a ladies' man with his unruly black hair and Irish blue eyes, Dylan O'Roarke could be a pain in the butt, Francey thought.

"Spare me the statistics, O'Roarke," she retorted. Then her memory returned. Breaking into the warehouse. A man on the floor. She'd lost her footing when she reached the wrought-iron staircase. "The victim?"

"He's fine," her father told her. "Some smoke inhalation."

"And a few bruises from being dropped," Dylan added gleefully.

"Oh, shit." Francey struggled to sit up. The action sent a bolt of pain through her arm. She looked at it. "What the hell?"

Her father sat on the bed and gently touched the plaster cast on her arm. "It's broken, kiddo."

Francey closed her eyes and sank into the pillow, recalling her trip to the hospital and her stint in emergency. Her head began to throb. She used an obscenity she rarely used in front of her father. He gave her a weak grin.

"How long?" she asked him.

A firefighter like his daughter and one of his sons, Ben Cordaro understood her concern. "You'll be out at least two months."

"Never."

"You will, honey."

Her older brothers, Nicky and Tony, came up behind their father. Nicky had Ben's dark good looks; Tony, the older, was fair, with taffy-colored hair.

Tony bent and kissed her. "Hi, kid. Took a nasty fall, huh?"

Francey nodded at his trademark gentle kindness. "I guess."

"Tough break, sis," Nicky said. "Excuse the pun." She gave him a pained look, like the ones they'd shared as children. "Hey, you can always go to the academy and work with Dad."

Francey rolled her eyes. Most firefighters dreaded an academy stint, missing all the action. "What are *you* doing here?"

"My crew was on at Sixteen's last night. While you were playing hero with the CEO of Templeton Industries, I was in the basement knocking down the fire."

Francey frowned. "The CEO of Templeton Industries?"

"Yeah. Alex Templeton was working late at the company warehouse and apparently fell asleep at his desk. When the fire got going, he was overcome by the carbon dioxide. You pulled him right out of the jaws of death," he said with a wiggle of his eyebrows.

"Dylan and I both got him out."

"That's right," Dylan put in. "Just because you're a battalion chief's daughter doesn't mean you get all the credit."

Male chuckles resounded through the room. "Is everybody here?" she asked.

"Yeah."

Adam, quiet and unassuming as always, approached the bed, along with Robbie. "You can always come in and cook for us while you're off," Adam teased.

The entire crew groaned. Francey's lack of culinary skills was well-known in the department.

Francey gazed at the men gathered around the hospital bed—her biological family and her other family, Group One from station house Quint/Midi Twelve. Except for Robbie, their crew had been together for years, and the men were like brothers to her. Right now they were cleaned up and dressed in civilian clothes. But Ed Knight's face was drawn and looked pale next to his gray hair; Robbie's youthful complexion was pasty; Adam's eyes, almost the same hue as his coffee-colored skin, were concerned; the harsh lines of Duke's rough exterior had softened; and Dylan, though he joked and quoted his infamous firefighter trivia, had creases in his forehead whenever he looked at her.

They were all worried. She smiled in appreciation.

"What time is it?" she asked. "We off?"

"It's about seven," the captain told her. "We came here as soon as our shift ended and our relief arrived."

"You remember the ambulance ride?" Dylan, a paramedic, as well as a firefighter, had accompanied her to the hospital.

"Yeah. You got a great bedside manner, O'Roarke. You kept yelling at me to wake up."

"He saves his tender side for his women," Adam said.

Francey glanced at Robbie. "You did good, kid, for your third fire."

The redheaded rookie gave her his Opie grin. They teased him about being right off *The Andy Griffith Show*. "Yeah?" No one in the Rockford Fire Department doled out unwarranted praise.

"Yeah."

"Jeez, France, I'm sorry you got hurt. Especially on your birthday."

"Well, at least you guys won't be able to pull any stupid over-the-hill pranks on me now that I'm in the hospital." When they were done with their trick—a full rotation of four days on, three off, four nights on and three days off—they'd planned to go to Pumpers, a firefighters' hangout, to break out the champagne.

She glanced at Captain Knight. "How'd it start? And where?"

"In the basement. We're not sure how. The alarm was called in by one of the Templetons, who was driving by the warehouse. The fire marshals have been there all night. They think maybe…"

The captain's voice trailed off as someone came through the door to Francey's room. She couldn't see around the guys, but tension rose in the room quicker than heated mercury.

Her crew backed away from the bed. Ben, Tony and Nicky stilled.

"Diana," her father said. He was turned half away from Francey. His face was blank, his voice carefully neutral—a sharp contrast to the warmth and concern in it only minutes before.

"How is she?" Diana's tone matched his. Pure coolness.

"See for yourself."

Ben stepped away, but Nicky blocked her path and glanced dramatically at his watch. "What, the queen's up before noon?"

"Nick, lay off." The admonishment came from Tony, who rested a hand on his brother's shoulder.

Francey couldn't see her mother yet—Nicky's muscular frame blocked her view—but she could hear her voice. "Hello, Nicky. Tony."

"Hi, Mom," Tony said.

Nicky only sneered.

Diana Cordaro Hathaway stepped into Francey's line of vision. Slim as always, her carriage regal, Diana wore her fairy-princess blond hair swept back from a face devoid of makeup. Even so, she looked a decade younger than fifty. And light-years away from the rest of the Cordaros. "Francesca." Her breathiness was pronounced.

"Hello, Diana."

Diana cleared her throat. "Are you all right?"

Despite her efforts to remain aloof, her mother's fearful tone wended its way into Francey's heart. "Yeah, I'm fine."

Impulsively Diana reached out to touch Francey's cast, but drew back her hand at Francey's frown. "Does it hurt?" Diana asked.

"They got me pretty doped up. I don't feel much pain."

"Are you injured anywhere else?"

"Just this bump on the head."

Diana examined it with the care of a nurse, then said, "Well, good."

From the corner of her eye, Francey saw the members of

her fire fighting group, including Captain Knight, sneak out and leave the dysfunctional Cordaro family alone. It was so quiet Francey could hear the muffled sounds of a hospital's morning routine outside the closed door—the elevator ping, the shrill of a phone, orders being given.

Her father broke the charged atmosphere. "How did you find out about Francey's accident?"

Diana's violet eyes, the only thing Francey had inherited from her, flickered with repressed anger. "I heard about the fire on the morning news. I called your mother to see if Francesca or Nicky was involved." A mother's censure colored Diana's tone. "You could have phoned me."

Ben's face hardened. "I could have."

"Why?" Nicky edged in front of Ben, facing Diana. "So you could play the loving parent? Just because you moved back here eight months ago doesn't mean you're part of our lives."

Diana's sharp intake of breath silenced her son's attack more quickly than an angry retort.

Tony grabbed his brother's arm. "Nick, don't."

Finally Ben said, "Nicky, go get us some coffee." When Nicky hesitated, her father stared him down, just as he used to do when the Cordaro children were little and balked at going to bed.

With a scathing glance at Diana, Nicky stalked out the door. Tony followed him, stopping to kiss Diana's cheek on the way out. Her father turned to her mother, and his face softened fractionally. "I should have called you. I'm not used to your being back in Rockford."

Diana held his gaze unblinkingly.

"I, um, know how much fire fighting worries you, Dee."

Her mother swallowed hard, then turned to Francey. Her eyes brimmed with feeling. "I was hoping to see you today, but not under these circumstances, of course." Diana drew in a deep breath. "Is there anything I can do for you?"

Francey studied the woman who'd walked out on her husband and children twenty-seven years ago. Every time she saw Diana, she was assailed by conflicting emotions. This morning she was too tired to deal with them. "No, Diana, there's nothing you can do for me now."

ALEX COUGHED like a three-pack-a-day smoker and shoved away the oxygen mask. He swore as the IV tugged on his arm.

"You've got to use the oxygen, Alex." His younger brother Richard's voice was strained, and his normally pale complexion was chalk-white. He'd never matched Alex's six-foot-plus height and broad shoulders, but today Richard's hunched posture made him look even smaller. And his blue eyes, though they hadn't sparkled like they used to in a long time, were clouded with anxiety and fatigue.

"I will, but I want some answers first. What happened at the warehouse?" Alex coughed again, deep spasms racking his body, shooting pain to his already sore extremities. He fell onto the pillows. The doctors had told him to expect a general malaise, but this exhaustion rivaled his bout with mono when he was a teenager.

"Son, your recovery is more important than the business." Jared Templeton, looking haggard and drawn, leaned on his wife, Maureen. Worry seemed to have erased the progress he'd made since his heart attack ten months ago.

Alex grabbed the mask, took a few deep breaths and lay back. All he could remember about that hellish night was being so tired he put his head down on the desk. He'd awakened in a haze of smoke, stumbled to the door and collapsed against it. They said that the small amount of oxygen he'd gotten from being on the floor probably saved his life. The next thing he knew, he was outside on the ground, his eyes stinging and so watery he could barely see, his head pounding like a jackhammer, his lungs ready to explode.

After a few moments on the oxygen, he set down the mask. "Where did it start?"

"In the basement." Richard's scowl was pronounced.

"Do they know how?"

"Not yet," his father told him.

"What happened to the new thirty-thousand-dollar sprinkler system we put in?"

"No one knows," Richard said. "When I tried to talk to the firemen—"

"You were at the warehouse? Why?"

"I was driving by on the expressway and saw the smoke. I called in the alarm." He glanced away for a moment, then back. "Anyway, it was such a zoo just putting out the fire and getting you two into ambulances that the firefighters didn't say much. What the hell *were* you doing there at midnight, anyway?"

Alex ignored the question. "Us two? Was someone else in the building?"

"No. The second person hurt was a firefighter."

"How badly?"

His mother answered. "A broken arm. A concussion. Apparently he fell down the steps after he dragged you out of the warehouse." Maureen Templeton had been through a lot in the past few years, and her steel core always surfaced. She lifted her chin and said, "He dropped you before he fell. That's why you have that bump on your head."

"Are you sure he's all right?"

"Yes," she said. "I inquired about him while they were admitting you after we got through with Emergency. He's in a room right down the hall." She drew a neatly folded paper from her pocket. "His name is Fran Cordaro."

Alex swallowed hard as the realization sank in. "I'd like to see him. He saved my life."

"We know, dear. But you look tired."

Alex closed his eyes. He *was* tired. Every part of his body hurt—especially his head. He could see bruises forming like different-size coins on his arms. "What time is it?"

"Seven-thirty."

Alex yawned.

His father's voice soothed him, as it had when Alex was a child and sick. "Why don't you rest? We'll go get some breakfast, then come back up."

"You don't have to stay," Alex said sleepily, wondering about the guy who'd pulled him out of the fire. What did you say to a man who'd risked his life for yours?

Then he felt soft lips on his forehead and two gentle pats on his arm before sleep claimed him.

LATE THAT AFTERNOON, Alex stuck his hands in his bathrobe pockets and hesitated in front of room 495. He'd slept, eaten some hospital food that reminded him of the mystery meat they used to serve in the Harvard cafeteria and, with the help of an orderly, taken a blessedly hot shower. After Richard retrieved pajamas and a robe for him, Alex convinced his mother to take his father home to rest. Richard had been harder to send off.

The brothers had gotten closer in the past two years. Richard had had a bout with drug abuse when he'd lived in the Midwest. After a painful divorce and some rehab, the only good that had come out of it was that he'd returned home to upstate New York and assumed a management position at Templeton Industries. Though Alex enjoyed playing big brother again, he wanted Richard to get some rest. His eyes were red from exhaustion. At last his brother cooperated and left around four.

About fifteen minutes later, Fire Marshal Bob Zeleny had paid Alex a visit.

"How are you feelin'?" the fire marshal asked. A big, burly man—the stereotypical image of a firefighter—he was dressed in a suit and tie, not a uniform. The bulge in his jacket told Alex he carried a gun. His streetwise dark eyes assessed Alex carefully.

"Better."

"I need to ask you some questions." Zeleny coughed, then cleared his throat. "What do you remember about last night?"

"Just that I was tired and put my head down on the desk."

"What time was that?"

"About midnight, I think."

"Why were you there?"

"I hadn't gotten a chance to look at the invoices for some circuit boards we'd built. I got there about nine to do it."

"Okay. So you put your head down about midnight. What next?"

"For some reason, I woke up. The room was filled with smoke."

Zeleny scribbled notes on a small leather-covered pad. "Some research studies say your sense of smell in sleep is still active and could wake you in case of a fire. Others don't support that view." He nodded. "Go ahead."

"I tried to get to the door but didn't make it out."

"Well, this helps us pinpoint the time of the fire."

"Why?"

"Our rigs arrived at the scene at twelve-fourteen. If you zonked out about midnight, you must've breathed in the carbon dioxide only a few minutes. Much longer, you'd be dead."

Alex's eyes widened at his candor.

The fire marshal shrugged. "Anyone else in the building?"

"Not that I know of."

"Cars in the lot when you got there?"

"I didn't see any."

"Richard Templeton your brother?"

"Yes. Why?"

"He called the alarm in. We talked with him last night but need to see him again."

"Look, what's this all about?"

"When the origin of the fire is unknown, it's my job to determine what happened."

"Is there some kind of trouble?"

"We'll let you know," Zeleny said, heading for the door.

Alex had been drained by the encounter. And still had the damn headache. He'd fallen asleep for another hour.

This was the first opportunity he'd had to visit the firefighter who saved his life. Fran Cordaro, the name on the door said. He wanted to see for himself that the guy was really all right. And thank him, of course.

Alex knocked. No answer. Maybe he was asleep. Edging open the door, Alex blinked to adjust to the dim light of the room. Rockford Memorial Hospital had just been refurbished—his family had donated some of the money for the renovations, along with building a new wing—and the rooms had been spruced up considerably. Rose-colored mini-blinds were half-closed against the late-afternoon April sunlight. He could barely make out the muted rose-and-blue-striped wallpaper and dark blue accent chair.

A figure lay motionless in the narrow bed. From the doorway, the man seemed slight, at least compared to him. Alex knew that some firefighters were small, but they were usually muscular and tough as nails.

He crossed to the bed. The guy's back was to him. Something wasn't right. In the filtered light, he saw the graceful slope of a back and the rounded curve of a hip. Damp dark brown hair came almost to the neckline of the hospital gown. Most firemen he'd seen sported military cuts.

The figure shifted.

Alex froze.

A skein of silky hair fell over the firefighter's face. A

long-fingered hand rested on the pillow. And full breasts stretched the cotton of the gown enticingly.

Damn, he'd gotten the wrong room.

But he could detect a faint acridity of smoke. And the name on the door matched the one his mother had given him.

Intrigued, Alex stepped closer.

The woman on the bed half turned to her back, uncovering her face.

Alex winced at the swollen purplish bruise near her temple and the long, angry scratches under her chin. Her mouth fell open slightly, and he noted the lush poutiness of her lips. She stirred, stretching one arm over her head, arching her back, burrowing her cheek into the pillows. Sucking in a breath at the unconscious sensuality of the gesture, he gaped at her.

Her eyes opened, and she blinked. "Dylan?" she said huskily. "Is that you?"

"No." Alex cleared his throat. "I...I'm Alex Templeton."

He could see her focus on him. She struggled to sit up and moaned. "Could you turn on a light or open the blinds a little? I can't see very well."

Alex crossed to the window and cracked open the blinds, then switched on a corner lamp. Coming back to the bed, he scrutinized her face again, clearer to him in the light. She'd managed to ease herself into a half-sitting position. The nasty bruise was worse from this vantage point; her cheek had swelled around it. But it was her eyes that snared him. They were huge, almost translucent and the oddest color, indigo fanning out to deep purple. He'd seen a sky in Saint-Tropez once that was layered with those colors.

When he realized he was staring, he coughed uncomfortably. "I was looking for the firefighter who saved my life last night.'' Though awareness had dawned on him, he said, "You're not him.''

"No." Her voice was laced with amusement. "But I'm her.''

"Yes, so I've guessed." He smiled. "What's Fran short for? Frances?''

"Francesca." The amusement spread from her eyes to her mouth. He couldn't stop staring at her face. He didn't think he'd ever seen such a perfect arrangement of features.

"You pulled me from the building.''

"Yep.''

Though he'd never thought of himself as sexist—and certainly the existence of female firefighters was not new—the idea was somehow unsettling that this attractive female had rescued him.

He shoved back the disconcerting feeling. "Well, what does a person say to someone who saved his life?''

Those violet eyes twinkled like amethyst. "How about thank you?''

Alex reached over and squeezed her hand. It was warm and surprisingly soft. "Thank you. For saving my life.''

"You're welcome." Her enjoyment of his surprise and discomfort at learning Fran wasn't a man was obvious in her mischievous grin. "You, um, don't look like your ego's handling this very well.''

"I think my ego will survive," he told her dryly. But the stutter in his heart, the restless stirring of his battered body, indicated that the rest of him might not deal with the incident quite as easily.

CHAPTER TWO

"MAY I SIT DOWN?"

Francey stared at Alex Templeton. Though she'd been awakened from a nap and was still fuzzy-headed, she was conscious enough to notice he was a very attractive man. Big. Muscular. Classic nose. Cleft chin. His eyes were grass green, and they watched her with interest. *Male* interest. Francey recognized the look, although she was rarely tempted to return it. Today was an exception.

"Sure. Pull up a seat."

His shoulders were stiff and his gait a little uneven as he dragged a chair to the bed.

"You're hurting, aren't you?"

Clearing his throat, he sank onto the chair. "My lungs still burn some. And this headache's got its claws in me."

"That's to be expected from smoke inhalation. But the rest of you—you're sore from where I dropped you."

He smiled, and Francey felt an unfamiliar sensation in her stomach. "I'm not complaining. You saved my life."

"I wish I could have done it without wiping the staircase with your face."

He smiled. "How did you fall?"

"You jerked unexpectedly when we got out on the landing. You're pretty heavy, and besides I had on forty pounds of goods and a pry tool stuck in my pocket. I lost my balance."

His smile vanished. "I caused your fall?" Spontaneously, it seemed, he reached out and brushed her cheek beside the bruise with his fingertips. She shivered involuntarily. He glanced at her cast. "And I did that?"

"No, of course not. Hazards of the profession."

"Does it hurt?"

"Yeah, when the painkiller wears off."

"I'm sorry." He sat back, then glanced around the room. Sunny daisies, fragrant roses and two big green plants had arrived. "You have a lot of friends."

"The fire department's like family. When one of us gets hurt, news spreads like wildfire, no pun intended."

"No pun taken." He studied a big pink and silver balloon swaying gracefully in the draft from the heat vent. "Is it your birthday?"

She sighed. "Yes."

"How old?"

"Thirty."

"Ah. A big one. Happy birthday." He waved his hand toward the flowers and balloons. "It was nice of your friends to send these."

She scowled at the plants, unimpressed. "I *wish* they'd sent food."

"Food?"

"Yeah. I can't cook, but I eat like a longshoreman. I'd sell my soul for some real, honest-to-goodness food instead of the imitation food from the hospital kitchen."

His eyebrows shot up. "Really? What would you eat if you could have anything you wanted? On your birthday?"

"Hm…something I don't have to cut." She held up her cast. "I know—seafood. Peter, the best cook in the fire department, makes this fancy shrimp and scallops dish when he subs at our station." She licked her lips.

Alex stared at her mouth. "I see. May I use your phone?"

Francey shrugged. "Yeah, sure."

He went to the phone, dialed a number and asked for a listing for the Rio. He winked at her as he made a second call. The gesture unnerved her. "Yes, Lawrence, this is Alex Templeton. I'd like to order dinner. No, it's not for business this time. Just for two." His laugh rumbled deeply in his chest. "Well, she *is* gorgeous. But she has a broken arm, and I'd like to pamper her. So make it good. Shrimp scampi, coquilles Saint Jacques and stuffed snapper. Maybe some of that white asparagus if you have it. And dessert. Can your driver deliver to Rockford Memorial?" After a few more instructions, he hung up.

Francey stared at him, then shook her head. "You do this kind of thing often?"

"Mostly for business meetings." He sat and smiled warmly. "Sound good?"

"Sounds wonderful. And expensive. I've been by the Rio."

"Hey, nothing's too good for the woman who saved my life."

"Put that way, I graciously accept."

He gave her a sideways glance; she got a good look at his square jaw. "There's a catch. You have to invite me to share it."

"Oh, I think I can endure that."

As they waited, he lounged in the chair, the soft cashmere of his bathrobe hugging his shoulders. She'd seen one like it on a patient when they went out for an emergency medical services call at the Hyatt Hotel. Dylan had told her how much the robe cost. Alex Templeton must be well-off.

"Would you like to rest before dinner arrives?" he asked her.

"No! I'm going to die of boredom." She lifted her arm, weighted by the plaster. "This is gonna kill me."

"You won't be able to work for a while."

"No."

"How long have you been a firefighter?"

"Eight years."

"Mind if I ask how you got into it?"

"Typical firefighter story. My great-grandfather, my grandpa, my dad and one of my brothers are firefighters. I've wanted to do this job as long as I can remember."

"What did your mother think of it?"

"My mother wasn't in the picture."

When he looked at her quizzically, she shrugged. It seemed as if he wanted to pursue the subject, but instead he asked, "Do you like it?"

"It's my life. I couldn't do anything else."

"Do you find it hard to be a woman in a traditionally male job?"

"It was tough at first. The men weren't too happy when women joined the department. But once a woman—or for that matter a man—proves herself on the line, the veterans accept her."

Alex settled more comfortably into his chair and asked, "And how did you prove yourself?"

He was beginning to make her feel nervous. She adjusted the sheet. "You sure you want to hear this?"

"Yes, of course."

She studied him to see if he meant what he said. Deciding he did, she said, "It was my fifth fire. My first roof. I was up high with an officer to ventilate." At his quizzical look, she explained. "Open the roof to let air out. The saw stuck, but I didn't panic. I got it going, made a clean cut through the shingles, knocked out the hole just in time for the ground firefighters to go in. I didn't lose it when the flames shot through the opening. I guess the guys realized I'd be okay. I think any of them would feel okay with me at his back."

"Well, you can save my life anytime, Francesca."

"It also helps that I can fix their cars."

"What?"

"I'm a mechanic, too. I was the top student in my auto mechanics class at East High School in the city."

He roared with laughter. She liked the way his eyes crinkled with mirth. "You must have driven the boys crazy."

"What do you mean?"

His green eyes turned smoky. "Francesca, have you looked in a mirror lately?"

She hadn't, but given his obvious appreciation, she was tempted to primp a bit. She stifled the urge by gripping the sheet. "Oh, well. That's always been a problem."

"Tough luck," he said dryly.

Trying not to show she liked his teasing, Francey rolled her eyes. Flirting with him probably wasn't a good idea, so she switched the subject. "Do you have any idea how the fire started?"

Alex shook his head, and his mouth took in a grim line. "The fire marshal came to see me today."

"What did he say?"

"That since they haven't determined an exact cause, it's suspicious."

"He stopped in here, too."

"Really?"

"Yeah. It's common practice to interview the firefighters on the scene. I imagine he's talked to all of us by now."

"Did you notice anything important?"

"Nah. I was too busy saving your hide." He smiled. "They really want to talk to the guys who knocked the fire down."

"Knocked it down?"

"Put it out."

"Ah." He appeared to study his hands, then said, "I can't believe this might not be an accident."

"Do you have any reason to believe it isn't?"

"No."

"Was anyone on the scene?"

"No."

Her eyes narrowed. "Who reported it?"

"My brother. He was driving by and saw the smoke."

"Oh."

"Something wrong?"

"No, no."

Alex leaned back and sighed. "Let's talk about something else."

"Sorry, I get carried away about my work."

"It's not that. The possibility that the fire was set intentionally is disturbing." He paused. "But fire fighting sounds fascinating. Tell me about the job—what you do, how you spend your days."

"You really want to know?"

"Yes." When she hesitated, he glanced at his watch. "And we've got about thirty more minutes before our food comes."

So Francey agreed, and for half an hour, she regaled him with tales of the characters in her department and some humorous stories about her stint at the fire academy. He listened attentively and asked questions. The best part was when he laughed.

She was just finishing an anecdote about one of the lieutenants when there was a knock on the door. "Come in," she called.

The Rio's deliveryman, in a waiter's black tux, entered the room and deposited their meal on a table, set out the plates, spoke with Alex, then left. Her mouth watered at the smell of fresh-baked bread, the sweet scent of seafood and the aroma of hazelnut coffee.

Alex dished up their food and brought a plate to her. "Your wish is my command, mademoiselle." There was no missing the sexy inflection of his tone. When he reached out to position her tray table, his tawny hair tumbled over his forehead. Her fingers itched to touch it. Was it soft and silky or springy and coarse?

Forcing herself to focus on the dish in front of her, she said, "This is unreal, Alex."

"Enjoy." When she glanced up, he was sitting and biting into a plump shrimp. Her eyes fixed on his perfectly straight teeth, his sculpted lips, the lower one fuller than the top. Jeez, she thought, tearing her gaze away, she'd never been distracted by a man's mouth before.

She gave herself a shake and dug into the seafood, the twice-baked potatoes, the perfectly done asparagus. "Tell me about yourself. I talked about me for half an hour."

"My life story's nowhere near as interesting as yours."

She cocked her head. Most men she knew outside the firehouse couldn't wait to talk about themselves. Some firemen, too, though as a group, they tended to be more reticent.

"What?" he asked at her quizzical gaze.

"Nothing. What does Templeton Industries make?"

"Electronic equipment for the utilities and process industries." At her puzzled look, he added, "Circuit boards, monitoring devices to measure temperature, pressure gauges..." He shrugged. "Sounds boring, doesn't it? Especially compared to your job."

The door opened, precluding her response.

"Oh, I'm sorry, Francesca. I didn't think you'd have company during the dinner hour." Diana stood in the doorway carrying a silver-wrapped package. Dressed in a taupe pantsuit, her golden hair swept back and held with a mother-of-pearl clip, she was elegance personified. And to boot she'd more than likely designed the outfit herself for her successful clothing business, Diana's Designs.

Alex stood. "Diana?"

She blinked, came a few steps closer. "Yes?"

"I'm Alex. Alex Templeton. Maureen's son."

"Of course—I recognize you now. Elise has spoken of you several times."

Francey stilled. "You two know each other?"

"Diana plays bridge with my mother once a month, and we run into each other occasionally at Bright Oaks Country Club."

Francey struggled to keep a lid on her disappointment.

"And you've played tennis doubles with Elise," Diana added.

Alex nodded.

The attraction Francey had felt between them for a few hours before Diana's arrival was abruptly doused.

Diana turned to Francey. "How do you know Alex, Francesca?"

"I pulled him out of a fire," she said tonelessly.

Alex was from her mother's world. That told it all. She didn't need his life story.

"How do you know Diana?" Alex asked her.

Francey didn't answer. After an uncomfortable silence, Diana said, "I'm her mother."

The air in the room seemed to grow heavy, and Francey felt the way she had the first time she'd taken a gulp of smoke into her lungs. No one spoke. Pushing away the remnants of her meal, Francey sank back into the pillow. *I should have known. I did know. The Rio. The cashmere robe. CEO of Templeton Industries. What was I thinking, flirting with him that way?*

He was from her mother's world, and as far as Francey was concerned, nothing could put him more off-limits.

IN THE HOSPITAL cafeteria, hot coffee sloshed over Diana's hand, stinging her skin. She set down the cup and wiped the spill with a napkin. Get a grip, she told herself. She'd stopped in to calm herself after her encounter with Francesca. Still shaken, she was in no shape to drive home.

At eight o'clock at night, the cafeteria was deserted except for a nurse who sat staring off into space, a cup in front of her. The drab beige walls and empty vinyl seats accented the ache inside Diana. So she repeated her mantra silently.

You have a mission. You can do it. You're older, stronger now.

But Francesca's injury and the fact that today was her birthday had eroded Diana's certainty that she could accomplish what she'd come back to Rockford to do—salvage her relationship with her sons and daughter.

Even though it's too late for Ben. Damn, she wasn't quick enough to short-circuit the thought. Usually she stopped herself from thinking about him, from wishing she could fix what had happened to them as a couple. But seeing him this morning, hearing him call her Dee, had made her memories excruciatingly painful. Every time she looked at his wary eyes and stiff posture she was reminded of what a first-class coward she was.

She forced her thoughts to her daughter. As usual, Francesca had been distant when Diana had raced to the hospital to make sure she was all right. But tonight, after Alex Templeton had left, her daughter had been more curt and close-mouthed than ever. Sometimes Diana wondered if she'd ever be able to scale the walls her two youngest children had built around themselves since she'd left Rockford. She'd done all right with Tony, her older son, managing to stay close to him over the years. Bolstered by that success, Diana told herself she could win back the other two if she was patient and tried hard enough. She took a sip of coffee. It tasted bitter, like a lot of things in life.

"Diana?"

Her pulse leaped at the deep baritone of her husband. Her *ex*-husband, she corrected herself. Carefully schooling her features into a mask of indifference, she looked into the craggy face of the man she'd loved since she was seventeen. "Hello, Ben."

"What are you doing here?" He'd always reminded her

of Robert De Niro, and since *Backdraft* was released, years after they divorced, the similarities were even more marked. His dark hair was cut short and sprinkled with gray. But his chocolate brown eyes were as knowing and watchful as ever. He was dressed in his fire-department uniform—a crisp white shirt that set off his olive complexion, dark blue pants, which hugged his still flat stomach. The battalion chief insignia was proudly flaunted on his shoulder.

I'm gonna do it, honey. I'm gonna be a battalion chief someday.

The memory made her cringe, just as the words had when he'd spoken them more than three decades ago. Right from the beginning, his work in such a dangerous profession had filled her with fear.

"Can I sit?" he asked when she didn't answer.

Say no. "All right."

A big man—over six feet with linebacker shoulders—he grunted as he lowered his frame into the chair across from her. "Why are you here?" he repeated.

"I came to see Francesca, of course. I didn't get to visit with her this morning."

"How is she tonight?"

"You haven't seen her?"

"No, Ma and Pa went up first. I needed coffee, so I came in here."

"You always need coffee."

The memory came, unbidden, unwanted. First thing in the morning he'd nuzzle her breasts with his beard-roughened chin, run his callused hand down her body and promise her paradise if she'd get him a mug of high test.

He frowned at her remark. "You should wait and see Ma. She'd like that."

Stalling for time, Diana took another sip of her coffee. She'd had lunch with Ben's mother yesterday, but she didn't tell him that. Just as she hadn't told him about the letters

Grace Cordaro and she had exchanged, the pictures sent, the times they got together when Diana was in town to visit the kids. She wouldn't tell him now, either. He'd just get angry. And spout more of the mean remarks he'd made to her since her return to Rockford. "Maybe I will. She'd like talking about the store."

Seeming to forget himself and his animosity toward her, Ben leaned back, linked his hands behind his head and smiled. His shirt stretched across his wide chest. "Yeah, she's proud as punch of your success. Remember how she taught you to sew?"

"On that old Singer."

"Seems like a lifetime ago."

Diana held his gaze. "It was."

He stared. "Today's Francey's birthday," he said huskily. "I remember when she was born."

Oh, Dee, a girl! There hasn't been a girl in the Cordaro family for decades. I love you so much, sweetheart.

Diana swallowed, her stomach knotting at the recollection. They'd been so happy. "Hard to believe she's thirty."

Ben nodded and stared at the woman across from him. She looked terrific. And because her beauty had sucked him in from day one, he said unkindly, "You look good, Diana. For fifty. Have a little cosmetic surgery?"

His ex-wife's eyes clouded with pain. He felt like a heel. "No, just the right moisturizing cream."

The comment reminded him vividly of the time she'd perched at the dressing table he'd made for her, in their cramped bedroom in his parents' attic. He'd opened her lotion bottle and rubbed it on her body, and then they made love on the hardwood floor. Damn, he couldn't afford this trip down memory lane!

"Well," he said, "you shouldn't have any trouble snagging another husband. Got any prospects?"

"I have no desire to remarry."

"No? Not like the last time?"

She angled her head. "It was ten years after our divorce before I married Nathan."

Nine years, three months and two days, to be exact, Ben thought. That was seventeen years ago. He'd gotten slobbering drunk the night he heard about her remarriage; his father had had to drag him to bed.

"Seemed quick to me." Because the memory punched him in the gut, he swallowed the last of his coffee, plunked the empty cup on the table and stood. "Well, I'm going up." He couldn't resist taking one last look at her. Her eyes were cool, her shoulders back, her chin lifted. Her debutante look. God, he hated it. "Maybe you should rethink your strategy about remarrying. You don't want to die a lonely woman."

She didn't respond, but her lower lip quivered and her hands were unsteady on the coffee cup. He thought about it all the way to the elevator, though he tried to steel himself against her—against the memories. But they wouldn't go away, like scenes from a movie that kept replaying in his mind. Once inside the elevator, he reached into his pocket and dug out his wallet. From its deepest recess, he pulled out a photo. Crinkled with age, and yellow, it was Diana's senior picture from high school. Blond hair so soft it made him long to touch it. Violet eyes so huge and simmering he got lost in them. He'd met her when the fire department had been called to Mercy High School. She'd been seventeen, he a cocky twenty-year-old rookie firefighter. A couple of coeds had been smoking in the john and had inadvertently started a fire in the waste container. Ben's squad had marched in, all brave and herolike, and put it out. The girls had crowded around them afterward as if they were movie stars, though the nuns were beside themselves trying to shoo the students inside. Diana had slipped her phone number into his turnout coat. Like a fool, he'd called her. When he found out how old she was, he'd backed off. But *she* hadn't. She'd pestered him with calls and letters until she turned legal, and once he'd agreed to take her out, it had been all over. Within two months, they were sleeping together.

The first time those violet eyes had sparkled with anticipation and a little bit of fear. The fear had made him say, "We shouldn't be doing this. You're too young."

She'd given him a siren's smile. "I want you to be my first."

He couldn't resist her. They'd gotten married a few months later. She was pregnant with Tony and deliriously happy. Given the circumstances, Ben had been right to marry her, but getting involved with her in the first place had been the worst mistake of his life.

The elevator doors opened on the fourth floor. Just as thinking about her now was a mistake. Why the hell had she come back to Rockford from New York City after her husband died? Why the hell couldn't she just leave them alone?

THE FOLLOWING AFTERNOON, Francey fell back onto the pillow consumed by a fit of giggling. She laughed so hard she bumped her cast on the side of the bed. "Ouch."

Chelsea Whitmore grinned. "Isn't it great?"

Behind her, Beth Winters leaned against the wall, shaking her head in disgust. "What am I going to do with you two?"

"Come read the card, Beth. You'll love it," Francey told her friend.

Beth pushed away from the wall and sat on the side of the bed opposite Chelsea. "All right, hand over the smut."

Francey did so. Chelsea's choice of birthday greeting had been typical of her. On the front, a dark-haired guy wearing skin-tight jeans, a baseball cap and nothing else held a baseball bat, muscular arms bulging. Below him it read, "Do you want to help me bake a cake for your birthday?" She watched Beth open the card. Inside, it said, "Or do you just want to lick the batter?"

Even Beth, who rarely laughed, whose smiles were as infrequent as eclipses, chuckled. Chelsea and Francey had come to accept their friend's seriousness, but that didn't mean they didn't worry about her.

"Oh, great," Beth said dryly. "We're reduced to adolescent cards."

"And great presents." Francey fingered the lavender silk tap pants and teddy in the box on her lap. "Thanks, Chels."

"Wear it for a special occasion." Chelsea winked at her friend.

Francey rolled her eyes. "I wish I had more opportunity."

"Your own fault. The guys pant after you wherever you go. Then they're devastated when you won't give them the time of day."

"Most men bore her," Beth said.

A man with tawny hair and laughing green eyes who didn't bore Francey flashed into her mind. Too bad he was off-limits.

"You should talk, Winters," Chelsea chided.

"I date," Beth said, haughtily lifting her chin. Beth's delicate features and tall slender body belied the fact that she was one of the toughest women Francey knew.

Chelsea and Francey exchanged knowing looks but said nothing. Beth dated older men whom she dumped as soon as they got serious.

"Speaking of men," Francey said, "how's Billy?"

Chelsea shrugged. "Okay, I guess." She scowled. "He's getting too serious, though."

Francey worried about Chelsea, too. She was dating a firefighter, something Francey refused to do after her broken engagement to Joey Santori, a fellow firefighter in Group Three in her station house and a guy who'd grown up in her neighborhood.

"Open my present," Beth said, changing the subject. Whenever the women launched into a powwow on their love lives, Beth got uncomfortable. They'd met when Francey and Chelsea had been in the academy and Beth had been their Emergency Medical Systems instructor. In the intervening eight years, they'd become good friends, but Francey felt she didn't really know Beth Winters and the quiet sadness that shrouded her.

Francey tore open a rectangular present wrapped in glittery gold paper. Inside she found a framed Mark Manwaring print entitled "Silent Heroes." Smoke-tinged firefighter gear rested on a bench— a rumpled turnout coat, bunker boots with the pants and suspenders falling over them, an ax and a helmet, out of which peeked thick brown gloves. Bright yellows and reds provided colorful accents. "Oh, Beth, it's beautiful. I've wanted one of these for so long." She reached out and squeezed Beth's hand. "Dylan has a couple of Manwaring prints in his house."

Beth scowled. "Boy Wonder would."

Francey chuckled. "Seen your nemesis lately?"

"Please," Beth said. "We just ate lunch. Don't make me ill."

Though they occasionally joked about it, no one went overboard teasing Beth about Dylan O'Roarke, or vice versa. The two had a serious personality conflict that dated back to Dylan's days in the academy. He was the one who had dubbed her Lizzie Borden, a name the recruits secretly bandied about when she was out of earshot. They'd clashed again when Dylan had gone to the academy to get his EMS training.

"I'll hang this over the fireplace as soon as Dad and Grandpa finish my mantel. Thanks, Beth."

"You're welcome. Happy thirtieth, one day late."

"Sorry we missed lunch yesterday," Francey said.

"You were a little incapacitated."

Francey held up her arm. "Yeah. Think I'll be off work more than two months?"

Beth shook her head. "I looked at the X rays. It's a hairline fracture. You should have the cast off in four weeks, then four weeks of physical therapy will give you back your strength." She smiled soothingly. "I'll bet it hurts."

"The painkillers help but I don't like taking so many."

"Well, take them, silly," Beth told her with the maternal concern she sometimes exhibited. "Anyway, you'll be good as new in a couple of months."

"Especially after we put you to work lifting weights," Chelsea told her, referring to the weight training they did together at the gym.

"Good. I can't fathom how I'm gonna stand...."

Francey's words trailed off as she was distracted by a movement in the doorway. Alex Templeton leaned against the jamb. Today he was dressed in street clothes—an off-white collarless shirt made of some gauzy material, the long sleeves rolled up his forearms. Doe-colored pants and Docksides shoes finished the outfit. His hair was damp and brushed off his face, highlighting his handsome features. A Greek god clothed in modern dress, she thought whimsically.

"Hello." His voice was still hoarse from smoke inhalation. "I didn't mean to intrude." He glanced at his watch. "I'm being discharged and I wanted to say goodbye."

Francey said, "Oh, sure." Quickly she made introductions.

Chelsea's appreciative gaze swept over Alex. Then she turned mischievous eyes on Francey. "We were just about to go get ice cream for the patient here. Come on, Beth."

"No, it's fine, you guys, I'm not—"

"See you in a bit," Chelsea sang as she exited, tugging Beth behind her.

Francey was seriously regretting her confession to her friends that she found the man whose life she'd saved attractive.

Alex approached the bed. "Having a party?"

She nodded.

He scanned the remains of the chicken Caesar salad, croissants and sparkling water the women had brought for her. "They fed you, too?"

"We were supposed to go out for lunch on my birthday." His eyes grew serious. "Oh." He stared at her arm.

"Alex, it wasn't your fault you were caught in a fire and I got hurt."

"I still feel bad."

Francey shifted on the bed, uncomfortable. Unfortunately the movement drew Alex's attention to her birthday gifts. Without asking permission, he leaned over. His scent, male and musky, ambushed her. He picked up the teddy. When he rubbed the strap between his fingers, Francey's stomach somersaulted. She could practically feel that slow, sensuous touch on her skin.

"Pretty," he said, flashing her a grin. "And very feminine." She could read the rest in his eyes. *Just like you.*

Stifling the urge to groan, Francey glanced away. After a moment, Alex dropped the silk and shifted his gaze to the firefighter print. "That's beautiful." Then he glanced behind him at the door. "Are they in the fire department?"

"Chelsea, the blonde, is. She works over at Engine Four."

"Engine Four?"

"That's the station house. They're referred to by the type and number of their rig."

"Oh."

"And Beth is an EMS trainer at the Rockford Fire Academy."

At his questioning look, Francey explained, "She trains EMTs—emergency medical technicians—and paramedics, as well as conducting certified first responder classes for recruits." Francey smiled. "She was my teacher and Chelsea's. Since there's so few women at the academy, we got to be friends.''

''That's nice. I haven't had time to make many friends since I came back to Rockford to work.''

''From where?'' Francey asked in spite of her decision to remain aloof.

''Boston. I had a job there for several years after I got out of business school.''

''Let me guess. Harvard.''

''Yes.''

He'd graduated from Harvard Business School, and she had an associate's degree in fire fighting from a community college, and that only because her father had insisted. The reminder of her and Alex's differences brought back her resolve.

Trying to hurry his departure, she asked, ''You're being discharged?''

''Yes.'' He seemed to search her face. ''I came to say goodbye.''

Goodbye was good. ''You should take it easy for a while.''

He shrugged. ''My family will hover, I'm sure.''

Family. Oh, God, Francey hadn't even thought there might be a wife in the picture. Now that she did, she could have kicked herself for not realizing a guy like him was almost certainly married. She refused to check out his hand for a wedding band.

''I was wondering if I might call you,'' Alex said.

With intentional frost in her voice, she asked, ''Wouldn't your *family* mind?''

''My parents and brother are grateful that you saved my life, Francesca. Why would they mind if I called to see you again?''

Without her consent, her eyes dropped to his left hand. He tracked her gaze. When she looked up, he was grinning.

"Do you think I'd ask to call you if I was married? For that matter, would I flirt with you so blatantly if I had a wife?"

Francey was enthralled by his seductive tone. "I, um…" Her breath caught when he raised his hand and brushed her hair off her forehead. She suppressed a shiver. "I don't know you well enough to answer that."

His eyes flickered with interest. He glanced at the lingerie, then at her face. "Well, I'd like to do something about that."

Steeling herself, she shook her head. "I don't think so, Alex."

He frowned, as if being refused was foreign to him. Francey was pretty sure it was. "May I ask why?"

"It's just not a good idea."

"Have I misread the signals?"

Inherently honest, she shook her head. "No. But I have reasons."

"I'd like to know them."

"Let's just leave it alone, okay?"

With masculine grace—and arrogance—he stuck his hands in his pockets and rocked back on his heels. "I'm not sure I want to accept that."

Francey stared him down. "I am." He angled his head. "Sure. That I don't want to see you again."

A petite redheaded nurse appeared at the door. "Sorry to interrupt. I've got to record your vitals." Francey watched the woman take a long sideways glance at Alex.

"That's okay," Francey said, grateful for the distraction, the reminder. Wondering if she would have given in to the challenge and sexual intensity in his eyes, she finished, "My visitor was just leaving." She pasted a fake smile on her face. "Take it easy, Alex."

His gaze narrowed on her. "You, too, Francesca. And thanks again. For saving my life." He strode out of the room with a curt nod.

As the nurse took her blood pressure, Francey squelched the disappointment rising inside her. She'd done the right thing. The smart thing. She was very sure it was *not* a good idea to let Alex Templeton into her life.

CHAPTER THREE

"THE SPRINKLER SYSTEM in the basement of the Templeton Industries warehouse was manually disconnected." Fire Marshal Bob Zeleny leaned back on his leather chair in his big downtown office. The tone of his smoke-husky voice was deceptively casual.

Alex, however, was openly incensed. *"What?"*

"When my people went in after the fire, the first thing we checked was the failure of the sprinklers. They didn't work because they'd been turned off."

"Why would someone turn them off?"

Zeleny's gaze narrowed on Alex, only to be interrupted by a fit of coughing. When it subsided, Zeleny said, "Sorry. You have any ideas?"

"No." Alex tried to remain calm. "What are you implying?"

"Not a thing. I'm simply conducting an investigation. That's my job."

"Does this happen often—people disconnect sprinkler systems?"

"All the time."

That made Alex feel better. "Why?"

"Are you a smoke-free company?"

"Yes, I implemented the policy when I came here two years ago."

"Somebody might be smoking in the basement and worry the system would go off."

"Why the hell would anyone risk that?"

"Addiction. It gets its claws into you and can eat you alive. Say somebody needed a smoke bad. He goes down to the basement during the day and dismantles the system, then he forgets to turn it back on. So when the fire started Friday night…" The fire marshal let that thought trail off. "Of course, there's always the possibility that someone torched the place. Turned off the system intentionally to aid the fire."

"Arson? You implied that the day after the fire."

"Yeah. We call it an incendiary fire. The sprinkler situation makes me even more suspicious." The man observed Alex closely. "You made any enemies lately, Templeton?"

Alex shifted in his seat, his navy blue suit suddenly feeling uncomfortable. He adjusted the knot of his tie. "We've been downsizing. There've been layoffs."

Zeleny stroked his chin. "Revenge is a common motive for arson."

"I can't believe it."

Zeleny coughed again and stood, signaling Alex that the meeting was over. "Well, in my preliminary report, I'm noting the absence of cause and the sprinkler deactivation. We'll definitely be going further with this. In the meantime, you might put together a list of people you've laid off and any other enemies you might've made."

Alex nodded and left. Preoccupied, he headed out of the Public Safety Building to his car, barely noticing the mild April afternoon. Driving through the city, he thought about the newest development in the bizarre events of last week.

Could someone possibly have set the fire? He'd kept himself from jumping to conclusions after his initial meeting with the fire marshal, hoping they'd find the cause was faulty wiring or something. He'd discussed it briefly with Richard yesterday. His brother had been questioned at length and was troubled by the implication of arson, too. He and Richard had decided to table discussion of the issue until they had more information, which the fire marshal said should take about a week. After what Alex had learned today, they had more reason to believe the cause of the fire was suspicious. God, he hated that idea. But Rockford was a big city—more than a million people—with a high crime rate. It could happen here.

Made any enemies lately? Other than the layoffs, had Alex made enemies since he'd come back to take over the presidency of Templeton Industries? Damn it, he hadn't had time to make any enemies *or* friends.

Which reminded him of the beautiful Ms. Francesca Cordaro. He'd told her he hadn't had time to make many friends since he'd come back to Rockford. That was four days ago, and her violet eyes and husky laughter had been haunting him ever since. He could still picture her, lounging in the bed, mussed in a way she might be after sex, the silky underwear nestled in her lap. He'd been having fantasies, X-rated fantasies, about that underwear and her in it.

She doesn't want to see you again, Templeton. Why can't you get that through your head?

As he maneuvered through the city streets, he tried to analyze why he couldn't accept the fact that Francesca wasn't interested. Well, hell, first of all, he'd felt the vibes from her. And she'd admitted to them. But that wasn't the only reason he was unwilling to acknowledge her brush-off. He thought back to his conversation with Richard. Alex had confided in his brother about Francesca rejecting his request to see her again.

"Why would you want to see her, anyway? She isn't exactly your type." His brother's disapproval was evident in his scowl and critical tone. Richard's reaction had surprised Alex. He'd attributed the vehement objection and Richard's other strange behavior to the fact that he looked like he hadn't been eating or sleeping well. Because of the fire, of course.

"That's *why*. I'm bored with *my type*. I'd like to spend time with a woman of substance, a woman who has a job and interests outside of me."

"Dammit, Alex, there are women who fit that bill and still have something in common with you."

"Yeah? I haven't met any since I left Boston."

"Because you hole up in that office all day and half the night." Richard stared past his shoulder. "How about Elise Hathaway? She's made no secret she's interested in you. And she works."

Alex thought about the wispy blond beauty, Diana Hathaway's daughter, who "helped out," as she put it, in her mother's shop. "She's Francesca's half sister, did you know that?"

Richard had rolled his eyes like a sulky teenager. "No, I didn't make the connection. In any case, you'd be better off with Elise...."

Thinking of Richard's advice, Alex pulled the Porsche into his reserved parking space at the Templeton Industries building. A relatively new brick-and-glass structure, located three blocks from the warehouse, the top floors were offices and the entire bottom level housed the factory. It was after seven and most people were gone. A good time to tackle his paperwork. It had piled up in the three days he'd been off because of the fire.

But once seated at the big oak desk he'd inherited from his father, he didn't dig into his work. Almost against his will, he ferreted out the clippings his secretary had left on his credenza. There had been several articles about the fire in the *Rockford Sentinel* over the past few days.

Though the damage to the warehouse had been extensive and would require weeks of cleanup, the paper had taken a whimsical view of the human interest side of the story. One headline read, "CEO rescued by female firefighter." A reporter had called it "the stuff of romance novels."

Several pictures of Francesca had appeared in the paper. On top was the one he liked best—a color photo of her in uniform. The light blue shirt stretched nicely across her breasts, and the tailored trousers showcased her long legs. Next in the pile was a blowup of her face, no doubt printed to show off her remarkable beauty. Slowly he traced his finger down the gentle curve of her hair, remembering the silken texture. He ran the pad of his thumb over her bottom lip, wondering how soft it would feel. And those eyes—they seemed alight with confidence and contentment.

Yes, he was definitely interested. And not willing to let her go. At least not without a fight. He smiled at himself and shook his head wryly. *Serves you right, Templeton. It's about time you were on the receiving end of it.*

As he put the clippings aside and picked up the insurance forms, he admitted that was another reason he didn't want to let Francesca Cordaro go. Pure male ego. He couldn't remember the last time a woman had turned him down. He glanced at the phone. The hospital had told him she was staying at her grandparents' house for a while. He could call her. Easy to find the number in the phone book, since she'd mentioned they lived on St. Paul Street. By now, the efforts he'd made all week to charm her had probably worked. He wondered what she was thinking.

FRANCEY WAS READY to scream, tear out her hair and commit murder. But, as Grace Cordaro plumped the pillows behind her for the thousandth time, Francey bit her lip and smiled wanly. "Thanks, Grandma."

Her grandmother, the saint who, along with her grandfather, had raised her from the time she was three, frowned. "I know you want to go home this weekend, but I really don't think you should." Grace smoothed a hand over Francey's dog, a tiny white Maltese named Killer, who lay asleep on the couch at Francey's feet, then turned away. "Talk to her, Jakey. She listens to you. She's not ready to stay by herself.''

Jake Scarlatta smiled at Grace. His family had lived next door to Grace and Gus; when his father—Ben Cordaro's best friend—had died in a fire, Ben had become Jake and his sisters' surrogate parent. But Jake had had a tough life being the only Scarlatta male and had taken on too much responsibility. Almost ten years older than Francey, he'd also fallen into the role of another older brother to her—as if two weren't enough. "I'll do my best, but she was always stubborn.''

"You boys spoiled her, that's why.''

Grace left in pretended offense, and Francey glared at Jake. "Thanks, Benedict Arnold. Grandma's hovering is driving me crazy.'' She stretched out her long legs, clothed in comfy gray sweats. "You could have stood up for me.''

"What, and risk getting cut out of Sunday dinner? Not on your life.''

She laughed good-naturedly, glancing at his tall, muscled physique, clothed today in a slate blue designer T-shirt and coordinated shorts. Jake's one weakness was his penchant for nice—read, expensive—clothes. Then she sobered. "Did you hear anything about the Templeton warehouse fire investigation at the station?''

"Not today. All I know is that it's a possible incendiary fire.'' He scrutinized her face. "Why, France?''

She averted her gaze, leaned over and scooped up Killer, then settled him comfortably in her lap. As she petted him, she said, "No reason.''

"Oh, sure,'' Jake said, his eyes glinting knowingly. Then he pointed to a wicker basket that sat on the coffee table. "This the latest?'' The basket was filled with expensive sweets—Godiva chocolates, Swiss candy, several kinds of mints and chocolate-covered cherries and peanuts.

"Don't start. Everybody's picking on me.''

"The guys on my group at the station are wondering," he began. When Jake had turned eighteen, he, too, joined the fire department and was a lieutenant on the opposite shift to Francey at Quint/Midi Twelve. "Did Templeton *really* send you a gourmet pizza from Gepetto's, all cut up in bite-size pieces?"

"Yep. It was so big I shared it with the nurses." Francey smiled in spite of herself. The night Alex had been discharged from the hospital, the huge pizza with everything on it had been delivered in time for dinner. The next day, a quart of her favorite Rocky Road ice cream arrived at noon. Then, the evening before she'd been released, he'd sent an expensive dry red wine along with a mouthwatering filet mignon, rare, just the way she liked it, done as a shish kebab so she didn't have to cut it. "This goody basket arrived here yesterday."

Jake plucked out a piece of the Godiva, popped it into his mouth and savored the dark, creamy chocolate. "He's smitten, like all of them."

Francey sighed. "I told him I wasn't interested."

Jake reached over and snatched the card peeking out from the sweets. Francey recalled the glib note. *Isn't the way to a woman's heart through her stomach? Or does that just apply to men?* As Jake read it, his dark eyebrows rose. "I guess he didn't hear you."

"He heard, all right, he's just not listening."

Jake's expression grew serious. He'd always understood her well, certainly better than her brothers. "Want to talk about it?"

"Maybe." She glanced into the den where her father lounged in his favorite recliner watching television with her grandparents, who were side by side on the couch. "Alex isn't my type, Jake. For obvious reasons."

Nodding, Jake tracked her gaze. "Has Ben said anything?"

"Of course. As soon as the gifts started to come, we had this heart-to-heart talk. He was more nervous than when he gave me the lecture on sex when I was fourteen. Which I'd already heard from you guys."

"It killed him when Diana left, France."

Francey noticed, but didn't bother to mention, the switch of topics. She was glad to avoid talking about Alex. "I don't remember much of the early years, but I know it was hard for him."

"I remember some of it. I was thirteen when they split." He rammed his fingers through his dark hair. "I couldn't understand it. They were more in love than any couple I've ever seen in my life. I was shocked, liked everybody else."

"I guess after I was born she completely lost it—you know, about the fire fighting and all. I heard Grandma call it a nervous breakdown."

"Well, whatever it was, it made her leave him. Ben was devastated. I don't think he's ever recovered."

"Because he's never remarried?"

"Yeah. And how he is when she's around. Especially since she came back here to live."

Frustrated, Francey sank into the pillows. "Diana is friends with Alex's mother. And he's dated Miss America."

Jake chuckled at the unflattering reference to Elise Hathaway. When Diana returned to Rockford and opened a store in a wealthy east side suburb, her stepdaughter, Elise, had come with her. Elise had taken an instant dislike to Francey—and vice versa.

"Well, it doesn't seem like Prince Charming's giving up," Jake said.

"Don't you have that backward?" She tried to lighten the mood. "*I* saved *him*."

Jake smiled at her. "Did I tell you how proud I am of you, kid?"

Francey returned the smile, basking in the warmth of her

family. "Yeah, buddy, you did." Shooting a quick look into the living room, she took in the sight of her dad and grandparents watching a rerun of *Emergency*. The homey, familiar scene made her even more determined to steer clear of Alex Templeton. Just as Diana's return to Rockford had created havoc in their lives, letting Alex Templeton into hers would only cause trouble.

Francey opened her mouth to ask Jake about the station house's firefighter trivia game when the phone rang.

FRANCESCA SAT across from Alex at Schaller's devouring a jumbo cheeseburger, French fries, onion rings and a chocolate milk shake while he pretended interest in his grilled chicken sandwich and coleslaw. Broken arm aside, she ate with gusto. He was mesmerized watching that lovely mouth consume the food he'd persuaded her to share with him at Rockford's popular lakeside diner. It had been easier than he thought it would be.

"Schaller's is open for the season?" she'd said when he'd identified himself on the phone the night before and asked her to go out for a casual supper.

"Yes. Just this week. Come with me tomorrow night."

She'd covered the mouthpiece, and he'd heard muffled voices. Was someone there with her, a boyfriend, perhaps? The idea only increased Alex's determination.

"I don't know, Alex," she said when she returned to the phone. "I told you it wasn't a good idea for us to go out."

"Give me one chance to change your mind."

She was silent.

"Please. I'm running out of places that deliver."

In spite of herself, she'd chuckled. "The food's been great. Thank you, but all this isn't necessary."

He pretended to take umbrage. "Are you saying that saving my life isn't worth a couple of dinners?"

"I wouldn't dream of saying that."

"Then let it be worth one more. Aren't you ready to get out of the house?"

She'd groaned. Apparently that had done it, because she'd agreed.

"Alex? Where are you?"

He gave her his most charming grin. "Thinking about how glad I am that you came with me tonight."

"We've got to talk about that."

"I know. Not while we eat, though. We'll walk along the shore after and talk." He frowned at her arm. "Do you have a sling?"

She cocked her head and stared at him. "Yeah."

"Why are you looking at me like that?"

Shrugging, she said, "Because you don't need to worry about me. I can take care of myself. I always do."

He filed that information away as he watched her bite into a French fry, her toothpaste-commercial teeth sinking into it with relish. As she swallowed, he studied the graceful curve of her throat visible above her oversize denim shirt and dark T-shirt.

"So," she said, "why did you come back to Rockford from Boston?"

Alex dug into his sandwich, and between bites, he answered, "To be with my family. Dad wasn't feeling well, and he'd always hoped I'd take over Templeton Industries eventually. When he was diagnosed with a weak heart, it was time to come home."

And we found out about Richard, he thought, but didn't tell Francesca. His brother's problems were private.

"Did you mind coming back?" She wiped her mouth with the napkin, drawing his eyes to those lovely lips. He wondered briefly if he'd ever get to taste them.

"Truthfully, I was ready for a change. The job I'd had in Boston was interesting, but I wanted to do something different. I just didn't expect to take over Templeton Industries so soon.''

''Why did you?''

''Dad had a heart attack.''

''Oh, I'm sorry. Is he all right?''

''I think so. Though the warehouse thing set him back some. But he was getting stronger every day.'' After a pause, he said, ''The fire's been hard on us all.''

''Have they determined the cause yet?''

Alex tossed his napkin on the table. ''No. The sprinkler system was deactivated, so there're some questions around that.''

''There always are in warehouse fires,'' she told him.

''So the fire marshal said. It's nerve-racking, not knowing what happened. And I'm a little worried about Dad.''

She reached over and squeezed his hand. Her fingers were strong and beautifully formed, like the rest of her. ''I hope they clear it up soon.''

''Thanks.''

She scowled. ''Look on the bright side. *You* were lucky. Five minutes more and you would have been dead.''

''Zeleny told me that, too. Coming so close has made me…reorder my priorities.''

''I see a lot of that in my job.''

Alex leaned back against the leather-covered booth. ''Are you ever afraid?''

She arched her delicate eyebrows. ''Afraid? Of fire?''

He laughed at her incredulity. ''A lot of people are afraid of fire, Francesca.''

''No. I'm not afraid. It'd be the kiss of death for a fire-fighter.''

''How can you *not* be afraid to walk into a burning building?''

''Because I know what I'm doing. So does my crew.''

She drained her milk shake and finished the cheeseburger. "I do worry about Dylan sometimes, though."

Dylan, is that you? he recalled her asking when he'd visited her.

"Dylan?" His tone was sharp and drew her attention to his face.

"One of the firefighters in my group. He takes a lot of risks."

"Don't all firefighters?" Alex stifled the urge to ask if Dylan was the reason she hadn't wanted to see *him*.

"No. Well, maybe calculated risks. But Dylan's done some things that are *too* risky. He never endangers anyone else, but he's gotten his hands slapped for jeopardizing his own life."

"What's he done?"

Francesca pondered for a minute. "The worst was last year when we were called to a fully involved fire."

"Fully involved?"

"Where the building's roaring—totally engulfed in flames. It has to be knocked down from the outside."

"I see."

She stared over his shoulder, clearly back at the fire. "A family member who'd gotten out told Dylan a baby was in the house. Before anyone could stop him, Dylan smashed through the picture window and dived into the living room." Her eyes were full of concern and a little bit of awe.

Alex leaned forward in his seat. Though he was dumbfounded by the firefighter's action, he was nonetheless impressed by the man's courage and selflessness. "Did he save the baby?"

Francey shook her head, sending waves of dark hair into her eyes. Absently she pushed it back. "It was too late." She bit her bottom lip. "It's hard to lose a kid. We're not the same afterward."

"I'll bet." He smiled gently. "It's important to concentrate on the ones you do save."

"I suppose. But you always second-guess yourself. If I'd turned left instead of right. If I'd looked closer at the burn pattern, stuff like that."

He waited. She shook off the regret. "Anyway, Dylan wasn't hurt, thank God." She smiled. "Though the Cap chewed him out something fierce. Threatened to put a reprimand in his folder the next time if he didn't shape up."

"Did he?"

"Nope. He got a reprimand, too." Francey clearly sided with Dylan. Alex realized he wanted to know more about her love life.

"You done?" he asked, flicking a gaze at her plate.

"Yes."

He paid the bill and escorted her to the foyer. She reached for her dark gray fleece-lined windbreaker from the coat rack. "Aren't you going to put the sling on first?" he asked her.

"Oh, yeah," she said, tugging it out of her pocket. Awkwardly she tried to loop it over her head one-handed. And winced. "Damn it."

"Hurt?" She nodded. "Here, let me help."

Taking the sling from her, he slipped it over her head and held it while she slid her arm in. "Just a second, it's caught in your hair." Dipping his fingers underneath the sling, he tugged loose the silken strands. They curled like silk ribbons around his fingers. The feel of them, combined with the way they smelled—lemony and fresh—made his body harden.

"Alex?"

He let go immediately. "Mmm?"

"Can you help me with my coat? I can't get the thing around my shoulders."

"I think I can force myself." He held up the jacket. Once

her good arm was in it and he'd pulled it over the other shoulder, he reached for the zipper.

"Um, I don't—"

He grinned. "Hey, it's windy out there, and you need this closed. It's big enough to fit over your sling and still do up."

His big hands were unsteady as he pulled the front together and attached the zipper. Tugging the tab up, he held his breath when he reached her breasts. Her gaze flew to his. He flushed. "I'm not getting fresh, honest. I just want to help." And he meant it. But the closeness of her lovely body was murder on his already wayward thoughts.

She nodded and looked away.

Once outside, he found he could breathe more easily. Alex loved the weather here in upstate New York, despite its severe winters, which could rival Siberia. In late April, it was about sixty-five degrees, and an unusually warm breeze blew off Lake Ontario. They headed to the shore and began to walk. The soft rhythm of the waves was soothing, but Alex was wired.

"Okay, shoot," she said.

He smiled at her candor. No demureness for this lady. So he matched it. "What's your relationship with Dylan?"

"Dylan? O'Roarke?"

"The hero."

"I told you, he's on my group. We're all close."

"How close are you to *him,* exactly?"

She threw him a sideways glance but kept walking. "What's this about, Alex?"

"I thought maybe it was because of him that you didn't want to see me."

She laughed. "Have you been turned down so few times that you assume there's another guy?"

Sticking his hands in his navy jacket, Alex tried to appear nonchalant. Her amusement rankled him. "I suppose so."

She shook her head. "There's nothing between Dylan and me except friendship."

"*Is* there someone else, then?"

"No."

"Oh." He stopped walking and captured her gaze. "Did I offend you somehow? By flirting?"

"No, I find you very charming."

"All right, then, just tell me why you don't want to see me."

Francey studied him. The wind ruffled his hair, which blew boyishly over his forehead. The twilight accented his high cheekbones. God, he was handsome. And desirable. Too desirable.

She drew a deep breath and started walking again, and he matched her long stride.

"My father's a firefighter. He married a woman from *your* world when he was twenty. It lasted six years. When it ended, their three children, me and my brothers, paid the price for their foolishness. I..." She hesitated, unaccustomed to sharing her feelings. "My older brother, Tony, is as nice as a saint and as forgiving as a priest. But it was hard for me and for Nicky. He's the most bitter—even blames his recent divorce on them. *I* learned a valuable lesson—oil and water don't mix. My parents should never have gotten together."

To his credit, Alex didn't object immediately. They walked a few yards and he remained silent, thoughtful. "I'm sorry about your parents," he said at last. "It must have been difficult."

He couldn't have responded better. She hated it when men belittled a concern or tried to rationalize what had happened or worse, tried to fix it. Unfortunately, Alex's reaction made him even more attractive.

"Was it money?" he asked.

"No, though there was never enough of that. I guess it

boiled down to her not being able to accept her husband being a firefighter. And it wasn't just the life-style. She also lived in fear of something happening to him.'' Francey shook her head. ''Ironic, huh? She loved him so much she had to leave him.''

''Because she couldn't stand his putting his life in danger.''

''Apparently she had a breakdown over it.''

''I'm sorry,'' he said again. ''Is that why you stayed with your father?''

''Partly. But I think it was mostly because we'd always lived with Grandma and Grandpa. Right after I was born, Diana had to go to work to help support the family, and Grandma took over with us kids. When Diana left, it would have been worse for us to go with her.'' She smiled. ''Dad tried to play fair, even said he admired Diana for her selflessness. But I know he's bitter, too, that she wasn't stronger.''

''You call her Diana.''

''Yeah, so does Nicky.''

''Why?''

''We stopped visiting her regularly when I was about thirteen, and for some reason, we stopped calling her Mom then, too. Tony still does, though.'' When he didn't respond, Francey added, ''Diana calls me Francesca, just like you do.''

He looked at her blankly. ''Doesn't everybody?''

''No, after Diana left, it got shortened to Francey.''

''I didn't realize. You'd told me Francesca when we first met.'' After a moment he asked, ''Do you mind?''

''No, not at all.'' In truth, it sounded sexy as hell when the soft syllables rolled off his tongue.

Unexpectedly, he reached over and brushed her cheek with his knuckles. It was a butterfly-light touch that she felt right to her toes. ''I can see where a little girl growing up without her mother might not have understood all of what happened.''

''Yeah, I guess. But I wasn't Orphan Annie, Alex. I had a wonderful childhood. Don't feel sorry for me.''

''I'm sorry you had that pain in your life, Francesca, that's all.''

Francey gulped. Alex Templeton was a lethal weapon. Lethally good-looking, sure, but the understanding in his eyes was far, far sexier. And more dangerous. ''My parents' divorce is why I can't start anything with you, Alex. It wouldn't be smart. We're too different. You'd have problems accepting my job—both the danger and the life-style.''

''So you'll never marry.''

''I probably will. But it will be someone who understands my world.'' She smiled. ''I'm sorry. It would have been… nice.''

His chuckle was very male, very confident. And very sexual. ''Oh, baby, it would have been a lot more than nice.''

That one remark, and the raw, husky way he said it, curled though her like a sip of good whiskey. It tempted her to take back her refusal to see him, tempted her to throw caution to the wind that rumpled his hair. She thought of his big hands doing up her zipper and the jolt of awareness that shot through her when his knuckles brushed her breasts. For a brief moment, she knew exactly what made her mother marry her father.

But Francey had always been practical, and it put her in good stead now. ''Yeah, I guess it would have been more than nice.''

They walked farther. Alex seemed deep in thought and, despite her determination, Francey was wrestling strongly with her attraction to him.

When they turned and headed to the restaurant, he brushed against her accidentally, zinging even more awareness through her. "So, does this mean we can't see each other at all?"

"What do you mean?" Her voice was a little shaky, and she could feel herself weakening.

He gave her an electrifying smile. "Maybe we could be friends."

She recalled his saying he'd made few friends since he'd come back from Boston. She glanced sideways at him looking for signs of deception. "You really don't have many people to spend time with, do you."

He shook his head.

"I still don't know, Alex. It doesn't sound like a very good idea," she repeated. Mostly to convince herself.

"Afraid you can't keep your hands off me?"

Yes. "No, of course not."

"Afraid I wouldn't abide by the bargain?"

She found herself getting caught up in his flirting like some naive schoolgirl. "Maybe."

He slapped his palm over his heart. "You wound me, Francesca."

"Oh, sure."

They strolled up the pier, around the restaurant and to his Porsche, their bodies grazing a few times; once he put his hand protectively on her back. The sleek gray of his car sparkled under the restaurant lights. He opened the door and settled her in, buckled her seat belt, then rounded the hood to the driver's side. Once in the car, he glanced at the dashboard clock. "It's early. Are you tired?

"You're kidding, right? I haven't done anything for days."

He smiled. "I don't live far from here. Come to my house with me. We'll talk more about this. Set some ground rules you can live with."

She shook her head. "I don't know, Alex...."

"If it doesn't work being friends, we can always stop.

What's the harm in giving it a shot?'' Somehow his little-boy wheedling was endearing.

The harm was clear in the coziness of his car, which smelled like expensive leather. In the dimness his hair looked dark, and his long lashes were silhouetted against his cheek. God, he was gorgeous. ''Okay. I'll go to your house and we'll talk. Maybe we can work something out.''

He leaned over and brushed her cheek with his lips. ''Good.''

That was going to be one of the ground rules, Francey decided. No physical contact. She liked it far too much.

ALEX'S HOUSE fit him to a tee. Nestled on the lake, with a wide expanse of beachfront, it was a three-story, cedar-sided structure with one entire wall of glass and decks facing the lake. He led her into a spacious living room on the second floor, with overstuffed couches in front of the windows, stereo equipment off to the side and a glossy, high-tech, open kitchen in the back. It looked like a feature in *Better Homes and Gardens.*

''This is beautiful, Alex.''

''I like it. It went up for sale just when I returned to Rockford.''

''Lucky you.''

''Would you like some coffee?''

''Sure.''

''How about dessert?''

She narrowed her eyes.

''Did you plan this all along?''

''What? To get you back here?''

''Yes.''

''Yes.''

''Well, at least you're honest.''

He sobered and tucked a loose strand of hair behind her ear. ''I'll always be honest with you, Francesca.''

"Okay. Let's make that rule number one."

He arched an eyebrow. "Should I write these down?"

She shook her head. "Not on *my* account. I'll remember them."

"Like the Ten Commandments, I'll bet," he muttered under his breath. "Sit. I'll get the food."

She sat on one of the plush, Indian-print couches. The sound of water lapping against rocks echoed to the house, creating a cozy atmosphere. She leaned back against the cushions, then removed her arm from the sling, rested it on the pillow and closed her eyes. She had to think about what she was doing. She couldn't afford to kid herself or let Alex kid himself about what was happening. This was a bad idea, given the sexual attraction that sizzled between them.

Then she told herself to relax. There was no reason she had to act on that attraction. Maybe he could just be a friendly diversion.

"Sleepy?"

Opening her eyes, she saw that he had set down a tray. The smell of flavored coffee—hazelnut—wafted up to her, reminding her of the dinner from the Rio. "No, just thinking." She surveyed the dessert. Small shell-shaped pastries were mounded on a plate in a hill of chocolate.

"Madeleines," she said.

"Huh?"

"They're called madeleines."

"Beautiful *and* smart."

"Rule number two, Alex. No flattery."

"I'll try to control myself."

So will I.

He poured her a mug of coffee. "Black, right?"

"Are you kidding? Cream and three sugars."

"I don't believe it." His gaze raked her. "How do you stay so slender?"

"I'm hardly a twig."

"Good. I don't like twigs."

She discounted that remark. "I work out every day. Sometimes twice a day. And I have good genes."

His gaze dropped to her jeans. "Yes, you do."

"Rule number—"

"—three," he finished for her. "No sexual innuendo."

She frowned slightly. "No bad puns."

"That'll have to be rule number four." Alex sank onto the couch and tested his coffee, his eyes on her all the while. She reached for a pastry and took a bite. "Mmm, these are heaven."

He continued to stare at her. She looked at him like a stern schoolteacher about to scold a pupil.

"Francesca, if rule number five is I can't look at you, this will never work."

"Okay. You can look. But you can't touch."

"Not even a friendly hug once in a while?"

"We'll see. Maybe."

"Does that cover it?"

"Not quite. What about women?"

"Women?"

"Are there any women in your life who might object to our friendship?"

He was about to answer when the doorbell rang.

"Expecting someone?"

He shook his head. "No. But my parents are treating me like I'm sixteen again. They've been stopping over to check on me. Maybe it's them. You could meet them."

"I'd like that." Alex got up and crossed to the door. She stood, too, ready to greet the Templetons.

When Alex pulled open the door, his mouth fell open.

"Hello, Alex."

Francey froze.

Framed by the high archway was a vision of loveliness. Shoulder-length blond hair that looked silvery in the moonlight. A pink light wool jacket with a delicate hood. Tailored pants and leather boots. All in all, the perfect complement to the way Alex was dressed. Francey resisted the urge to smooth her jeans and man's work shirt.

For a moment, no one spoke.

The woman's gaze shifted beyond Alex and landed on Francey. She finally exclaimed, "Well, if it isn't my sister, the firefighter!"

CHAPTER FOUR

ALEX PULLED the Porsche into the driveway of Francesca's house, an older home on a city street with a wide front yard and a white picket fence. Killing the engine, he turned toward her. She was staring ahead, silhouetted in the light from the street lamp and deep in thought.

"How long have you lived here?" he asked, nodding toward the two-story house.

She unbuckled her seat belt and turned to face him. "Since I got into the department. About eight years."

"Do you like living in the city?"

"Yeah. There's a lot going on within walking distance. Park Avenue's close, and they have lots of restaurants, shops and activities in the summer. I also run in the park nearby." She glanced at the house. "It's close to Dad's place and Nicky's new apartment. And there's a yard for my dog."

"You have a dog?"

"Uh-huh. A little white Maltese. Dad says he's more of a toy than a dog, but he was abandoned near the station and I couldn't resist taking him home."

Since she made no move to get out of the car, he wondered if she was bothered by the scene with Elise and wanted to talk about it. After he'd gotten rid of Elise—rather abruptly—Francesca had grabbed her jacket and asked him to drive her home. Their easy camaraderie had been shattered. On the way back, they'd made stilted small talk.

"I'm sorry if Elise upset you," he said.

Francesca leaned back against the door and closed her eyes. "She always upsets me."

"Want to talk about it?"

"There's not much to say." Her fingers twisted the cord at the bottom of her jacket.

"If we're going to be friends, Francesca, we should be able to confide in each other."

She peered at him, her eyes luminous in the light from the street lamp. "Do you really want that? To be friends? Or is it just a come-on?"

"If I can't have any more, yes, I want that." When he said the words, he realized they were true. He really would give being just friends a shot. Right now she looked like she could use one. "How about you?" he asked.

"Yeah, I guess I want to try it."

"Okay, tell me about your sister."

Francesca grimaced as if she'd tasted something sour. "She's not my sister."

"What?"

"Diana married her father, Nathan Hathaway, when I was twelve and Elise was ten."

"But she looks just like…" He trailed off.

"Go ahead, you can finish it. She looks just like Diana. More than I do."

"Ah, yes, she does."

"Sometimes I think that kind of freaked her out. Made her think she was Diana's biological daughter and I was the interloper."

"Why would she think that?"

"She hates me."

He waited, sensing Francesca needed to gather her thoughts.

With a short huff of a sigh, she said, "You know, I don't talk about this much. Not to anybody."

"Oh, well, then, I'll be the friend you can talk to about your mother."

"It doesn't take a rocket scientist to figure out why Elise hates me," she said, staring over his shoulder. "She was young when Diana married her father. Her own mother was dead, so she latched onto mine like a leech. I'd visited Diana often before she remarried, but afterward, Elise was so rotten to me that I made excuses and stopped going to New York. Since she and Diana came to live here, I've bumped into her at my brother Tony's a couple of times. She still looks at me like I'm a cockroach."

"Why did they come here to live?"

"Nathan Hathaway died over a year ago, so for Diana it was just a move back home, I suppose. As for Elise, apparently she was at loose ends after her failed marriage. She had no work experience, so she tagged along."

He nodded.

Restless, Francesca shifted in the seat. "Now that Elise has the wrong impression about you and me, it'll be worse."

"There's nothing between Elise and me except some tennis games and a few drinks at the club."

Francesca sighed. "From what I saw tonight, she doesn't seem to see it that way. And bumping into me at your house will make her resent me even more."

"I'm sorry if I've caused you trouble."

"It's not that. I was just making an observation."

He sighed, then touched her sleeve in a comforting gesture. "If seeing me, even as a friend, causes you problems, maybe it's not what's best for you."

Francesca gazed at him, her eyes wide. "Thanks for thinking of me first, Alex. But I don't let anybody run my life. Especially Elise." She studied him for a moment. "I think I *want* to try being friends with you. If we can stick to it, that is."

"We can." Again, he found that he meant it. "I promise."

Her smile melted his heart. "So, if you're not dating her, who are you dating?" she asked him.

"No one."

"Why?"

He shook his head.

"Come on. I shared. Fess up."

"You'll think I'm arrogant."

"I already do."

"Thanks a lot."

"We said we'd be honest."

"All right. Most of the women I know bore me. I *did* date in Boston, was even engaged after college. But it didn't work out."

"I was engaged, too. Right out of high school."

"Who was he?"

"A guy I grew up with."

"Let me guess. He's a firefighter, too."

"Yeah."

"Well, we have something in common. Broken engagements. No steady dates. Time on our hands. Looks like a perfect setup for a friendship."

"Maybe." She grinned, then glanced at the house. "I'd better go in. Thanks for tonight. I had a good time. Before Elise."

He reached for his door handle. "I'll see you to the door."

She stopped him with a firm grip on his arm. "No, this isn't a date."

"Well, just to make sure you're safe, then."

At first her features softened; she'd told him she was unused to people looking after her. Then she shook her head. "Are we forgetting who saved whose life, Mr. Templeton?"

"God forbid," he said.

She chuckled.

"I'll call you," he said.

Pushing open the door, she threw him a wiseass grin. "Or I'll call you." And then she was gone.

Alex sat where he was and watched her dash to her house in a graceful, athletic jog, then take the porch steps two at a time to reach the front door. It took her only seconds to unlock it, despite her cast, then she was inside. She didn't once look back. He wished she had.

He started the car but didn't pull out of the driveway right away. Instead, he stared at her house, trying to be honest with himself.

Did he mean what he'd said about being friends?

Yes.

Was he going to try to seduce her into more?

He hoped not. He found that kind of dissembling unpalatable.

Could he keep his hands off her?

He'd sure as hell try. That was the best he could do.

FRANCEY LEANED against the rig as Adam checked the water tank. Her group at Quint/Midi Twelve had just come on the night shift, and they'd invited her for dinner. It had been two weeks since the accident, and she was going stir-crazy. The only good thing was that her arm had stopped hurting. Now it just itched like hell.

"Any action last night?" she asked, smoothing her jeans and tugging at her red cotton shirt. She wasn't used to being out of uniform here.

"Two EMS runs, and a supposed gas leak at the Towers."

Francey smiled at the mention of the local senior citizens' apartment complex, Dutch Towers, three blocks from the fire house. As happened in many fire stations, Quint/Midi Twelve was plagued with summonses from the elderly, who often overreacted to problems, got scared when little things went wrong or were just plain lonely. "Who called that one in?" she asked.

"Sergio again." Adam referred to one of the widowers who lived in a ground-floor apartment by himself. "Mrs. Lowe knows Jake's schedule," he told her, smiling indulgently about the old woman who seemed to need the fire department whenever Jake Scarlatta was on duty.

"The captain have a talk with Sergio?"

"Nah. When we got there, the old man looked so sad Ed didn't have the heart. He made a time to come over and play a game of checkers with him, instead."

"You guys are saps."

"Yeah, look who's talking. The last time you were on and Dutch Towers called us, you spent thirty minutes with Mr. Steed checking out birds with his binoculars."

"You were all busy with the broken pipe. It didn't hurt to do a little bird-watching with him. And it was a beautiful morning."

Francey felt strong hands grip her shoulders from behind. "Hi, gorgeous." She turned to see Dylan grinning at her. He was the only one in her group—in the department, really—who didn't treat her with kid gloves. When women had joined the fire service, all firefighters had been given a crash course in sexual harassment and how to treat females in the station house. Like a rebellious schoolboy, Dylan ignored most of the suggestions about language and touching, yet for some reason, his lack of caution made her the most comfortable with him.

"Hi, buddy."

He sniffed. "Mmm, smell that. Peter's outdoing himself tonight. Just for you."

"What is it?"

"I don't know. Smells like that fancy seafood dish again." Dylan caught a glimpse of Adam trying to straighten a hose that had gotten twisted. "Let me help you with that."

As Francey watched the guys untangle the two-incher, heavenly scents reached the bay. It reminded her of another seafood dinner and Alex Templeton—whom she'd been seeing a lot of.

First there was the dinner at Schaller's. The following Sunday, he'd taken her to a movie, a stupid cop show, and he'd teased her about the female police officer being the bad guy. He'd brought lunch over one day, too—enough sweet and sour Chinese takeout to feed an army. The food had been delicious, and his visit had broken up her day, which had seemed interminable. Last night he'd shown up with the latest Kevin Costner video along with popcorn and Pepsi.

Everyone she knew was working or too busy, and Alex had really helped pass the time. She hoped she was returning the favor by distracting him from the slow progress of the fire investigation. It seemed to him to be dragging out forever, but Francey was able to reassure him that these things took time.

Every time she'd seen him, he'd been a perfect gentleman. Once or twice she'd catch him looking at her, something sexual shimmering in his eyes, but he'd banished the look when he knew he'd been found out, so she guessed that was okay. Anyway, fair was fair—she glanced at him with more than just friendly appreciation, too.

She loved the way he moved, with a loose-limbed confidence and easy grace. And he had a terrific smile. It crinkled the corners of his eyes and made his whole face light up. But she appreciated other things about him, too—his dry sense of humor, his interesting experiences, his work ethic.

"Yo...Francesca? I said we were done. Where were you?"

"Nowhere," she said to Dylan. "Come on, I want my chance at the firefighter trivia game."

"You missed two rounds."

"I know. Who won?"

"Jake, both times."

"He's been reading up on firefighter lore again, hasn't he?"

"He said he wasn't."

Leading her out of the bay to the spacious common room, Dylan crossed to the bulletin board and a big gray metal desk in the corner. Francey could hear the guys cooking in the kitchen, which was off to the right; to the left, some good-natured joking came from a workout area with weight machines, a treadmill and Ping-Pong table. At six o'clock at night, no one was in the bunk room in the back of the station.

Dylan took down a typed page that had been tacked to the cork board. "Read 'em and weep, sweetheart," he said in a poor imitation of Humphrey Bogart.

As Francey perused the questions, an announcement came over the PA system. She and Dylan stilled immediately.

"Quint/Midi Five," Dylan said after listening carefully to the fire call that went to every station. "Not for us."

Francey looked at the paper and read the questions. Who set up the first volunteer fire department? That one was easy. Benjamin Franklin. What year was the first SCBA gear used for fire fighting and where did this happen? She knew it was Boston, because her grandfather had told her. But she couldn't recall the year. What nationally known artist got his ideas from his membership in volunteer fire fighting? Francey had no idea. True or false—did the dispatcher who was on in 1871 when Mrs. O'Leary's cow started the Chicago fire strum his guitar for his family instead of answering the call?

"Jeez, Dyl, these last two are hard."

"Nobody'll play if they're not. That's how we got the thirty-inch TV and new treadmill."

He sat on the desk and picked up *Report from Engine Company 82*, the most popular anecdotal book written about fire fighting. Dylan consumed firemanic material—fiction, nonfiction, magazines like *Firehouse* and manuals with the latest equipment or memorabilia in them. The information about fire fighting that he absorbed from these sources formed the content of their two-week rotation trivia game.

Dylan posed four questions. Everybody in each group— there were four groups at every fire station—got a shot at answering them for a dollar apiece. At the end of the rotation, whoever had the most right got a third of the profits. Another third went to raising money to purchase station house equipment. The rest they saved to give a whopper of a Christmas party for the School of the Immaculate Conception for Down's syndrome kids. Because next to fire fighting, Dylan O'Roarke loved Christmas and kids the most. This routine had gone on for five years.

She told him her guesses for the first two—which were correct.

"Give up on the others?"

"Yeah."

"Courier and Ives is the artist. And the last one is true. The jerk was showing off for his lady friend and didn't hear the call."

"Dinner!" Robbie yelled from the hall on his way to the office to get the captain.

When they reached the kitchen and sat down to eat, Francey found she was ravenous. Instead of seafood, tonight's feast consisted of chicken cordon bleu, green beans, wild rice and crusty Italian bread.

Just as they dug in, another call blared from the PA system. Everyone listened. "It's Thirteen's," the captain said, and they relaxed.

"So, France," Robbie asked between bites, "how long can you string this injury out? We sure like having Huff here."

She glared at Robbie. Peter Huff, an ex-cop, was thirty-five. He'd been a bit older than most recruits when he joined the RFD, and was a floater, which meant he substituted at various stations when needed. He'd been assigned to Quint/Midi Twelve for the duration of her convalescence. Blond and blue-eyed, he was a good firefighter if somewhat cool and distant. Furthermore, he could cook like a five-star-restaurant chef.

"Watch your mouth, probie," she said to Robbie. "I'm never gonna make the two months," she told the crew.

"You will," Ed Knight assured her.

"Yeah, kid," Dylan said. "You can do it."

Another call came over the speaker. Again everybody paused. And again it wasn't for them.

"That guy you saved seems to be payin' a lot of attention to you," Peter said teasingly. "We heard about all the food he sent you."

Francey laughed.

Duke Russo frowned. "I hear the Templeton warehouse fire might be arson."

"So they say."

"Did you know that arson is the leading cause of fire in the nation?" Dylan asked chomping on a piece of bread.

"Now look what you started, Russo," the Captain groused.

"It accounts for fourteen percent of all fire injuries and is the second leading cause of fire deaths."

Robbie threw his napkin at Dylan, though it was well-known the probie thought Dylan walked on water.

"And it's the leading cause of property damage."

"So help me, O'Roarke," the Cap told him getting up to get more ice tea. "I'll give you johns to clean for a week if you don't stop quoting those damned statistics of yours."

The banter felt good. Along with firefighters' notorious black humor, Francey had missed their razzing each other the most.

The crew decided to clean up before dessert. Robbie was washing the last of the dishes, Francey was putting them away and Dylan was reading to them about the newest imaging devices available—at an exorbitant cost—which allowed firefighters to see through smoke, when the PA system came on again. This time, it was for Quint/Midi 12.

All banter and joking stopped, as if someone had abruptly shut off the TV. Everyone raced to the bay. Out of habit, Francey followed.

They bounded to the rigs, kicking off their boots, which went flying all over the place. One of Adam's hit her in the arm.

"Sorry, France…too bad, kid…tough luck…" They tossed the words out while they donned their gear, mounted the trucks and buckled up. As driver of the Quint, Dylan waited just until the door of the bay rose to where he'd marked a big red line on the wall—he'd measured how far they had to wait for the truck to clear the height—and then he tore out of the station. The Midi followed right behind.

When they were gone, Francey crossed to the button and pushed it to close the overhead door; it squeaked down, then banged shut on the concrete with a loud thunk. Then there was silence. For a moment, Francey was stunned by the stillness in the station house. She'd never been alone here before. Her heart sank. The call was for a fire. She was missing a *fire*.

For two weeks she'd resisted feeling sorry for herself. Even when she couldn't get the cap off the bottle of painkillers or when she had trouble zipping up her jeans, she'd taken it in stride. Injuries were part of the business, though she'd rarely had one that kept her out of work. Her brothers had taught her to be tough, to roll with the punches.

She made her way to the kitchen, finished putting away the dishes, stored the dessert in the refrigerator and turned off the lights. She listened carefully to the PA and heard that

Quint/Midi Twelve had a working fire in a store on University Avenue.

Dejected, she made her way into the common room, thinking she'd wait for the guys to get back. She dropped onto the couch and picked up Dylan's *Engine 82*, but she couldn't concentrate on the stories.

The phone was right next to her. Hmm. Chelsea was at the gym tonight. Beth was out of town at a conference. Her grandparents were at bingo. Tony was probably having dinner with Erin and the kids. Dad was bowling. Maybe Jake was home.

She wondered what Alex was doing.

Glancing down at the clock, she stared at the numbers. Seven.

She could call him. See if he was busy. Maybe he'd meet her at Pumpers for a drink. He could console her about missing a fire, and she could take his mind off the snail-paced investigation into his warehouse fire.

Hey, she thought as she picked up the phone, what are friends for?

STIFLING A GROAN, Alex eased himself into the hundred-and-four degree water and settled onto the bench. He laid his head against a specially designed headrest that fit onto the corner of the hot tub built into his deck. Before he closed his eyes, he glanced at the perfectly cloudless sky, just turning dark. Several stars winked at him.

Every one of his muscles screamed in protest at his earlier mistreatment. He'd acted like a sixteen-year-old jock and overdone the exercising. Not only had this been the first opportunity he'd had to work out since he'd recovered from the injuries he'd sustained in the warehouse fire, but he'd been pitifully out of shape before that. Since he returned to Rockford two years ago, he'd let his fitness routine go completely by the wayside.

You didn't have to try to recoup in one night, jerk, he told himself. But he'd been struggling to keep the demons at bay and hadn't been careful about how many sit-ups he'd done or how long he'd run on his newly purchased treadmill.

Sighing as the soothing water bubbled around him and drained the tension from his muscles, he acknowledged what he'd been reluctant to admit. He was depressed. Though it rarely happened to him, he knew the signs—and he knew why. The root of his funk was threefold. The warehouse fire investigation was stalled; he was winded after five minutes on a treadmill; and his personal life, he'd come to realize in the past couple of weeks, was a desert with no oasis in sight.

He could call Francesca.

No, not a good idea. They'd had a pleasant two weeks, and he'd thoroughly enjoyed her company. But not once had she initiated contact with him, and that had bored a little hole in his heart. Maybe he was pushing too hard for the friendship. Too bad, because he liked being with her. She had a dry, sometimes black sense of humor, she respected hard work, and she didn't want to talk about herself all the time. Her lack of concern with her appearance was refreshing—and ironic, given how her looks stopped a guy in his tracks. Alex had found that if he could get past those looks, he could appreciate her for who she was inside and value her as a friend. Still, he'd wait until she called him this time.

Her stepsister, Elise Hathaway, had called him several times—just to see how he was, she'd said. She'd stepped up her campaign big time to snag his interest. As Francesca said, it didn't take a rocket scientist to figure out why. The phone had rung earlier, and Alex had let the machine pick it up, because he feared it was Elise. No one had left a message.

"Hi."

Alex's eyes snapped open. Before him stood Francesca. The wind ruffled her hair, her windbreaker was open—she probably couldn't zip it alone—and she was dressed comfortably in jeans and a red shirt that complemented her complexion. Bathed in the soft glow of the deck lights, she was utterly lovely. "Well, this is a surprise," he said.

She hesitated. "Is it okay? To drop in?"

"More than okay. I was just thinking how you've never called me, not even once." His look was scolding. "Like friends do."

Giving him a half smile, she came closer. "I called. Earlier, from the station house, but there was no answer. I didn't feel like going home, so I thought I'd take a drive by the lake." She shrugged. "Well, out here, to see if you were home."

He noted the tension in her jaw and the little catch in her voice. "You were at the fire station?"

She nodded.

"Did you have a nice visit?"

"I guess." Absently, she crossed to the hot tub and sat on the edge. She ran her fingers through the water. "Feels good."

"Want to join me?"

"I'd love to. But I don't have anything to wear. And this cast…"

He nodded at the French doors to the right of the Jacuzzi. "There's a bathroom off the deck. It's got towels and extra swimsuits in the closet. Something'll fit. And you can sit in the tub with your arm on the ledge."

"I won't ask you what you're doing with spare women's suits," she said, rising, "but I'll take you up on the offer." She headed to the door.

He called out, "Hey, if you need any help—with zippers and stuff—let me know."

"Rule number three, Templeton," she yelled before she disappeared behind the door.

"No sexual innuendo." He chuckled. Suddenly he felt a lot better. Francesca Cordaro was a mood-altering drug.

The high lasted until she emerged from the bathroom a few minutes later. The vision of her kicked him in the stomach and made him suck in his breath. She'd chosen a plain navy racing suit one of his cousins had left behind. But beauty-pageant queens didn't look half as good in their designer suits. The red trim on the top accented firm breasts that needed no support. The spandex dipped into her waist nicely; the French cut emphasized legs so long they could wrap…. He closed his eyes and swallowed hard. "What have I done to deserve this?"

She'd drawn close enough to hear, and she smiled wryly. "Serves you right," she said.

He opened his eyes and angled his head at her questioningly.

"You look pretty tempting there yourself, all bare-chested and rumpled."

"I do?"

"Yeah." She was eyeing the tub, puzzling over how best to get in.

"You have no heart telling me that," Alex said, warmed more by the simple compliment than the outright passes he'd gotten from other women.

"At least I have a sense of humor about all this."

"Is it worth it, Francesca?"

Her head came up. "Yes. I've really enjoyed these two weeks." When he stared at her, her smile slipped, and for a minute she looked like a shy schoolgirl, not a thirty-year-old woman. "Haven't you?"

"I've enjoyed them, too." He saw her shiver. "Get in before you get chilled. It's warm for April, but not that warm."

As she swung her legs over the side, he said, "Sit in the

corner, across from me. There's a headrest there. Just make sure you keep your cast out the water.''

"Yes, Dad," she said, laughing.

"No wisecracks, woman. There's a built-in mechanism in men that makes them want to take care of their women.''

"You turning caveman on me, Templeton?'' She sighed as she slid into the water as far as the cast would allow. "Oh, God, this is sinful.''

For a brief moment Alex was overcome by pure lust. He imagined her sighing with the pleasure he could give her, moaning with it, begging for more.

In a nanosecond, his body responded. *Focus on something else,* he told himself. Something that would douse his ardor. "What did you do at the station?''

"I had dinner with my group. Peter Huff, the floater, is taking my place, and he's a gourmet cook. The meal was something else.''

Alex frowned. He felt a spurt of jealousy—for their cook, for God's sake. "You must adore him.''

"I adore his cooking." Then she fell silent. "They got called to a fire just as we finished dinner," she finally said.

He detected the unhappiness in her voice. Though he didn't understand the mentality of *wanting* to walk into burning buildings, he'd learned from her over the past two weeks that firefighters devoted their lives to putting out fires and they hated to miss an opportunity to do their job. "And you feel bad?''

"Yep.''

"Want to talk about it?''

"Nope." She changed the subject. "Any news on the investigation?''

He hesitated, but then answered, "It's stopped.''

"Stopped?''

"Only temporarily. Bob Zeleny was admitted to the hospital today with pneumonia.''

She sat up straighter, and her lovely eyes widened with concern. "Oh, no, that's terrible."

"I hope it's not too serious. He seems like a good man."

"He is. He has a nice family, too. His son's a lieutenant at Engine Fourteen."

Alex remembered her telling him that the fire department was like family. No wonder she looked so grim.

After a moment he said, "You're hair's getting wet. Want to pin it up?"

"No, it'll dry." She sighed. "Poor Bob. So many fire-fighters develop breathing problems."

"Even though you wear the masks?"

"Yeah. Exposure to smoke happens after the fire. We're supposed to leave our breathing masks on for the overhaul—when we make sure the fire's out—but not everyone does."

"Doesn't sound safe to me."

"Nothing's safe about the whole business."

Her cavalier attitude about her safety bothered him. He started to mention it when she said, "Are they still questioning people?"

"I believe so. Zeleny's assistant said he'd be in touch after he reviewed the case."

"Your brother, too?"

Alex nodded. "Why?"

"No reason."

"Francesca?"

"I've been thinking about something, Alex, and every time I've seen you, I thought I should tell you. Their questioning your brother—well, the marshals often zero in on the person who calls in the alarm, the one who's at the scene."

"Why?"

"More times than not, he's the one who set the fire."

"*What?*" Alex sat forward.

"Look, I'm not telling you this to worry you. Or to accuse

anyone. As your friend, I just thought you should be prepared for what might come up.''

"I had no idea." He jammed a hand through his hair. "Why would someone remain on the scene who'd set it?"

"To see the results of his handiwork. Sometimes it's a vanity fire, where a person helps the firemen and gets praise."

"Richard would never hurt the company or the family."

"No, I'm sure he wouldn't." She gave him a reassuring smile. "I just thought you should have all the information. I'm sorry if I upset you."

"No, it's all right. I'm not upset. I *am* worried about my family, though, in this whole mess. Dad, mainly."

"You love your family, don't you?"

"Of course. Don't you love yours?"

"Yeah."

"Including Diana?"

Her shoulders stiffened, and she sat up straighter. Some of the light went out of her face. "I don't know Diana well anymore."

"Do you wish you did?"

"Truthfully?"

"Hey, that's rule number one."

"Lately I've been wondering if I've been too harsh on her. Probably because I'm off work and have time to think about it."

"Want some *friendly* advice?" he asked, raising his arms to the rim of the tub and lounging back again.

"Sure."

"When my father got sick, I regretted not having come back to Rockford sooner. But I was lucky—Dad recovered and I've been able to spend lots of time with him. Second chances aren't always there when we're ready for them."

"I'll think about it." Moved by his insight, Francey gazed

at Alex and noticed the deep creases bracketing his mouth and lining his forehead. "You look tired."

"I'm exhausted. I worked out tonight and I can barely move."

"Really? I usually feel great after I work out."

"I'm not surprised. You can probably bench press more than me, too," he grumbled.

"Probably."

"I'm out of shape. Since I came back to Rockford, I let my exercise regimen slip. And I haven't been eating well."

"Eating well is highly overrated," she teased.

"Maybe, but exercise isn't."

"Why haven't you kept up with it?"

He rubbed his hands over his face wearily. "Because I've been working my fanny off trying to learn the business, keep up sales and negotiate differences among the executive staff."

"I guess that's why you haven't dated much, either."

The searing look he gave her overheated her more than the hot tub. "That's *one* reason."

She splashed some water at him. "Watch it, buddy, no flirting. Rule number two."

"You make me forget myself, Francesca."

"Why'd you get back to the exercising tonight?"

"It had something to do with almost losing my life in a fire. And a woman who's in better shape than I am." He looked thoughtful for a minute. "In some ways, it's disconcerting to learn a woman is stronger and better conditioned than you."

"I know. Dennis, a lieutenant I worked under when I was subbing, told me once that women coming into the fire department made men question their masculinity—if a woman could do the job, what did that say about how manly they were."

"I can understand that. I had some of those feelings when you saved my life."

"Are you always this honest, Alex?"

"I thought that was rule number one."

She chuckled. "Anyway, it's a good idea to get back in shape. We could work out together, if you like."

"Don't tell me you're working out with a broken arm."

"Why wouldn't I?"

He shook his head, looking like a lieutenant explaining something simple to a rookie for the fourth time.

"Actually, I'm working out more. The better shape I'm in, the less physical therapy I'll need. And the doctor said I could start running as soon as I get a lighter cast."

Alex's eyebrows formed a vee. "I don't think that's a good idea."

"It's a necessity. If I want to be back on the line in six weeks, I've got to stay in shape."

"Well, I think it's foolish. What if you reinjure your arm?"

She scowled. No one, not even her brothers, questioned her about her activities; it felt odd to have someone worry about her. "I won't. I'm careful. Anyway, I've been doing most of my stuff at Chelsea's gym, and she's there a lot."

"Chelsea's gym? I thought she was a firefighter."

"She is. She also owns the Weight Room over on University Avenue. Lots of firefighters have other jobs."

He sighed, relieved. "Then she can watch you there. Who will you run with?"

"I hadn't planned to run with anybody."

"What if you fall?"

"Alex!"

"Friends worry about each other. Humor me. Run with me for a while. Just until I see you're okay doing it."

"I don't know... I plan to run in the mornings."

"Good. I'll run before work."

When she was silent, he gave her his killer grin. The one that had probably charmed the pants off scores of women. Literally. "Look," he said in a seductive voice, an intentionally seductive voice she'd heard from on-screen movie stars. "*I'm* responsible for your injury, so let me do this. I'll feel better about everything. And it'll help me get back in shape. We'll both benefit."

"Oh, all right," she said, trying to deny the appeal of having him worry about her, trying not to be thankful for having someone to spend time with. "I suppose it wouldn't hurt."

"Good girl." He glanced his watch. "I haven't eaten. I don't suppose you're hungry."

"Who, me, hungry?"

He chuckled.

"What did you have in mind?" she asked hopefully.

"Cottage cheese and salad?"

"Oh, God, rabbit food. No thanks. But you go ahead."

"How about if I order you a pizza?"

"With everything on it?"

"I think I can manage that."

She stood up. "All right, let's go."

He stayed where he was.

"Alex?"

"Ah, Francesca, I think you'd better get out first. Go in and get changed."

She cocked her head and shivered, rubbing the gooseflesh that formed on her arms. "Why?"

He gave her long, scorching stare, then the corners of his mouth curved up. "Well, I didn't expect you to come here tonight."

"I know that."

"And I, that is, when I don't have company, I..."

"Spit it out Alex."

"All right. I don't have any swim trunks on, Francesca. I'm naked."

CHAPTER FIVE

CLOTHES WERE STREWN everywhere in Francey's bed-room—jeans draped over the chair in the corner, blouses covering the queen-size bed and underwear piled on the floor. The mess was worse than when she was a teenager. Francey sat on the thick beige rug next to one of the stacks and sighed. Killer curled up at her sneakered feet, and she petted him absently. She was hopeless when it came to or-ganizing her house. Probably because she didn't care much about housework or furniture or clothes. Sometimes she wished she could go naked....

I don't have any swim trunks on, Francesca. I'm naked.

The image came out of nowhere, and Francey felt the heat rush through her just as it had when Alex had announced his state to her. She'd been in the hot tub for a good half hour with a naked man. A sexy naked man right out of the pages of *Playgirl*. And she hadn't even known it. He'd got-ten a big kick out of her faked indignation, and they'd both ended up laughing about it.

Get back to work, she told herself. *And get your mind off Alex Templeton's soaking wet, naked body.* She'd just stood up when the doorbell rang. Killer scrambled to his feet and barked. Thankful for an excuse to postpone cleaning, Fran-cey told the dog to stay and bounded out of the room; she reached the door after the second ring. Whipping it open, she came face-to-face with Diana.

"Hello, Francesca." Her mother's voice was hesitant.

"Hi, Diana." Francey's voice was cool.

Her mother bit her lip, and her eyes clouded. The eyes that Francey had inherited.

You have beautiful eyes, honey. Just like your mother's. I always loved her eyes. Her father's words came back to her, a fleeting moment from her childhood when Ben Cordaro had gotten nostalgic. The memory softened Francey's attitude.

"Come in," she said a little more warmly, and led Diana into the living room. As usual, her mother looked stunning. She wore a dark green skirt that fell to just above her knees and a matching jacket that skimmed her hips. A mint green top peeked from underneath. A frothy looking scarf graced her neck. Next to her, Francey, in an ancient sweatshirt she'd stolen from Nicky and frayed jeans, felt like Raggedy Ann.

Diana put down the shopping bag she carried and turned to her daughter. "How are you today?"

"Bored to tears." Francey glanced up the stairs to where sixties music blared from the radio. "I'm reduced to cleaning out closets and drawers."

Diana smiled, and for a minute Francey had a flash of other smiles, as her mother leaned over her bed or swabbed a scraped knee; other smiles that had always made her feel better. "You sound like it's a prison sentence," Diana said.

"It is." Francey held up her arm. "This whole thing is."

A wrinkle marred Diana's brow. "Is the break healing?"

"Yeah, this is the third week. After four, I can get a lighter cast."

"Speaking of casts, I brought you something."

Francey looked at the bag. "Something to eat?"

"No." Diana laughed. It was a girlish, musical sound, again one Francey remembered from years ago.

"Let's sit," Francey said, moving to the worn corduroy couch.

When they were settled, Diana held out the package. Her hand trembled. "I should have done this right after you broke your arm, but I didn't think of it. When some new things arrived at the store this morning, I realized…. Well, just open it.''

Giving her mother a weak grin, Francey reached into the bag. Clothing fell onto her lap. In various colors were light-weight camisoles, some lacy, some satiny, all very feminine. ''Oh.''

''You see,'' Diana said, speaking fast, almost breathlessly, ''since your arm is broken, I realized you couldn't fasten a bra. So I thought maybe these would work for a while.''

Francey stared at the underwear. A rush of a memory blindsided her—needing her first bra, shyly informing her father, who valiantly told her not to be embarrassed, he'd take her to the store that day. Francey had been nine. ''Well, what a *motherly* thing to do,'' she said, the bite in her tone intentional.

When Francey looked up, her mother's face had paled and the dark green color no longer flattered her. But she held her daughter's gaze. ''Yes, Francesca, it is. That's why I did it.'' Francey stared at her. ''I missed doing many *motherly* things when you were growing up.'' She reached over and squeezed Francey's hand. ''I…I'd hoped we could do some together now.''

Francey swallowed hard, more touched by the gesture than she wanted to be. For a long moment she warred with herself. Then she recalled Alex's comment. *When my father got sick, I regretted not having come back to Rockford sooner. Second chances aren't always there when we're ready for them.*

It tipped the scales. ''Sometimes,'' Francey whispered, ''I want that, too.''

Diana's eyes misted. Francey's throat closed up. Neither woman moved for long seconds. Then Diana said, ''Well, maybe I could help up there, too.'' She indicated the stairs.

"Now, there's an offer I can't refuse." Francey stood, grasping the camisoles, and led Diana up the steps.

When they got to her bedroom, a little white blur made a running leap for Francey but zigzagged to Diana when he saw her. Her mother bent down and scooped up the dog. "Well, who's this?"

"This is Killer."

Diana's laugh wafted through the room. "He's beautiful."

Francey snorted and crossed to the bed. "Dad doesn't think so. He says he's a poor excuse for a dog."

"Your dad loves big dogs. When I first met him, he had this golden retriever named Copper. She used to sleep with us...." Diana's voice trailed off, causing Francey to glance at her. Her mother took a deep breath, then shook her head, sending soft blond waves tumbling forward. "Well, no matter." She nuzzled Killer. "*I* like you, baby."

"He's getting hair on you."

Diana shrugged, and even that motion was graceful. "All the clothes I design are wash-and-wear." She set the dog down and surveyed the room. "Now, what are we doing here?"

"Trying to sort out my clothes. Nicky and Tony came by last night, moved all the furniture and helped me clean and dust. Today I'm tackling my closets. I've got stuff here from when I was eighteen. Some of it needs to be thrown out and everything else needs reorganizing." She shook her head, feeling like a rookie at her first EMS call. "I can reposition a hose in its bed faster than anyone in the house and clean my turnout gear in record time, but I can't seem to get this bedroom in order."

"Well, why don't we start with the stuff on the bed?" Diana smiled indulgently, like a mother would at her little girl. "That way, if we don't finish, at least you'll have a place to sleep."

It took three hours to sort through Francey's clothes, the

ones on the bed and still in the closet, as well as the dresser drawers, deciding which to keep and which to bag for charity. They chatted companionably as they worked. Periodically Diana commented on the sixties music and what she remembered happening in her life when the songs had been popular. Francey made small talk about the kind of music she liked and what they listened to at the firehouse. They stopped at four for some of the cookies and flavored coffee Alex had sent and at five had only the lingerie left to put in order.

"All right," Diana said, eyeing the drawer space. She'd long since discarded her jacket and shoes. Standing with her hands on her hips by the two dressers, she scrutinized them. "Let's put bras and camisoles in one drawer, socks and stockings in one, panties in another...." She reached out and ran her palm over the smooth oak surface of one of the bureaus. "These are lovely pieces. Where did you get them?"

As she separated underwear on the bed according to Diana's suggestions, Francey said, "Dad made them for me."

"He's still doing carpentry?"

"Yeah, more so, now that he's off the line."

Diana fell silent. Francey looked at her and saw that her face was white again, her hand slowly, almost lovingly, rubbing the surface of the furniture. "Diana?"

Giving her head a quick shake, Diana turned. "Sorry. That just reminded me of something. Here, let me help you with that."

It reminded her of Dad, Francey thought. Diana didn't mention him, but Francey was sure she was right. It made her think of Alex, of how she knew why her mother had succumbed to her father despite knowing that she shouldn't.

Diana crossed to the bed and sat. She picked up a pair of red lace panties. "You have some pretty things."

"Those are mostly gifts from Chelsea."

"Chelsea?"

"A girlfriend of mine who thinks wearing white cotton is a crime."

Diana's brows arched. "Isn't it?"

Francey giggled.

"I'd like to meet your friend sometime," Diana said, holding up the lavender teddy Francey had gotten for her birthday.

"Well, having a slumber party?"

Both women jumped at the sound of a booming male voice. Ben Cordaro filled the bedroom doorway, his big frame spanning its width.

"Dad? What are you doing here?"

His eyes were riveted on her mother. Diana had frozen, clutching the purple silk to her chest. Finally Francey's father glanced at his watch. "It's six o'clock."

Francey looked at him blankly, then slapped her forehead with her hand. "I forgot. I was going to softball practice with you to watch the teams. Jeez, I'm becoming an airhead." She turned to Diana to explain. But the expression on her mother's face halted her words.

Diana told herself to stop staring. But the vision of her ex-husband dressed like he was twenty again mesmerized her. He wore tight-fitting faded blue jeans, battered Nikes and a navy blue fire department T-shirt. A Buffalo Bills cap rested on his head.

Ben held Diana's gaze for a moment, his dark eyes glowering. "What's going on here?"

"Diana was helping me clean out my clothes."

"So I see." Ben's gaze hardened. "I knocked but no one answered. I tried the door, came in and heard the music." He scowled at the basket he'd set at his feet. "This was delivered when I was on the front porch."

"What is it?" Francey asked.

"Another Templeton bribe, probably."

"Bribe?" Diana said.

"Seems like hotshot Templeton is flooding my little girl with gifts." He threw his daughter a warning look; Diana remembered those looks stopping even toddlers in their tracks. "I don't like this, France."

Francey crossed to him, kissed him on the cheek and said, "I know, Dad. Let me see what it is."

She picked up the basket, returned to the bed and sat, then untied the pink ribbon at the top of the gift and tugged off the crinkly purple cellophane. Scents of baked pastry and cinnamon and nutmeg wafted to her from several small loaves of tightly wrapped bread, muffins and Danishes. A card from Stavistano's bakery read, "For breakfast tomorrow. Maybe I can join you? Alex."

"At least the man has good taste," Diana said.

Francey laughed. "Yeah, he does."

Diana looked up, feeling Ben's gaze on her. His hands were fisted at his side.

"Well, I should be going," Diana said with a glibness she didn't feel. "Since you've got plans with your father."

"Oh, yeah. We play on the fire department softball teams." Francey's smile was genuine. "Hey, thanks for helping me with this." She waved her hand to encompass the room.

For a moment, Diana allowed herself to bask in the warmth of her daughter's gratitude. She reached over and smoothed Francey's hair. It was the exact texture of Ben's. "I loved every minute of it." Diana donned her shoes and jacket, picked up her purse and crossed to the door.

Ben didn't move out of the doorway immediately. She drew up close enough to him to smell his aftershave. It was different from the one he used to wear—a little spicy, citrusy. She was forced to angle her head at him; she'd forgotten how much bigger he was than she. He stared down, his arm braced against the jamb. Finally he stepped aside, and as she went by, her shoulder brushed his bicep. It was rock hard, and she remembered those arms, braced on either side of her, as he drove into her.

The memory spurred her to hurry out and flee down the stairs. She yanked open the front door and stepped onto the porch, then stopped when she got to the railing, leaned on it and took in a deep breath. She felt a strong hand on her arm.

"Just a minute," Ben said. "I want to talk to you."

BEN HELD ON tight to Diana's arm, trying not to notice the softness beneath his fingers. She'd put on a little weight over the years. Unfortunately, he always liked her best when she'd been well-rounded, the way she was during and after a pregnancy—and now.

She pivoted and gazed at him, those violet eyes wide and surprised. "About what?"

Slowly he eased his grip on her and dropped his hand. She stepped back, and the distancing gesture made him angry. He remembered when she used to try to crawl inside his skin. "That was a pretty chummy scene I walked into. What are you up to?"

"Up to?" Her voice had turned cold, something else he hated.

"Yeah, up to. What do you want from us?"

Diana averted her face. She adjusted the strap of her purse over her shoulder, then tossed her head. She reminded Ben of a probie gathering his courage to face a fire. "I don't want anything from you, Ben. Except maybe some forgiveness. My children are another story."

"What do you want from them?"

"The same thing I've always wanted. To be part of their lives."

"Yeah, well, are you sticking around this time?"

"What does that mean?"

"It means, sweetheart, that the last time you said that, I let Francey visit you, encouraged her to build some kind of relationship with you, and it didn't work."

He could still see his daughter at thirteen, teary-eyed and trembling, getting off the plane. *I don't want to go back, Dad. Please don't make me.*

"It worked until she refused to come visit."

"And why was that?"

Diana's shoulders slumped. He had her cornered like a trapped animal, and he knew it. She swallowed hard. "It was Elise. I couldn't control that, Ben."

The catch in her voice defused his anger. He leaned against a porch pillar. Diana looked at him with those kiss-me-senseless eyes and that don't-be-mad expression that had always won arguments quicker than any words. "I know that, Dee."

The wind picked up and whipped the scarf she'd looped around her neck into her face. The material looked silky and smooth, just like her skin. He stared at her throat a minute. Which was a mistake, because he was bombarded by memories of planting kisses up and down it....

"Listen, I can handle your seeing her, like you do Tony. It's probably good for Francey to have some sort of mother-daughter relationship with you." He hesitated, then added, "I think Nicky's another story. You'll never get through to him."

Diana raised her chin. "I'm not giving up on either one of them."

"All right. Just don't encourage Francey with this Templeton thing."

"What do you mean?"

"I mean, the guy's sniffing after her big time. Pulling out all the stops. I don't want it to happen, is all. So don't go telling her he's got good taste or he's a nice guy."

"He is."

"I don't give a shit."

She arched a brow.

"Goddamn it, Diana. Don't you see what could happen here?"

"Francesca could fall in love and live happily ever after."

"What the hell's the matter with you? There's no happily ever after. Especially not between two people who are so different." He reached out, grasped the ends of her scarf and pulled her closer. "Or have you forgotten?"

He expected her to cower.

She didn't.

Instead, she lifted her hand and ran her palm down his cheek. "I haven't forgotten anything."

He wanted to lean into her touch, let her soothe away all the years of loneliness. Because of that, he summoned images he knew would stop him—Francey getting her period, and how he stumbled through the whole thing; shopping for her first prom dress and having no idea what was too old for her; watching her graduate from the fire academy without a wife by his side.

He yanked on the scarf. "Well, you better remember it all, Mrs. Hathaway. Because we gave each other nothing but grief. We paid a high price for being hot for each other, and I'll be damned if I'll let my daughter make the same mistake." He let Diana go.

Again she surprised him. She stepped back, and her gaze and voice were confident. "Being married to you was the best part of my life, Ben. I was a fool to walk out on it. Especially since I worried about you, anyway. As far as Francesca is concerned, she's a totally different person from either of us. She's stronger than I ever was. And she's more flexible than you were capable of being. If she wants a man who's different from her, she's woman enough to handle it. Even if I wasn't."

With that, his ex-wife turned and gracefully descended the

steps. Ben watched her until she got into her black Mercedes and pulled out of the driveway.

A swift wave of sadness enveloped him. He sank onto the porch swing and buried his face in his hands. So much lost. He thought he'd gotten over it.

Apparently not.

IF NOTHING ELSE, Alex thought, knowing Francesca Cordaro was an exercise in humility. First she'd rejected his offer of a romantic relationship. Now she outshone him at the gym where he'd gone with her to work out three times this week. As Alex gulped for breath on the treadmill like an out-of-shape old man and struggled to keep his arms in motion, she did leg squats across the room—with weights strapped to her upper arms. Forget about her broken arm, which peeked out from a ragged fire department T-shirt. She ran circles around anything he could do.

"Winded?"

Alex looked up to find Chelsea next to him. The gym owner wore snappy hot pink shorts and a matching tank top under a zippered sweatshirt emblazoned with the Weight Room logo. Francey had told him Chelsea gravitated toward unusual clothing. Though blondes weren't his type, he could nonetheless appreciate her beauty.

"Yeah, I'm winded." He scowled. "Still."

"You can't recoup quickly, Alex. Forgoing your exercise routine lost you a lot of stamina and quite a bit of strength." She reached out and pinched his waist. "At least you didn't go to flab," she said, smiling to take the sting out of her words.

Alex had come to like Chelsea the few times they'd met. She'd was a serious and sensible trainer and set up a practical but demanding program for him; he'd followed all her advice.

Why wouldn't he? She was in great shape. Francesca said

Chelsea was a competitive weight lifter, and her lithe muscles attested to that. Jeez, was everybody Francesca knew in terrific shape? A few of the male firefighters also came to this gym to work out, and they made Alex feel like a slug.

Across the room, Francesca finished the squats and sat at the universal to do leg raises. She handled the weights like they were toys.

"How much can she do on that one?" Alex winced at his petulant tone.

"About one-fifty," Chelsea said, biting back a smile.

He shook his head.

"Can I ask you something personal?"

Tearing his eyes away from Francesca's nicely muscled thighs accented by her khaki shorts, Alex looked at Chelsea. "Of course."

"Are you serious about this friendship thing with her?"

"Absolutely." He cocked his head. "Why?"

Chelsea shrugged. "Because sometimes you look at her like you want to eat her up."

"Sometimes I want to," he said lightly. "But she's not interested. So I'm settling for friends."

"I'd hate to see her get hurt."

"How could I hurt her?"

"It has something to do with the way she looks at you, too."

Alex slowed his pace on the treadmill, feeling the sweat soak through his T-shirt. "Chelsea, Francesca and I have both admitted to the attraction between us. She's against pursuing it. I think we're both bound to wish the circumstances were different, but I don't want to give her up because of it."

Chelsea nodded, watching Francesca's face redden. "No more than twenty, Cordaro," she yelled across the room. "You've only been back a week."

Francesca saluted Chelsea like an obedient soldier and

smiled at Alex. His heart rate spiked over the target Chelsea had set for him. "Can I ask *you* something?"

"Sure."

"Do you think she's right? To shy away from anything more than friendship with me?"

"For her she is. Francey was devastated by her mother leaving. And, if you ask me, Ben Cordaro still suffers over it. I don't blame her for avoiding a similar heartbreak." She smiled at Alex, her blue eyes sparkling. "I'd go for it, though."

"Why?"

"Life's too short to be so cautious. As a firefighter, I've learned that." Her gaze was snagged by another customer. "Oops, I'd better go help Esmerelda. She's got the wrong weight. See you later, Alex."

Alex wound down his treadmill stint, got off the equipment and crossed to Francesca, who'd just finished her leg raises.

"Hi," she said, grunting out the word.

"Hi."

Sweat trickled down her cheek. She'd tied her hair in some kind of knot, but several strands had come loose and framed her lovely face. He looked away.

"You okay?"

"Yeah. But could you go to the other side of the room while I do the bench press?"

She chuckled. "Alex, you're not still upset that I can lift more weight than you, are you?"

"Fifty pounds more."

She reached out and tweaked his arm. "Hey, you'll get there. Dylan can bench more than me now."

Dylan, again. "Is there anything Dylan *can't* do?" he asked irritably, stretching out on the bench.

She grinned and lifted her eyebrows. "According to the women he dates, there isn't." She scanned Alex's supine body. "I imagine you could keep up with him just fine in that department."

"Now, Francesca," he said, trying to ignore the warmth that spread through him at the compliment, "rule number two…"

"Of course, I forgot myself. See ya," she said over her shoulder as she headed for the treadmill.

Twenty minutes later she was covered with perspiration and chatting with Esmerelda, who'd come to walk on the machine next to hers. Alex was about done with his workout, so he wandered over to them. The two women were deep in conversation. He plucked a free weight from a rack behind the machines and halfheartedly attempted some bicep curls as he eavesdropped.

"It really ticks me off that they can eat so much and not gain an ounce," Esmerelda said, her face beet red.

"Slow down, Ezzy. Yeah, it ticks me off, too."

"Women have it tough in every way."

Out of the corner of his eye, Alex saw Esmerelda eyeing Francey's body. "Don't you get tired of eating salad and yogurt just to look like you do?"

"Uh-huh."

Alex dropped the barbell, and it clanged against the other weights. Francey glanced at him. The conspiratorial wink she gave him overheated his already sweaty body. She turned to her friend. "But, Ezzy, I don't watch what I eat to look like this. I do it for my health, not vanity."

"Yeah, I know. You've said that before."

"You're doing great on this program. But do it for yourself, not for how you look to others."

Alex wiped his face with the towel he'd roped around his neck. He crossed to the women. "Well, I'm heading for the showers. You almost done?"

Francey gave him a smile that would curl any man's toes. "Yeah, I'll meet you at the desk in ten minutes."

Alex ambled off toward the men's locker room. For the first time since he'd asked Francesca to be friends, he wondered if he could hold up his end of the deal. Something inside him had shifted when he'd heard her lie outright to Esmerelda just to make the overweight woman feel better. Francesca was beautiful on the outside, but more importantly on the inside, where it counted.

Alex was startled at the strange sensation he felt in his belly. The longing to have more from her than friendship was painful. He hadn't bargained on that. He hadn't *foreseen* that. Probably because it had never happened to him. All his life, he'd rarely hurt for something he couldn't have, because he usually got everything he wanted.

Maybe he needed a date, he thought as he opened the locker-room door. His accountant had been showing a lot of interest in him these days. Maybe it was time to try to get his mind off the beautiful firefighter who'd saved his life.

Alex wasn't a masochist, and he didn't like the pain he felt tonight at all.

FRANCEY SWUNG her pickup truck into the parking lot of Pumpers and let the engine idle for a minute. There'd been an odd sound in it since she'd left the Weight Room. She smoothed her hand over the restored leather interior of the Red Devil, as she'd dubbed her truck—it was what firefighters called a fire. "Come on, baby, stop making that sound. I can't work on you with this arm."

The truck began to behave the way it should, and Francey sighed. She switched off the engine; silence surrounded her. But she didn't get out of the cab immediately. Instead, she laid her head back on the seat and closed her eyes, thinking about Alex.

She'd come out of the locker room to find him helping Esmerelda into her coat.

"You aren't really interested, are you, Alex?" Esmerelda had asked him.

"Of course I am. I told you we're looking into new cafeteria facilities for my company." He'd pulled out his wallet, withdrawn a business card and handed it to her. "Call me."

Esmerelda had flushed. "All right."

Francey had grasped his arm and leaned close for a minute as they walked out of the gym together. "That was nice of you."

He peered at her. "Why? I *am* thinking about revamping the food service at Templeton Industries."

"Well, you've made her night. She was practically swooning at your feet."

"I hardly notice when women do that anymore," he said dryly.

Francey bet women did swoon over Alex. By their cars, his hair damp, his cheeks ruddy from working out, a dark green thermal shirt peeking out from under a light jacket, he looked healthy and very male. "Watch it. There won't be room for you and your ego in your Porsche."

He smiled, but the smile was tinged with a certain melancholy.

She said, "Are you all right?"

"Sure."

"I'm going to stop at Pumpers. Want to come?"

"Pumpers?"

"It's a bar about three blocks from here."

"Don't tell me, it's a firefighters' bar."

"How'd you guess?"

Again he smiled with the same melancholy.

"I'll buy you a beer," she said.

"I don't drink beer."

"Ah, well, nobody's perfect. I could probably spring for a—what? Jack Daniel's?"

"Johnny Walker."

"Okay, I'll buy you a Scotch."

"No, I don't think so." He checked his watch. "I've got some calls to make."

"At nine o'clock at night? A little late for business."

His gaze sober, he reached over and snapped the top two buttons on her jacket. "Who said it was business?"

Her heart lurched a little. "A date?"

"I think rule number five should be that we don't share details of our love lives."

She'd ignored the sinking feeling in her stomach and swallowed hard. "Oh, sure. Okay."

"He's calling a woman right now," she said aloud into the interior of her truck. "I wonder if it's Miss America." The thought of Alex with Elise made her want to puke, so she shoved it away. Like most firefighters, Francey was very good at blocking things. She'd done it all her life. She repressed the pain of growing up motherless. Or losing a victim in a fire. Some things shouldn't be dwelled on.

She exited the truck and made her way into Pumpers. Long and narrow, it was a neat little bar. Pictures and fire memorabilia covered every inch of the walls. Francey's recruit-class photo was on the left near the doorway, and one of Dylan's many commendations was framed above one of the booths. Laminated newspaper articles were scattered throughout. The owner, Jimmy McKenna, mopped up the long mahogany bar. He kept the place as spotless as the firehouse he once worked in.

At the end of the bar, her father sat on a stool talking to Jake Scarlatta. She made her way toward them. "I'm glad this year's recruit class at the academy is almost over," she heard her father tell Jake. "It's been a tough one."

"Well, like you always said, if you didn't want a recruit at Francey's back, then he shouldn't graduate the academy."

"Talking about me?"

Her father swiveled and Jake peered at her. She gave Ben a peck on the cheek.

His face was drawn, his eyes bloodshot; he was more dressed up than usual, in a navy sports coat and gray slacks. Jake wore a casual taupe linen blazer over a brown T-shirt and slacks. "Going somewhere, you two?"

"We just got back from Jessie's concert," Jake told her. After Jake's divorce five years ago, he'd gotten joint custody of his daughter, Jessica, and moved back into his childhood home next door to the Cordaros. Jessie spent more time there than with his fussy ex-wife. She was a bright spot in Jake's life, just as Francey was in Ben's.

Francey glanced at the drinks on the bar. Each man had a beer in front of him. Next to her father's was an upside-down shot glass. "Hitting the hard stuff, Dad?"

"Just a couple."

Her gaze snapped to Jake, who shrugged like an innocent bystander. "I'm driving," was all he said.

Francey took the stool next to Ben. They made small talk and after a few minutes, Jake slid off his stool and announced, "There's Joey. I need to talk to him about something." He picked up his beer, squeezed Francey's shoulder and left the Cordaros alone.

For a moment Francey stared at her father, the person she loved more than anyone in the world. "You okay, Dad?"

"Yeah. Why wouldn't I be?"

Because you're drinking hard liquor. Her eye caught a pack of cigarettes half-hidden under the napkin. She picked it up. "These yours?"

He grabbed it out of her hand. "You're not supposed to see those, little girl."

"Dad, you only smoke when you're stressed out."

"I used to smoke all the time. Until I met your mother."

Francey cocked her head. "Really? How'd she get you to stop?"

Her father's face softened. He fingered the cigarette pack. "I can't tell you that, honey. It's too personal." Ben took a swig of beer and upended the shot glass. Jimmy came over and refilled it with whiskey. "Hi, France. What'll ya have?"

"Hi, Jimmy. Just a beer." She named a popular brand.

Ben tossed the whiskey down in one swallow. "Your mother was so easy to please, you know," he said after Jimmy brought Francey's beer. "Everything I did made her happy."

Francey's heart constricted at the raw pain in her father's tone. "Everything except the fire fighting."

He nodded. His eyes got a faraway look in them. After a minute he shook off the mood. "Did you have a good time with her yesterday?"

"Yeah. She…she said she wants to spend more time with me."

"I know. She told me that when I talked to her on the porch."

"You were yelling at her."

"You heard us?"

"Not the words. Just the tone. What were you talking about?"

"Alex Templeton."

"Really?"

Ben shook a cigarette out of the pack, lit it and took a long drag. "I told her not to encourage you with him."

"Dad, Alex and I are just friends."

Ben reached over and tucked a strand of hair behind her ear; the gesture reminded her of when he used to brush her hair as a child. "Honey, that's the oldest trick in the book. He's just biding his time till he can get you in the sack."

"No, he's not. We're really working at being friends."

"Why?"

If I can't have any more, yes, I want that. Instead of telling her father the reason Alex had given her, she said, "Dad, don't you think I learned my lesson from you and Diana?"

"I hope so."

"Well, I did. She made you miserable."

Gazing into space, Ben said hoarsely, "She made me happier than I've been in my whole life."

Francey almost dropped her beer. *"What?"*

"It was her leaving that killed me." He stared over the bar. "This is the liquor talking." Stubbing out the cigarette, he shook his head.

"No, I want to hear it."

Ben swiveled on the stool and faced her fully. "Francey, I tried to be fair about this when you were growing up, but I know you've always resented your mother for leaving."

"With good reason."

"No, not really."

"Then tell me about it."

Ben sighed. "Diana and I were happier than anybody could have imagined. She was a good mother and an even better wife. When she left she took a piece of me with her."

"Is that why you never remarried?"

"Partly."

"I never heard the whole story about her leaving. Want to tell me?"

"You really want to hear?"

"Yeah."

He braced his arms on the bar and stared ahead. "She hated the danger of fire fighting. I didn't know that until we'd been married for at least a year. One night I came home after a fire that had been on the news. I found her rocking Tony in his room, tears streaming down her face. She was terror stricken. From then on, I tried to keep everything from her. Later, just before we split up, I realized that only made things worse."

"She was weak, Dad. Other women handle it."

"I know. Maybe she *was* weak, but whatever it was, she couldn't take it. This went on for six years. It was the only thing we fought about."

"I don't remember you ever fighting."

"You were too little." He shook his head. "You know, it was after you were born that she got worse. Somehow, having a girl made her even more frightened."

"What happened at the end?"

Ben shuddered, and Francey reached out to squeeze his arm. "I came home one morning after a nasty fire. It had gone on for hours, and I was beat. It was March, but colder than a bitch. I pulled into the driveway and your mother—" he swallowed hard "—was sitting on the front porch. Shivering. No coat on." Her father's voice caught. "God knows how long she'd been there. Her lips were blue, her hands like ice. Tears had almost frozen on her cheeks."

"Why was she there?"

"She was waiting for me. She was out of her mind with worry. Hadn't even noticed the cold."

"What did you do?"

"I took her to Emergency. They treated her for exposure. Then I called her parents."

"I don't remember them."

"You were little when they died in that plane crash on one of their jaunts to Europe. They were never really pleased that their princess had married a blue-collar guy like me, but to give them credit, they didn't interfere—until that morning."

Francey watched him like a student hanging on her teacher's next words.

"It was her father," Ben continued. "He was outraged by his daughter's state. First he yelled. Then...then he got tears in his eyes. He begged me let him take her home—*his* home—get her some help."

Francey threaded her hair restlessly. "Help?"

"Yeah. They put her in a private clinic until she recuperated physically. Then they kept her for a few weeks for psychological help." Ben took a swallow of his beer. "When she came back, she was never the same. She was as fragile as a china doll." He closed his eyes briefly. "She left about a month later for good—at the suggestion of the doctors and the strong urging of her father."

"He shouldn't have interfered."

Ben faced her, his eyes blazing. "I'd do the same for you, Francey. I'd take you away from a man who was destroying you."

Francey stared at him. "Dad, it's not that way with Alex and me." But a chill stole over her when she remembered the times she understood the attraction—and its inevitability—between her mother and father. Because she felt it for Alex.

"I hope to God it's not, honey. I couldn't bear for you to feel what I felt when I lost your mother."

Squeezing her arm gently, he turned away, signaled the bartender for another shot and lit another cigarette.

CHAPTER SIX

THE BREEZE WAS COOL, but it felt good. So did the early morning May sunshine that beat down on him. This was the fourth time he'd run with Francesca, and he was left gasping for air only half the time. The week at Chelsea's gym and building up his miles these few days had given him some stamina.

"How you holding up, big guy?" Francesca asked from beside him, her breathing heavy but not strained. At least she was sweating.

"Fine. It hardly feels like my chest is being ripped apart at all anymore. I can even speak a little now as we run."

She chuckled. "You're a good sport."

"Tell that to my screaming muscles."

Frowning, she asked, "Are you really overdoing it? We can slow down."

"Not on your life. My ego can't handle it." They rounded a corner and hit a grassy incline in Highland Park, a city track of land with bike trails and paths for runners. They didn't talk again until the were at the top of hill.

"So," she said casually, "how was your date this weekend?"

He hesitated. "I thought we weren't going to discuss this."

"I wasn't asking for the intimate details."

Good, Alex mused, because there weren't any. But the date *had* done him some good. His accountant, Stephanie Pittman, a pretty brunette, was a witty, interesting woman who'd enjoyed dinner at the Rio with him and a play afterward. Alex had enjoyed it, too. The only dark spot had been when he'd kissed her good-night; he wasn't into it, wasn't excited by it. Well, he figured philosophically, it usually took him time to get into the physical part of a relationship; he was thirty-six, not sixteen, and he chose his sexual partners carefully after he'd known them awhile.

"It was very pleasant," he replied. But Francey wasn't paying attention. She was staring into the trees that bordered the park. "Aren't those lovely?" She pointed to some tulips peeking through the dirt.

"Mmm," he said, and couldn't help smiling at how she looked. No designer clothes for her, like the dark green Ralph Lauren running suit he wore. Instead, she'd donned baggy gray sweats, but very good running shoes; her arm hugged her body in a sling. "Cast feeling okay?"

"Yeah, sure." She lifted the sling away from her chest and held it up like a trophy. "This new one's lighter. I can take a shower a lot easier now."

As he'd forcefully done every time a sexual image of Francesca popped into his mind, he banished it. He wasn't allowing *any* fantasies of her these days, especially one of warm water sluicing over that knock-'em-dead body. And there'd been no sexual innuendo from either of them. After the night at Chelsea's gym, Alex had tried even harder to keep things light and maintain some distance from her. He'd sensed a shift in her, too, as if she'd experienced a renewed determination to be just friends. As they neared Park Avenue, they slowed to a jog.

"Want to stop for coffee at Charley's Frog Pond?" she asked.

They'd gone to the local diner once after a run this week and chatted well into the morning; Alex had been late for work for the first time in months. He stalled his answer by checking his watch, trying to decide if he should chance the extra time with her. Sometimes it was better to limit his exposure to her.

"It's okay, though, if you're in a hurry," she said. "I have other things to do."

"You're really bored, aren't you?"

They fell into a fast walk. "It's better since I offered to go into the schools and do some fire-safety education. I'll be at East High this afternoon to talk to their fire fighting class about being a female on the line." She referred to an innovative program—a two-year course in fire fighting for city kids—at her old high school.

"You know, some people would just enjoy the time off."

She threw him a sideways glance. "Oh, look who's talking. Mr. Works-All-Hours Templeton. You were at the warehouse at midnight when the fire broke out."

"Yes, well, there's a lot to do." He slowed to a lazy walk. "Come on, I'll buy you a coffee and maybe even split a plate of your favorite frittata with you."

"Split it?" she said, stopping short with shock. "You mean, like, share my food?"

He laughed and hooked an arm around her neck to give her a brief brotherly hug. "You, lady, are something else."

In Charley's Frog Pond they settled into the booth. Francey studied the little diner. It sported frog wallpaper, toad statues and waitresses who wore frog T-shirts. She loved the place.

"So, what's going on this week with you?" she asked him.

In the month since the fire, they'd gotten into the habit of sharing their schedules. Though Francey had resolved even more strongly after her talk with her dad to be just friends— she hardly noticed anymore what Alex looked like in a pair of shorts and how sexy his mussed hair was when it fell into his eyes—she wasn't able to give up the friendship. Nor did she want to. She liked Alex and was sure she could keep the relationship platonic. She'd done it with men all her life, hadn't she? Jeez, she spent ninety-five percent of her time with men on a professional or friendship level.

"This week?" He sipped his favorite hazelnut coffee. "Well, the warehouse is finally cleaned up, so I'm overseeing its reopening."

"What's going on with the investigation?"

"I'm told they're still interviewing people who had access to the building, neighbors, et cetera. But it's slower than it should be because Zeleny is still out."

"He's home from the hospital, Dylan said."

"I'm glad to hear it."

Impulsively she reached out and touched Alex's hand. She was surprised when he turned his over and linked their fingers. "I hope this is settled soon," she told him.

"So do I." He squeezed her hand, then let it go and reached for his mug. "In the meantime, I have to take a trip to Philadelphia. We're thinking about buying a company there and I'm meeting with the president on Friday."

"Buying a company?"

"Yes. They make the same processing products we do, and if we buy them, we can shift their manufacturing to Rockford and double our output."

"When would you go?"

"Thursday night, probably."

"Philadelphia's a great city."

"Have you been there?"

"Only when I was little. But I've read books about the city and its fire department. My grandparents grew up there. Grandpa took us to see the Fireman's Hall Museum near Independence Square when it opened. I was about five."

The frittata arrived, and Alex placed the plate between them. She looked at it like it was ambrosia. "Try to save some for me, okay?" he teased as she dug in.

She took a big bite of potatoes and hot, spicy sausage. "Oh, this is bliss."

"Tell me about the fire museum. I'm considering staying over the weekend."

She frowned, but caught herself before she said anything. If he wanted to be away for a few days, that was his business. She just hadn't realized how much she'd come to count on seeing him.

"It's an old restored firehouse on Quarry Street. They have all sorts of fire fighting memorabilia—old helmets, fire marks, displays of early fire wagons. I don't remember it all—I've been meaning to go back sometime. Grandpa's father, my great-grandfather, was a Philadelphia firefighter. There's a plaque with his name on it somewhere there, I think."

"Why haven't you gone back as an adult?"

"Too busy, I guess."

"You should go now, when you're off work."

She bit into a piece of Italian bread, heavily buttered. It tasted like Grandma's homemade. "Yeah, I hadn't thought about it in years." Alex was quiet; she looked up from the food. He was staring at her, his brows forming a vee. It was his deep-in-thought look. "What is it?"

"I was trying to decide whether or not to ask you to come with me."

"You seem…troubled by the thought."

He let out a heavy breath, and his face grew serious. It was the expression of guy about to break up with his girlfriend. "I am. I'm struggling very hard to keep this friendship in line, Francesca."

She put down her fork and held his gaze. "So am I."

"Think we could spend a few days together as friends?"

"I'm doing fine with it," she told him. Her conscience taunted that it had been hard for her. But she'd done it. And the thought of getting out of town for a few days rivaled a gourmet meal. And she'd love to see the museum. And Alex was such good company. And…all right, she was making excuses. "It's not the best idea in the world, I guess."

"You're probably right."

She toyed with a crust of bread. "Do you, um, would you *want* me to go with you?"

"Of course I want you to go. It would be fun to have company."

"But?"

"Well, as you said, it might be too much contact. Given the fact that we're trying to keep it cool between us."

She swallowed a protest.

"On the other hand," he said lightly, "we're both adults. We should be able to manage a few days together without ripping each other's clothes off."

A blinding flash of desire swept through Francey as she pictured being naked with Alex. It stunned her into silence.

"Why don't you think about it?" he suggested.

She cleared her throat. "All right. So you're leaving Thursday night?"

"Yes."

"You're probably flying."

"I'd drive if you went with me."

"Okay, I'll think about it. I'll tell you tomorrow morning when we run."

IT FELT RIGHT to be in her uniform again, Francey thought as she perched on the edge of a desk in a classroom at her alma mater, East High School, in front of six firefighters-in-training. They looked so young, so wide-eyed. God, had she ever been this eager? She glanced at Beth Winters, who'd come to address the class about EMS. The two of them had done their presentations and were fielding questions from the students.

A slim, small-boned girl had her hand raised. Francey

wondered if she'd have the strength to lift hoses and other fire-suppression equipment. "Yes?"

"What do you wear to bed at the firehouse?"

Almost every group she'd talked to asked her this question. It seemed silly to Francey. "Same thing the guys do. Gym shorts and a T-shirt."

"Don't the men's wives mind your sleeping in the same room with them?"

"I've been with my group for eight years. I don't think anybody worries about it," she said dryly. "Some of the wives and girlfriends are even glad to see women in the department. They think it civilizes the men."

"All right." The instructor, a smiling, gray-haired volunteer firefighter from a suburb of Rockford, called for their attention. "One more question."

"Did you ever lose anybody in a fire?" a student asked Francey.

"Yes." Francey felt her insides grow cold at the thought of the charred body she'd carried out of a four-alarm fire. "You all will, too. It's horrible. You feel like you should have done something to prevent it." She cleared her throat. "And you can't forget it. The job has a lot of downs—that's the big one."

After the teacher thanked Beth and Francey for coming, they headed to their cars. Francey glanced at her watch. "Do you have plans for dinner, Beth?"

Beth smiled. "It's only four o'clock, Francey."

"Well, we could have a drink first and eat at five."

"Sure, I'm done at the academy for the day. Let's go."

Five minutes later they were seated at Minx's, a cozy, two-room restaurant only a block from Quint/Midi Twelve and a little farther from the academy. Beth sipped a glass of wine, and Francey drank a beer.

"How are you faring without work?" Beth asked.

"Good." She held up her arm. "The cast comes off next

week, so there's a light at the end of the tunnel. I should be back on the line maybe by the end of May.''

"Super. Been working out?''

"Yeah, at Chelsea's. And I've been running every day.''

Beth's auburn eyebrows knitted. "Be careful. Your balance will be off from the arm. I'd hate to see you injured from a fall while you were running.''

"We're taking it easy.''

"We?''

"I'm running with Alex.''

"I thought you weren't going to see him.''

"I wasn't.'' She hesitated. "He suggested we run together, mostly to watch over me, I think. It's worked out well.'' At Beth's frown, Francey added, "We're just friends, Beth. We're not letting it go any further.''

"Good.''

"You don't like him?''

"I have no opinion one way or the other of him. You decided he wasn't good for you. Your reasons are sound. It's important to make rational decisions and stick to them.'' Beth's clinical diagnosis of the situation didn't match the turmoil Francey felt over her decision.

"I think I'm doing that by controlling when and where I see him.''

"What do you mean?''

"He's going to Philadelphia at the end of the week. I'd love to see the fire museum there. We talked about my going with him.'' Francey took a swallow of beer. "I've decided not to go. It would be tempting fate.''

Beth nodded. "Good girl. You can't be too careful.''

Francey usually disagreed with that. She'd always felt Beth Winters was way too cautious about life. "In this case you're right.'' She picked up a menu. "Now, let's eat.''

ALEX SANK BACK into his leather office chair, his mouth agape. "What?"

The fresh-faced investigator who was filling in for Bob Zeleny shifted uncomfortably in his seat, an understudy unsure of his role. "The fire was *not* accidental. We've gone over all the data, and our report will state that it was an intentional fire."

"Arson?"

"Fire Marshal Zeleny will have to determine whether or not there was criminal intent. But the burn pattern and the charring indicate that the fire itself was started on purpose."

"What else could it be if it's not arson?" Richard leaned forward in his seat. His face was drawn and rather pale.

"Again, Fire Marshal Zeleny will have to decide that. I can't say for sure someone wanted to burn the building down. All I can say is that the evidence shows the fire was lit intentionally with a device. We found the remains of some metal that looked like an electric fire starter."

"You must have *some* ideas." Alex struggled to keep the frustration out of his voice.

"I'm sorry, Mr. Templeton. You insisted on an update, and this is all I can give you." The investigator raked a hand through his short crop of hair. "I probably shouldn't have told you this much until the fire marshal draws some conclusions." He stood and snapped his briefcase shut. "Fire Marshal Zeleny will be in touch. We're not going any further because he's expected to be back next week sometime."

After the investigator left, Richard loosened the knot of his tie and swore. "What the hell does this mean?"

Alex rubbed the bridge of his nose where a headache was trying its damnedest to take root. "I can't believe it."

Standing, Richard prowled the office. He'd been tense lately. Alex had played golf with him on Saturday, and his brother had seemed distracted and quiet.

"You doing all right?" Alex asked, studying him.

"What do you mean?"

"I'm concerned about you. You seem anxious. Tense."

"Why wouldn't I be? This goddamned investigation is taking forever."

"Francesca says it's common for investigations to drag on like this."

Richard stopped in his tracks. "Francesca? I thought you'd decided not to see her."

"I'm not seeing her romantically. I'm spending some time with her as a friend."

"Give me a break, Alex. No one wants to be friends with a woman like her."

"A woman like her?" Alex battled his temper. "You haven't even met her."

"She's a woman in an all-male profession." At Alex's raised eyebrows, Richard added, "She sleeps with a group of men every night. How many of them has she boffed, do you think?"

Lurching forward, Alex slapped his hand on the desk. "I don't ever want to hear anything like that out of your mouth again." The buzzer sounded on Alex's phone. He glared at Richard for a second, then picked it up. "Templeton."

"Alex, this is Mike, at the guard station out front. There's a woman here to see you." He lowered his voice. "A real looker. She said if I called you, you'd see her. Name's Francey Cordaro."

"Yes, of course I'll see her." He eyed Richard, who was leaning sulkily on the doorjamb. "Show her back, would you, Mike?"

When Alex replaced the receiver, Richard walked to the window and stared out. After a long minute, he turned to face Alex and jammed his hands in the pockets of his expensive suit. "Look, I'm sorry if I was out of line. Ever since I was little I hated getting you mad. Or disappointing you. This thing with the fire is making me crazy.''

''You're my brother, Richard, and I'm glad you're concerned about me, about the family again. But my relationship with Francesca isn't anything to worry about.'' He glanced to the doorway, then at Richard. ''Let's table it now. She's coming in here any minute.''

As Alex stood and shrugged into his sport coat, Francey appeared in the doorway. She glanced at Richard. ''Excuse me, the guard brought me back here. I didn't mean to intrude.''

''You didn't.'' Alex came out from behind the desk as she entered the room. Richard stepped toward the door. ''I'd like you to meet my brother. Francesca, this is Richard Templeton.''

She held out her hand. ''Nice to meet you.''

Alex watched Richard rein in his surprise. ''You, too, Francesca. I owe you for saving Alex's life.'' He turned to Alex with a give-me-a-break expression on his face. Alex didn't need to be a mind reader to know his brother's thoughts. *How could you be friends with anyone who looked like Francesca?* And God, she looked good tonight. Even the navy slacks of her uniform accented those long legs. And the light blue shirt didn't disguise her full breasts.

''Well, I'll be going.'' Richard turned to Francesca. ''Good to have met you.''

When Richard left, Alex focused on Francesca. ''This is a surprise. I didn't expect to see you. Sit down.''

She took a nearby chair. ''I had dinner with Beth a couple of blocks away and decided to visit you, knowing you'd probably still be working.'' She glanced at her watch. ''It's seven o'clock, Alex.''

He dropped into the chair Zeleny's assistant vacated. ''It's been a hell of a day.''

Francey observed him carefully. ''Want to talk about it?''

He did. Especially to someone who knew the circumstances. Briefly he filled her in on the latest development, then finished, "What could be a reason other than arson that a fire was intentionally set with an electric starter?"

Francey shrugged. "There's a lot of them."

"Give me one."

"Could be a homeless person found a door open and came in for warmth. He started a fire and it got out of hand."

"It wasn't cold that night."

"No, but it had been raining earlier. He'd have been cold and wet from that."

"Still…"

"I've seen it happen. I've actually been called to a fire where that was the case."

Alex leaned back, closed his eyes and massaged the tense muscles in his neck. "Well, that makes me feel a little better." He glanced at her. "You do that a lot."

"What?"

"Make me feel better."

"I do?" Her smile lit up the room.

"Yes." He held her gaze. "Do it again this weekend. Come with me to Philadelphia. Distract me from all of this." He motioned around the room with his hand. "Make me feel better about it."

She hesitated. "Well, it's what I came to talk to you about."

"Say yes." He gave her an ingratiating grin. "Please."

She stared at him. He couldn't read her expression. "I…" Then, almost resignedly, she said, "All right, I'll go."

ALEX CLICKED the shutter of his camera, capturing Francesca's image as she spoke to the curator of Philadelphia's Firemen's Hall Museum. Herb MacGregor, a line firefighter who oversaw the restored firehouse, had snagged her as soon as they walked in. Alex leaned against the wall and watched her chat animatedly with him. She'd been just as energetic and interesting on the trip down. He hadn't laughed so much in years.

"*Where* did you get that book?" he'd asked as she read aloud from a book called *Firefighters: Humorous Stories and Jokes.*

"Dylan brought it over last night."

"It's dumb. Read me some more."

"All right, let me see." She'd flipped through the pages as Alex steered his Porsche down Route 17. He rarely drove long distances anymore, but this trip had proved to be pure pleasure. Francesca had entertained him for three hours, and time had flown by.

"Oh, my God," she'd gasped.

"Come on, woman. Aloud."

"All right." She cleared her throat. "Why do firefighters make such good lovers?"

Alex practically swallowed his tongue to keep from saying, *Because they're just like you.* Interesting. Funny. Beautiful. And sexy as hell. "I, um, don't know. Why?"

"There's a list." She giggled.

"You aren't embarrassed, are you, Francesca?"

"Not after what I hear at the fire station. The guys are like adolescents once they get going. Okay, one—because all firemen are hung like hose." Alex rolled his eyes. "Two—because female firefighters do it on their knees."

Alex laughed. "Now that has possibilities...."

She sniffed in pretended offense. "Number three, because firefighters always come in emergencies." She chuckled, and so did Alex.

Closing the book, she'd stretched the seat belt and swiveled to the side, the new cast hardly an impediment anymore. "Okay, tell me a businessman's joke."

"I don't know any."

"Sure you do. Come on, just one."

Alex strove to remember some of the funny stories and humor that made their way to him. "Oh, yeah, I do know one. It's about a salesman, but all businessmen are basically salesmen, so it counts. These three guys, a doctor, an architect and a salesman, decided to have a contest to see whose dog was the best. They tied up a bag of bones and hung it overhead. The doctor started. He stood up and said, 'Okay, Scalpel, go get 'em.' Scalpel ran to the bag of bones, yanked it down and made a full-size, anatomically correct skeleton. Then the architect got up. 'Okay, Slide Rule, go get 'em.' Slide Rule ran to the bones, got the bag down and built a three-story house out of them. Then the salesman—"

Francesca interrupted, "The businessman."

"The businessman lazed back and said, 'Okay, Expense Account, go get 'em.' Expense Account bounded to the bones, wrestled them down, ate the whole bag, screwed the other two dogs and took the afternoon off."

Francey had giggled again....

From across the room, he saw her approach him. "Firefighter MacGregor has some documents he wants to show me in the back. Do you want to come with me?"

"Is this like a smoke eater's version of showing you his etchings?"

"Stop." She batted his arm playfully. "You wanna come?"

"No, I'll pass." He indicated a small bench to the left. "I'll sit here and make some notes from this morning's meeting."

"All right, but don't go through the displays without me."

"I'll try to stop myself."

When she was gone, he sat and pulled out a notepad. He hadn't had time to record his impressions of the meeting with Scientific Equipment about buying their company. He'd conferred with the president all morning, had lunch with the executives, but the plum of his day had been meeting Francesca at the museum at one o'clock.

The night before, they'd decided he'd keep his appointment in the morning and meet her here for the afternoon.

The night before, when they'd arrived at the Warwick Hotel where he'd reserved a suite for them...

Francesca had stood at the concierge desk and stared at him. "A suite?"

"Yes. I always stay in a suite. It has a couple of bedrooms and a living room and kitchenette."

"Fine. How much is it?"

Alex folded his arms. "Why?"

"Because I want to pay my share."

Struggling to keep a straight face, Alex shook his head. "Francesca, I'm paying for the rooms."

"Not for mine." She turned to the concierge and, in a move that would have made Susan B. Anthony proud, pulled her credit card out of her backpack and handed it to him. When he hesitated, she asked, "You do know how to split the bill, don't you?"

The man had looked at Alex, and when he'd nodded, said graciously, "Yes, of course."

Once they followed the bellman to their suite, Alex faced her. "Is it okay if I get the tip?"

"Sure," she said, "I'll get the next one." When the bellman left, she gave him an arch look. "Don't worry, Alex, I won't embarrass you. I know what a good tip is."

He'd grinned at her. "Sweetheart, the last thing you do is embarrass me. Now, trampling on my ego is another thing. Don't you know the man is supposed to pay?"

"That's Neanderthal, Templeton. This is the nineties." Then her violet eyes grew huge and serious. "I didn't think, though.... Did I—downstairs, were you embarrassed?"

He crossed to her and ran his knuckles down her cheek.

"Not in the least. But I insist I treat for dinner tomorrow night. I've got a special place in mind."

"I never refuse a free meal." Then she drew back. "But how about tonight? I'm starved."

"Surprise, surprise." He picked up the room service menu. "Here. Order for us both while I shower."

He'd gone into one of the bedrooms, shaking his head. She was simply enchanting. Everything she did pleased him. He'd purposely quelled the little jolt of pain that shot through him when he admitted how much he liked her. He wasn't going to brood because he couldn't have more. He was going to enjoy what he had.

They'd eaten rare, juicy steaks and baked potatoes with gobs of sour cream, drank a bottle of dry red wine and watched some TV before they turned in. If he'd gone to bed alone and frustrated, it was worth having her with him. He'd slept surprisingly well and looked forward to the day with her....

"Sorry I was so long." She glanced at his pad. "No notes?"

He smiled. "Oh, I guess I was just thinking. Come on, I'm dying to see this place."

She angled her head at him. "Are you really?"

"Sure, why not?"

"Why are you? Firefighting isn't an interest of yours."

He stood and tugged on a lock of her hair. "No, but it's one of yours. So I want to see this museum."

Smiling at the compliment, she headed across the room. The wall opposite the entryway was long and curved. Painted on it was a mural of an early bucket brigade—life-size images of firemen, buckets, wagons and horses, all silhouetted in black. Beneath the painting was a glass-enclosed case of fire artifacts. She painstakingly read each plaque.

"What would these be used for?" Alex asked, pointing to a group of fire marks.

"They indicated which houses had insurance and which company would reimburse the fire department."

Down a small incline was the bay that housed the old-time trucks. A brass pole was in the corner. "Ah, the famous fire pole," Alex said, running his hand over it.

"Yeah. An accident waiting to happen."

"What do you mean?"

"The first fire poles were wood. Splinters were murder."

"Is that why they got rid of them?"

"No, 'cause next they went to brass. They stopped using those because of the sprains firefighters got when they slid down." She shook her head. "I guess the designers of fire-houses thought it would be quicker to use a pole, but waking up from a dead sleep and reacting in minutes is tough enough. To slide down a pole from the second floor—it's nuts."

"Get over there by it, I'll take your picture."

Laughing, she scooted over to the pole, grasped it and wrapped her leg around it—her long, better-than-a-Rockette's leg, outlined perfectly in black spandex leggings. He groaned and snapped the picture.

Patiently she led Alex around the old pumpers and ladder trucks, pushed the More Information button every time she saw one and listened attentively to each speech.

"I didn't know Dalmatians were firehouse dogs because they got along with horses," she said. "I wonder if Dylan knows that."

Dylan, again. Alex was getting to hate a man he'd never met. "Dylan?"

"Yeah, he has this beautiful Dalmatian named Quint."

"Quint, after your…rig, right?"

She threw a friendly arm around his back. "You catch on fast, buddy."

He squeezed her firm waist through her pink oversize shirt and felt his heart rate speed up. "I try, Francesca."

Alex admired the architecture of the restored firehouse as they trekked upstairs. Everything was brick; two circular staircases led to what simulated old-fashioned firehouse quarters, along with other displays. Covering the wall of one staircase was a huge mural of a famous Philadelphia fire. Alex snapped a photo of Francesca studying it, as if she was picturing being there. As he stared at the raging flames and clouds of dense smoke, he tried to imagine her in the midst of it. Out of nowhere, a blast of fear hit him like a sucker punch to the gut. The danger she faced daily was staggering. It took him the climb of the rest of the steps to get over it.

When they reached the top, Francesca turned to check out the window. A huge half-moon of stained glass separated the two staircases. It was an explosion of colors—cherry red, indigo blue, shades of yellows all fanning out as a background of fire.

"Oh, Alex, look!" He stared at the design. Woven into the glass were firefighters in the act of various rescues. In the center, a man carried a young child. To the right was a raised ladder with a firefighter at the top and one at the bottom. Opposite that, several men aimed a stream of water at the fire, shown bursting everywhere in the background.

"It's breathtaking," she said, staring at the artwork as if it were the Sistine Chapel ceiling.

Throughout the afternoon, Alex took several shots of her, mostly funny ones—perched on top of a quilted, circular ring that looked like a trampoline but was one of the original nets used to rescue victims; sidling up to a dummy of a firefighter who appeared to be talking to her; seated at the smooth oak desk in the simulated chief's office wearing an antique helmet; at the highly polished wheel of a fire-boat reconstruction. She tried to take pictures of him, but he refused. She teased him about fearing he couldn't measure up to the dummy firefighters' muscles.

When they entered the last room, Francesca's enthusiasm

was still high. It was a hodgepodge of displays—sprinklers, posters, ancient fire hydrants, or plugs, as they were called. She stopped short in front of one of the walls. A quote from Shakespeare's *Julius Caesar* was scripted in almost foot-tall letters. "The coward dies a thousand deaths, the valiant dies but once."

Underneath it were hundreds of small brass plaques. Thoughtfully Francesca stared at the wall. "This is what I remembered about my great-grandfather."

There's a plaque there somewhere with his name on it.

"I didn't know he died in a fire," Alex said.

She nodded and edged closer to the wall. He followed her. Starting at the left, she read each nameplate. Alex looked over her shoulder, noting the repetitive dates on several of them. More than one firefighter died in many of the fires. He felt his stomach knot.

When she reached the middle, she lifted her hand and touched one of the small plates. It read, "Lieutenant Francis Benjamin Cordaro, 7/17/21." A quick scan told Alex no one had died with him.

Alex squeezed her arm. "Do you know how it happened?"

"He went in after some of his brothers. Two had gone down."

"They get out?"

She nodded. "Yes, but he didn't."

"He was a real hero." Alex looked at her. He was entranced by her shining eyes and the reverence on her face. "You all are." And he meant it. He'd never realized before just how much.

Her gaze drifted to a poem on the wall above the plaques. "Not everybody thinks so."

He tracked her gaze. Framed and hung was a poem called "What Firemen Face…"

"Most people think like that poem says—firefighters are a bunch of uneducated, beer-swilling jerks."

"Not most people." Though, Alex was ashamed to admit, he *had* believed the stereotype of a typical firefighter before he'd been rescued by one.

He inched closer to read the poem. It reflected the popular prejudice about how firemen earned their pay—hours with no calls, night shifts they slept through, many days off at a time. Then it reflected the horrors they'd all faced at one time or another—ice-covered clothes and equipment, volcanic heat, people trapped in burning buildings or crushed cars, losing a child...

Alex's throat closed as he read the words. He pictured the woman beside him on a spongy roof or inside a building, timbers falling around her, or trying to extricate someone pinned by a steering wheel. Images right out of a horror film raced through his mind, immobilizing him. When he could, he turned to her. "These things have happened to you, haven't they?"

Her violet eyes filled with feeling. "Yes." She pointed to one line about a victim trapped in a car. "Just last year, on a routine EMS call, I climbed in the car to administer some first aid—the guy was bleeding too much to wait to get him out. When I got in, the vehicle shifted, and I was trapped until we could get more help. The man—" she looked at Alex "—he died anyway. I was in there with him for a long time when he was dead."

Alex reached out and pulled her to him. She went willingly. "It was awful. The smell of blood and urine. Death literally staring me in the face. I thought I was going to be sick. Afterward, my dad and Dylan tried to get me to talk about it...but I couldn't." She burrowed into Alex. "I've never told anyone about it till now."

He held on to her tightly. "Thanks for sharing it with me," he said after a moment, his lips in her hair. Inside, he battled the flood of emotion he felt for the woman he held close. "Do you have any idea how special you are?"

She shook her head but stayed where she was. "I'm not."

"Oh, yes, sweetheart, you are. You most definitely are."

CHAPTER SEVEN

"COME ON, hit me, Francey, baby." Her brother Nicky held her gaze as Francey shot him a card across the scarred oak table. With the ease of a hustler, she dealt three cards each to the other guys in her monthly poker group.

"Aw, hell," Ed Knight said when he examined his hand.

"You always did have a good poker face," Gus Cordaro, Francey's grandfather, told her captain dryly. Francey guessed that someday her dad would have her grandpa's full head of gray hair. She wished he would also have Gus's twinkling brown eyes, but Ben's attitude toward life was far too sober.

Tossing his cards into the pile, Ed scraped back his chair and stood. "I'm folding, anyway. Why prolong the agony? Anybody want a beer?"

"There's more in the cooler I brought over from next door." Jake Scarlatta pointed to the ice chest that sat against the wall of the den. He turned to Ben. "Thanks for switching to your place at the last minute."

Ben glanced up from his hand. "No problem. I know what it's like to have a teenage daughter." He winked at Francey. "They take over the house."

Jake laughed. "Yeah, but I'll bet Francey never threw a makeup party. Hell, there were a dozen seventeen-year-olds putting all this goop on their faces in my living room. No wonder her mother wouldn't let her have the party at *her* condo."

"Are you kidding?" Tony said, studying his hand. "We

could hardly get France to wear a dress to church on Sunday.''

Francey rolled her eyes. ''See what you missed by raising a tomboy, Dad?'' Though Francey had, she admitted to herself, considered using some makeup lately. God, what had gotten into her?

Alex. Who hadn't called or come over in three whole days. It was the longest she'd gone without seeing him since she'd come home from the hospital after the warehouse fire.

And she missed him. A lot.

Let it go, girl. You know it's for the best. Her mother had known that about her father. And look what happened because Diana gave in.

''Francey, you with us?'' Nicky asked.

''Sure.''

''Your bet, honey,'' Ben told her.

''Oh.'' She squinted at her hand and tossed in a chip. ''I call.''

The bet went around the table again. When Sean O'Roarke, an older, more wiry version of his son, Dylan, raised a quarter, Francey folded. ''I'm out.'' So were Jake, Nicky and Ben.

As the two remaining players studied their cards, Francey leaned back in her chair and thought about Alex again. Something had happened to him at the museum. After several hours of sight-seeing, they'd gone to the hotel to relax. Alex had been quiet as they had a snack and watched the news. When they'd changed for dinner and she'd come out of her bedroom, his reaction had bolstered her feminine pride, especially given his unusual mood. His jaw had dropped, and for a moment he was speechless.

''That outfit ought to be illegal,'' he'd finally said, nodding to the knee-length black lace dress she'd bought to go to the annual fireman's ball last year. The neckline scooped just low enough in the front to hint at her curves, and the back hugged her fanny nicely. She'd matched it with not-too-uncomfortable heels.

"Hey, rule number three—no flattery."

Shadows had crossed his face, but he shook them off. "It's only flattery if it isn't true. I'd better go get a stick or something. I'll be beating off the guys at L'Auberge."

"Well, get one for me, too," she'd joked. "For the women. I'll need one." Francey eyed the way his charcoal suit was cut to fit his wide shoulders and lean frame. "Nice rags, Templeton."

He'd been less moody at dinner. After a couple of glasses of wine, he'd loosened up, encouraged her to try new dishes and danced with her to the soft rock band the restaurant featured. She remembered how big and masculine his hand felt on her back and how his cologne sent tingles of awareness through her. How he'd held her hand tightly to help support the cast.

It was during one particularly slow song that he drew back and stared at her. His eyes were forest green, their pupils dilated. His lips were a thin, hard line. "I think we'd better go."

She'd been so lost in the sensation of being held against his rock-hard chest that she'd stared at him with a glazed expression. Finally recognizing his reaction to their close-ness—and her own—she'd murmured, "Yeah, I guess we'd better…"

"France, come on, get with it." Nicky's annoyed voice halted her daydreaming.

She scanned the table; all the guys were staring at her. "Oh, sorry."

She stayed with them through two rousing games of seven card stud and one of follow the queen. When she raked in the last pot, Gus said, "That's my girl. I knew you'd do me proud when you were five and I taught you this game."

"What am I, Grandpa—chopped liver?" Nicky asked.

Tony grinned at Nicky's perpetual harangue about being the middle child who never got enough attention.

"*You're* in the hole, kid," Gus said easily. "Nothin' there to be proud about."

In the next hand Francey folded early, so her mind zeroed right back to Alex again, like a laser finding its target.

When they'd returned to the Warwick Hotel, Alex had said he was tired and disappeared into his bedroom. Francey changed into sweats. She was edgy and anxious—like her skin didn't fit right, Grandma used to say—and she knew she wouldn't sleep. She'd flicked on the TV. One of the movie offerings was *When Harry Met Sally*. Against her better judgment, she chose it. She told herself she'd only watch a little of the film about best friends becoming lovers. Because she wanted to stretch out, she opened up the sofa bed and got on top of it with pillows and the remote.

After a half hour, when Francey was glued to the story, Alex wandered out of the bedroom, wearing low-slung navy sweatpants. And nothing else. His chest was sprinkled with dark blond hair over a road map of muscles.

She quelled the reaction to gape. "Can't sleep?"

"No." He eyes flared when he saw the sofa bed was open. "I was going to watch TV with you, but…"

She patted the mattress beside her. "Don't be silly. I pulled out the bed because it was more comfortable." When he just stood there, she grinned mischievously. "I'll push it back in if you don't think you can control yourself on a bed with me."

He didn't smile.

"Alex? What is it?"

His look was dark and brooding. "Nothing." He crossed to the side table and poured himself a generous Scotch. "Want something?"

"No, thanks."

He returned to the bed, eased onto it, lay back against the

pillows and stared at the TV. When he recognized the movie, he glanced sideways at her. "Why are you watching this?"

"It was on." She handed him the remote. "Here, change it."

Immediately he switched to a talk show. After a few tense moments, they laughed at one of Letterman's jokes, and Francey felt herself relax.

Too much. The next thing she'd known, the sun was filtering through the windows, and her head was pillowed on a naked male chest that felt warm and—

"Damn it, Francey, get with it," Nicky scolded for the third time and muttered under his breath, "girls…"

She closed her eyes briefly, feeling her face flush as if she'd gotten caught parking with a guy in the back seat of his car. "Deal me out of this one. I've got a call to make."

Tony stood when she did. "I'm out, too. I told Erin I'd be home early because the baby isn't feeling well."

"Anything serious?" Ben asked.

"Nah, just a cold."

Francey left the table as Tony got his coat and said his goodbyes. She couldn't concentrate on poker. She wanted to know what was wrong with Alex. In the kitchen she grabbed a beer and stood in front of the open window, letting the breeze cool her face, looking for answers in the backyard where she'd played as a child. Things had been easier then.

"Hey, kid, you all right?" Tony leaned against the doorjamb, jacket on, jangling car keys in his hand.

She glanced at him. "Yeah. I hope the baby's okay."

He crossed to her, placed his hand on her neck and squeezed. The brotherly gesture soothed her. "I'm here, you know, if you need to talk. It must be hard for you to be off work."

"It's not that." She turned to him, stood on her toes and kissed his cheek. "Go home to Erin. She needs you."

He kissed her hair. "The offer stands, anytime."

When Tony left, Francey sipped her beer and thought about Tony and his family. She wondered if she'd ever have that—a man she could care about as much as her brother cared about his wife. A man who interested her as much as Alex...

On Saturday morning, they'd ignored the fact that they'd slept together Friday night and avoided mentioning that, obviously, after Francey had fallen asleep, Alex had turned off the lights and TV and returned to the sofa bed—instead of going to his own. And on the long drive home, he'd been so withdrawn she danced around his mood for a while and finally fell silent.

Torn, Francey's gaze traveled to the phone. She'd called him four times since they'd gotten back to Rockford. Twice she'd left messages. It was obvious he was avoiding her. Why?

At her house Saturday night, he'd insisted on walking her to the door, chivalrous as always. After stowing her things inside, she'd turned to him. "You want to come in?"

He checked his watch. "No, I don't think so."

"Got a hot date?"

Anger turned his eyes dark, as if she'd said something inappropriate.

"Alex, what is it?"

"Nothing."

"You seem...angry."

He'd stared at her; the wind had ruffled his hair, and her hands itched to smooth it. "Give me a hug goodbye."

She cocked her head. They'd been good about limiting physical contact—up until this weekend, that is. There'd been a lot of touching in Philadelphia. It had seemed natural enough, but it had made her skin sizzle at times, so it had probably been a bad idea. At her hesitation, he said, "Damn it, Francesca, you slept in my arms last night. What's a little hug?"

Even though it was awkward with the cast, Francey reached up and wound her arms around his neck. God, he always felt so good. He drew her to him, his strong body seeking hers. Their chests, hips and legs were in perfect alignment, like they'd been designed for each other. She felt his lips in her hair, then he squeezed tight and let go. "I can't run for the next few days," he said, stepping back.

Surprise momentarily silenced her. "Oh, okay."

"And I'll be busy at work, so don't plan on meeting me at Chelsea's."

That did it. "Alex, something's wrong. Tell me."

He shook his head. "We'll talk in a few days."

She reached out and gripped his arm. "Alex—"

Firmly he'd put his fingers to her mouth. But the quelling gesture became a caress. His thumb swept her lips, and she felt a strong surge of desire all the way to her toes. "Shh," he'd said hoarsely. "In a few days."

And then he was gone...

And he hadn't called. She'd tried to call him a couple of times, left a message, but still he hadn't called back.

Francey crossed to the phone, punched out his number and waited through six rings. "This is Alex Templeton. Leave a message."

"Alex," she said into the mouthpiece, "it's Francey again. It's about nine. I'm at Dad's but I'll be home by ten. Call me back tonight." She hesitated. "Please. We need to talk."

Slowly she hung up the receiver.

Turning, she came face-to-face with her father, who loomed in the kitchen doorway. "I came out to see if you were all right." He scowled at the phone. "What's going on, France?"

Before she could answer, the back door flew open. Francey's grandmother burst through it, saying, "And then he tripped over his feet, trying to get another glimpse of you."

Behind her was Diana. "You're exaggerating, Grace. Men haven't tripped over their feet for me in—"

Both women stopped abruptly when they saw Francey and her father.

"Ben, Francey, what are you doing here?" Diana asked.

Francey glanced at her father. His face was granite-hard. His eyes burned with hostility. "I could ask you the same question."

Grace said, "I had dinner with Diana at Antoinetta's. We came back here so I could show her the new dress I made." She raised her chin. "I thought you and Gus were next door at Jake's playing poker."

"It got changed to here. Jessie preempted us with some party." Ben's eyes fastened on Diana, who looked soft and feminine in various shades of pink. "Since when did you two start having cozy suppers together?"

Very deliberately Diana stepped in front of Grace. "Don't be angry with your mother for seeing me, Ben. I asked her to go out."

"Diana, we don't have to defend—" Grace began.

Gently Diana put a hand on Grace's arm. "No sense in his being angry with us both."

Ben's hands were clenched at his sides, and his chest expanded as if he was hefting hose. "I'm not angry at you, Diana."

She glanced pointedly at his fists.

He said, "I don't care enough about you anymore to be angry."

Diana recoiled as if he'd struck her. Her face went ashen.

Francey swallowed hard. She leaned into the wall and felt the phone at her back. The phone she'd just used to call Alex. Suddenly she was besieged with regret for having made the contact. Before her was living proof of why she shouldn't be calling Alex, shouldn't be thinking of him at all.

WHAT A SAP you are, Alex chided himself as he sat on Francesca's porch Tuesday night. *You're acting like a lovesick teenager over a girl who won't give you the time of day.* Damn it. This was as bad as his impulse to crawl onto the sofa bed with her Friday night. He'd given in to that bit of foolishness because he'd come to accept the fact that he'd never have the opportunity to hold her through the night again.

To distract himself, he studied the yard. Yellow and white flowers had been planted along the walk and in fat boxes on the porch. Their scent permeated the night air. She'd obviously been busy for the past three days. Of course. He'd never met a woman who had more trouble sitting still. Or a braver woman. Or a more admirable one. Or one he wanted more.

"Which is what brought you here in the first place, jerk," he muttered.

He checked his watch again. He could leave before she got home. Wait. Think this over. But he'd been pondering it for three days with more seriousness than international peace talks. And tonight was the last straw. The photos of the museum trip had come back. He'd sat at his kitchen table, in the bright overhead light so he could see them clearly, and studied each one, alternately laughing at the poses she'd struck and wanting to put his fist through the wall because he couldn't have her—*really* have her. It was his startling anger that spurred him to action. Never in his life had he reacted like that to a woman. Then, when she'd called, and he'd been reduced to listening to her voice on the machine several times, he'd decided to take matters in hand.

And so he sat on her porch at nine o'clock at night, waiting for her to return from her father's so she could break his heart. Inside, her dog scratched and whimpered at the front window, sensing someone was out here. A door slammed across the street and a pair of teenagers exited a beat-up Pontiac, giggling and razzing each other. Then he saw them stop and kiss in the driveway, a long, full-body smooch. Alex turned his head away.

The Red Devil pulled in next to his Porsche ten minutes later. Francesca killed the engine, climbed out of her truck and headed toward him. "Alex, hi." She was a little breathless and a lot gorgeous. In the light from the front porch, he could see she wore a pink T-shirt, broken-in jeans and Docksides without socks. She'd tied her hair on top of her head, like she did when they worked out, and soft tendrils framed her face, accenting her wide, translucent eyes.

"You got my message?" she asked.

He nodded. "All of them."

"Finally decided to talk to me?"

He smiled in spite of the battle waging in his heart. Most women he knew would dance around the issue, or pout, but not Francesca. Cut to the quick, that was her. "Can we go inside? I *do* want to talk to you, and it's getting chilly out here." He scowled. "You should have worn a jacket."

At her door, Killer greeted them with barking and nipping at their feet. Francesca nuzzled her dog, then disappeared into the kitchen to send him out to the backyard. While she was gone, Alex stood by the fireplace, staring at the Manwaring print over the mantel. A birthday present. Like the lacy purple underwear she'd received. He wondered if she'd worn it yet. And for whom.

"Can I get you something?" He pivoted; she stood about ten feet away, holding an ice bucket. Her smile was unsure as she nodded to a cabinet to the right of the fireplace. "I bought some Johnny Walker."

For me. How ironic. "Sure."

She made quick work of pouring him a drink and handed him the glass. "Want to sit?"

"No, but you go ahead."

She took a chair opposite the couch and stared at him. Those violet eyes sucked him in like a whirlpool.

"I'm going away tomorrow," he said simply.

"Again?"

"Yes."

"Where?"

"There's a trade show in Boston. It will be good for the business for me to meet with the reps." At her puzzled expression, he explained, "The people who sell our products."

"How long does it last?"

"Until Friday."

"You'll be back then?"

"No, I'm staying over the weekend. I phoned some people I knew from school who still live there. We're getting together."

Frowning, she plucked at a pillow on the sofa. "Oh. Sort of like *The Big Chill*."

"Yes, I guess."

She raised her arm and smiled weakly. "I'm getting my cast off tomorrow."

"Terrific."

"What's this all about Alex? Going away again. Not returning my calls. The deep freeze for three days after. Just tell me what's happening. Be honest with me."

He hadn't expected it to be this hard. But the catch in her voice, the frown wrinkling her lovely brow disconcerted him. Taking a deep breath, he said, "This isn't working for me, Francesca."

"What isn't?"

"This situation. Between you and me." He took a swallow of Scotch. It helped. "I know I said we'd be friends. That I could do it. And I've tried. But it's not working...for me."

"This comes as a surprise."

"Does it?"

"Um, yes. I thought…I thought we *were* friends."

"Oh, we are."

She frowned. He was being clumsy about this. Not his usual glib style.

He plunged in, his stomach churning like it had the first time he scuba dived. "We *are* friends, but it's not enough for me anymore."

She stared at him, shredding his control with a look.

It firmed his resolve. "I thought I could do it. But I can't. I know I said I could, but I was wrong."

God, this wasn't coming out right. He couldn't express the revelation he'd had at the fire museum when he realized the danger she was in on the job. It was really quite simple— his recognition of her vulnerability drove home how precious she was. And it made him want her more. It made him *yearn* for her. A romantic word for a painful feeling.

"I'm not saying this well, I guess. The point is, I *am* your friend. I cherish spending time with you. I look forward to seeing you every day." He set the glass on a nearby table and crossed to her. Reaching down, he drew her up to stand before him, so lovely, so much what he wanted in a woman that it weakened him. "But I want more."

He saw her swallow hard.

Slowly he lifted his hand and tucked a tendril of hair behind her ear, letting his knuckles graze her cheek.

She shivered. Leaned into his caress.

"I want to be your friend, Francesca, but I want to be your lover, too. I'm attracted to you. I want to act on that attraction." He could hear the huskiness in his voice. "I want to touch you the way a man touches a woman."

Her eyes dilated and her breath speeded up.

But she stepped back. "We discussed this, Alex."

That was true. Though she showed all the signs of arousal, he was, after all, the one to renege on their agreement. So he stepped back, too. "I know we did. I was wrong to think

I could keep this relationship just friends. It's why I haven't called you. It's why I'm going away for a few days. To try to get some perspective on this. When I'm with you, these feelings intensify." He cleared his throat. "And now it hurts to be with you."

She looked stricken. "I'm sorry I've hurt you."

He didn't answer her. Instead, he memorized the slight upturn of her nose, how her bottom lip was a little fuller than the top, the dimple in her cheek when she frowned.

"These people you're seeing?" she finally said. "Are they all from Harvard?"

"Yes."

"Frat brothers?"

He nodded. "Some."

"Women, too? Who you knew back then?"

His heart lurched. Her question confirmed she felt something for him—something beyond friendship. He guessed he knew all along she did. But to hear her admit it… "If you're asking if I'm going to rekindle old flames, the answer is, I don't know. I am going out with Suzanne on her yacht Saturday."

"Suzanne?"

"The woman I was engaged to. She married a few years after we broke our engagement, but she's divorced now."

"How convenient."

He smiled sadly.

"I'll be staying at the Hyatt in downtown Boston. If you need me, I'll be there until Friday."

She didn't ask where he'd be staying after that.

Shoving his hands in his pockets, he sighed. "I guess I'll be going."

She stared at him, stood stone-statue still.

He studied her for a minute, bombarded by the reality of not seeing her again, of the fact that she didn't ask him to stay, didn't throw herself at him and tell him she'd been wrong, ask him not to go Boston, not to go to another woman.

And because the pain of her rejection was unlike any he'd ever known, he reached for her. "Oh, hell, what do I have to lose?"

As he'd done a thousand times in his fantasies, he framed her face with his hands and lowered his mouth to hers. The touch electrified him.

She hesitated a moment, then leaned forward. It was all the encouragement he needed. He grasped her shoulders, pulled her to him, molded them hip to hip, chest to breast and demanded entrance to her mouth. She opened for him like a flower blooming before the sun. And, God, she tasted honey-sweet, like he knew she would. He ravaged her lips while his hands slid around and cupped her bottom. She moaned, and he let himself go, thinking if this was all he was ever going to have of her, he'd take it greedily.

But before it became irrevocable, before something happened that he knew was an unconscionable betrayal of their friendship, he pulled back. Somewhere in the passion-drugged haze of his mind, he knew she didn't really want this. For a minute she swayed into him, her eyes closed. He righted her, and she looked at him.

Though the fist of desire lodged in his throat, he managed to whisper around it, "Think of me, Francesca." And with one last brush of his thumb over her lips, he left her.

"GODDAMN SON OF A BITCH." Francey slammed the silverware drawer shut and swore some more. She was wired and tense and mad as hell. She hadn't fallen asleep until dawn; she'd dragged herself out of bed at nine o'clock this morning only because Dylan was taking her to the doctor's to get her cast off and to lunch afterward.

Think of me, Francesca.

Damn him. *Damn* him. She'd thought of nothing else for

twelve hours. She leaned against the kitchen counter, closed her eyes and rubbed them wearily.

Please, God, don't let me do this, she prayed, remembering her mother and father facing each other in the kitchen last night. Remembering the tangible pain arcing between them.

But she couldn't stop the images of Alex. The kiss was branded on her mind. She lifted a finger to her lips. She could still feel his mouth on hers. She could still feel his arms around her and his arousal pressing insistently against her.

She wanted him. This wasn't the first time she'd admitted that, but around two in the morning, she came to terms with the depth and breadth and all-consuming nature of her feelings. Around four she found the strength to tell herself it didn't matter, that involvement with a man from Diana's world wasn't worth the risk. And she feared that, like Diana with her father, he'd never be able to accept her job as a firefighter. He seemed to have a Victorian-male protective streak that would prevent that.

The bell chimed and, grateful for the distraction, she strode to the door and opened it.

"Hi, doll, ready to get sprung from that cast?"

She smiled at her friend. "Yeah, Dylan, come in."

"It's turned nasty out there," he said, shaking rain from his black hair and plucking at his navy slicker. "You need a coat."

She grabbed a red windbreaker from the closet and tugged it on. She could get into jackets more easily with the lighter cast but still had trouble with the zippers.

Hey, if you need any help with zippers and stuff, let me know.

"You okay?" Dylan asked.

"Yeah."

He tipped her chin and studied her face, a brotherly gesture that made her eyes sting. "Didn't get much sleep last night?"

She shook her head.

"Hot date?"

Tears welled in her eyes. God, she really *must* be tired. She couldn't remember the last time she'd cried.

"France, what is it?"

"Nothing. Let's go get this thing off."

Dylan accepted her reluctance to talk and baited her with firefighter trivia on the trek to the doctor's office. As the windshield wipers beat rhythmically and the rain spattered on the roof, Francey began to relax.

"True or false—the reason Irishmen became firefighters was because many American businesses refused to hire Irish immigrants."

"True."

He smiled. "Right. What's the ratio of career versus volunteer firefighters in the U.S.?"

Francey sighed. "Two to one, volunteers higher?"

"Nope, two hundred and sixty thousand career, seven hundred and ninety-five thousand volunteer. A little more than three to one. All right, last question," he said as they pulled into the doctor's parking lot. "What's the highest award for valor in the Chicago Fire Department?"

"The Lambert Award."

"No fair. You've been reading Jake's books again."

She tried to smile but failed.

Shedding the cast, at least, was a relief. She was grateful that most of her convalescence was over. But on the way to DeLuca's Diner—a restaurant that used to belong to a good friend of Jake's before he left town and was now a firefighters' hangout—she listened halfheartedly while Dylan entertained her with stories about the recent events in the department. She paid more attention when he told her that any day now he expected the results of the lieutenant's exam he'd taken.

After their food was delivered and they began eating, Dylan gave an exasperated sigh. "Okay, I've done everything I can think of to make you smile. You got the cast off, and even that didn't cheer you up. What's goin' on?"

Toying with her club sandwich, she shook her head. "Nothing."

"Francey, come on, you're not eating. The world must be about to end." He scowled. "No one's sick, are they? Gus or Grace? Your dad?"

"No, no, nothing that big."

Dylan leaned back, his Tom Cruise eyes sparkling with awareness. "Aha, it's love."

"Love?"

"Yeah, I recognize the signs."

"You've never been in love in your life."

"Doesn't mean I don't recognize it when I see it."

"I'm *not* in love." Even to her own ears, the words sounded pathetically whiny.

Dylan watched her.

"It's Alex," she said.

Thankfully, Dylan didn't tease. "What about him?"

"He wants more."

"Honey, he's wanted more from day one."

"I know. But now he won't settle for less."

"It was only a matter of time, France," Dylan said, taking a big bite of his hamburger. "It was bound to get to this point."

She stared at him. "Why? Things were fine the way they were."

"Were they?"

"What do you mean?"

He shook his head. "Women! Do you have any idea how

much you talk about Alex Templeton? And the way your
eyes glow when you do it?''

"You're such a romantic, Dylan. You don't see things
clearly."

"Yes, I do. It's okay if you don't choose to act on your
feelings, but it'd help to admit them."

"I can't act on them. My father did and he was miserable.
I think he's *still* suffering from it."

"You and Alex aren't your parents."

"I know, but it's too great a risk."

"Life without risks isn't worth living."

"Spoken like a true firefighter."

He grinned.

"I'm scared."

Dylan threw up his hands. "This from one of six women
out of five hundred firefighters in the Rockford Fire Department? This from a person who faces flames without a
quiver? I'm shocked."

"Emotional risks are worse."

"No, they're just different."

"What do you think I should do?"

He arched a brow. "If you want him, take him."

"As simple as that."

"Uh-huh. It'll work itself out."

"Since when did you get so smart about all this stuff?"
she asked, annoyed.

"Since I dated a psychologist," he said.

She smiled begrudgingly. "You're something else."

Dylan shrugged, ate six French fries at once and was
about to make a retort when his eyes strayed to the door.
And went as cold as frozen steel. When Francey tracked his
gaze, she saw that Beth Winters had entered DeLuca's with
one of the battalion chiefs from the academy. Francey waved
to her. Beth frowned; she turned, said something to her com-
panion, then headed their way.

"Damn," Dylan muttered.

Beth reached their table. "Hi, Francey." She smiled at her friend, then tilted her head, glancing at Dylan. "O'Roarke."

"*Ms.* Winters."

Pointedly ignoring Dylan, Beth turned to Francey and smiled warmly. "Got it off, I see."

"This morning."

"Happy?"

"Yeah."

"Good. Well, I won't interrupt your lunch. I'll call you."

Dylan watched her go, his brow furrowed, his usually smiling mouth a grim line. "I can't for the life of me see how you and Lizzie Borden are friends."

"And I can't understand this antagonism between you two."

His eyes were flinty. It was so unlike Dylan that Francey knew better than to tease him. "It goes way back. I don't want to talk about it." He glanced at the clock. "Look, I'm going over to Dutch Towers to carry some boxes out to the storage bins for Mrs. MacKenzie. Want to come?"

Francey smiled at her friend. He spent a lot of his off time at the senior citizens' complex reading to the older people, helping out with chores. Francey wasn't quite sure why, but she thought it had something to do with his grandmother, who'd died when Dylan was young. That and Beth Winters were the only things Dylan wasn't anxious to talk about.

"Sure, I'll come with you."

A half hour later, in Mrs. MacKenzie's living room, Francey waited as Dylan carted boxes to the basement and the old woman fixed them tea. The apartment smelled of yeast and spaghetti sauce. It was neat and clean, no dust on the framed photos spread over her coffee table. They were of her eight kids and her husband of fifty years, who'd been dead a decade. Francey was examining a picture of the young bride and groom on their wedding day when the old woman brought in the tea. "Looking at my Rory?"

Francey put the picture down. "He was a handsome devil."

Mrs. MacKenzie's eyes lit from within. "He was a devil in more ways than one." She handed Francey a cup and gazed lovingly at the picture. "I was four months along in that photo."

Francey choked on the tea she'd just sipped; it spilled all over her face and shirt. Wiping her mouth she said, "Four months *along?*"

"Yes, dear. You know, I was expecting."

"Mrs. MacKenzie!"

"I had to get him to marry me somehow." The old woman settled herself on a faded flowered divan.

Francey sank down on a rocker across from her. "He didn't want to marry you?"

"No. And he wouldn't have if I hadn't seen to it. He didn't have any prospects. He thought I deserved better than a man who dropped out of school in the sixth grade to support his family."

"What happened?"

"I didn't agree." Her smile gave Francey a glimpse of the beautiful young woman she must have been. "I won. We had nine children."

"Nine? I though you had eight."

"I lost one. Miscarriage at six months. Almost killed my Rory."

"You had a good marriage, then?"

Her eyes got dreamy. "Yes, and every time he sent me red roses on our anniversary—one for each year we were together—I reminded him of how I had to trick him into marriage."

"Did he ever regret it? Marrying you when...when he knew he shouldn't."

"Of course he should have, dear. When you love someone, there aren't any shouldn'ts."

FRANCEY PROWLED the house for two days like a caged lion.

On Wednesday night she sat in her living room, haunted by the hurt look in Alex's eyes when he'd told her he wanted more from her. *When I'm with you, these feelings intensify. And now, it hurts to be around you.*

That was it, she told herself. Remember the pain they could cause each other—*were* causing each other. Just like Dad and Diana.

But in bed, as she tried to sleep, the memory of that kiss was so vivid she felt like she was reliving it, the way his lips took hers as if he had every right to her, the way she'd responded. She'd been surprised at his forceful passion. Excited by it.

"So what?" she said aloud. "That's not enough. It wasn't for my parents—look what happened to them."

Thursday morning she ran and worked out with weights at Chelsea's gym. She picked a time when she could avoid seeing anyone she knew. She needed to think. At the gym, she recalled Alex with Ezzy. *I hardly notice anymore when women swoon at my feet.* Hell, if he'd kissed them all the way he'd kissed her, it was no wonder.

The thought led her to admit where he was, to imagine who he was seeing. She finally managed to banish that image.

But late that afternoon, it came back. *I'm going out with Suzanne on her yacht. She's divorced now....* Was he with Suzanne last night? Tonight? She knew he'd be at the Hyatt until tomorrow. Then he'd be with Suzanne. Touching her intimately. "So let him," she said as she reorganized her kitchen cupboards, denting soup cans and crushing boxes of cookies. "It's for the best."

Thursday night, she climbed into the bathtub at about

nine, hoping to soak away the fatigue that enveloped her from two nights with little sleep. But as she laid her head against the old claw-footed tub, she was swamped with memories of Alex—sitting naked in his hot tub, zipping up her jacket, sweat trickling down his forehead as they ran, at the fire museum, holding her as she confided things she'd never told anyone else.

It was ten o'clock when she tumbled into bed, wearing sexless cotton pajamas that Chelsea would have relegated to the Salvation Army. She fought with the pillows for an hour, struggling to block out her father's ragged claim. *She made me happier than I've ever been in my life.* Dylan's advice. *Life without risks isn't worth living.* And Mrs. MacKenzie's belief. *When you love someone, there aren't any shouldn'ts.*

"You don't *love* him," she told herself in the darkness. "You've only known him just over four weeks."

She glanced at the phone, then the clock. Eleven. She cared about him. The thought of not seeing him again twisted her inside out. The thought of him kissing Suzanne, who was probably some delicate blond flower like Elise, made her sick to her stomach.

She snatched up the phone and dialed information. She got the number of the Boston Hyatt, punched it out and tapped her hand impatiently on the mattress as she waited. Finally, she was connected to his room.

The phone rang. Five, six, ten times. Francey hung up. Oh, God, she'd waited too long. He wasn't there. He was with Suzanne.

She sat for fifteen minutes holding the phone on her lap. Then she called Boston again. Still no answer. Damn. An hour later and three more calls under her belt, she flung the phone to the floor. Stabbing her pillow viciously only sent a jarring pain up her newly uncasted arm. It brought tears to her eyes. She wiped them away, refusing to let any fall. She jerked off the light and lay down, willing herself to sleep. Firefighters were notorious for zonking out and waking up in seconds, and she willed the blissful oblivion to overtake her.

It didn't. At two o'clock, she tore off the blankets, picked up the tangled phone from the floor and dialed the Hyatt again. "One more time," she said aloud, pacing the floor as the phone rang on his end. And rang. And rang.

She was about to hang up when she heard a click and a deep, slurred male voice mumbled, "Hello."

Swallowing the emotion rising in her throat, Francey closed her eyes and breathed in deeply. "Alex. It's me. Francesca."

Dead silence. For too long.

Oh, God, was he with someone, there, at the hotel?

Finally he spoke. "Just a minute."

An eternity later, he was back on the line. "Francesca." The word was a caress, like his hand stroking her naked back.

"Hi."

"Hi." Amusement laced his voice.

Why not? she thought irritably. He'd won. She began to wonder how much she'd have to grovel. She paced. "I, um, I've been trying to reach you all night."

"All night, huh?"

"Yeah. I gave up at twelve and threw the phone across the room."

"Hmm. Now why is that?"

A lot. She was going to have to grovel a lot.

"Where were you?" she asked, attempting to keep the suspicion out of her voice.

His chuckle told her just how unsuccessful she'd been. "I was at dinner."

All right, so she'd ask. "With who?"

"A friend."

Plopping down on the bed, she rammed a hand through

her hair. "Damn it, Alex, just tell me. Were you with Suzanne tonight?"

He waited a moment. "No, I don't think I'll tell you quite yet, Francesca. Not until you tell *me* a few things."

More than a lot, damn him.

Fine. She'd do it. "Are you done with your business tomorrow?" She studied the ceiling, wishing she'd paid better attention to how women flirted. She needed pointers right now.

"Yes, I'll be finished about five."

"Then you could come back here tomorrow night, couldn't you?"

Again, he answered with infuriating calm. "I could. But I told you Tuesday night I had plans for the weekend."

"You told me a lot of things Tuesday night." Her voice turned husky, and she ground her heels into the bed.

"Yes, I did."

"Did you mean them?"

A long pause. "I meant every word."

Oh, God. Still, silence on his end. "Come home tomorrow night, Alex. Come here."

"Why, Francesca?"

"Because I want you to. I want to be with you...like a woman wants to be with a man." Though parroting his words from the other night felt awkward, she wanted her meaning to be clear.

She heard him draw in a breath. "Oh, sweetheart, do you know what it means to me to hear you say that?"

Relief flooded her, momentarily making her speechless. Her whole body sank into the mattress. "I think I do. But this isn't easy for me, Alex. I'm scared."

"Of me?"

"No, of how I feel about you. Of what it will lead to between us. Do you think...do you think we could take it slow? Just at first?"

She heard a very male chuckle and answered it with a smile. "I suppose I could control myself for a while longer."

Now that the constricting band of emotion that had gripped his heart since he'd walked out of her house on Tuesday had began to loosen, Alex relaxed. He fell onto the bed that only hours ago had felt so empty he'd gone down to the bar and had three Scotches just to be able to sleep. Staring at the whirling ceiling fan, he tried internalize what had happened. He'd won. Francesca had given in.

"I can control myself, but I want to kiss you again," he told her, imagining where she was, what she was wearing.

He heard her draw in a breath. Oh, this was going to be fun.

"I want to touch you, Francesca. And hold you against me."

She cleared her throat. "Alex."

"Do you want that? Say it."

"Yes, I want you to touch me."

"Where?"

"Where?"

He chuckled. "Uh-huh."

"Well, I think we should be in the house."

He laughed aloud, though he felt hotter than when she dragged him out of that burning building. "I meant where on your body, love."

"I know that's what you meant. I always joke when I'm nervous."

"Are you nervous?"

He heard her chuckle. "Yes. I'm not used to this kind of talk."

"What kind of talk?"

"This…sexual banter."

"Good."

"Good?"

"Yes. Good. I'm glad you're not used to it. We'll take it slow, but I can't wait to introduce you to all kinds of…things."

After a moment, she whispered softly, "Me, too. I can't wait, either."

CHAPTER EIGHT

DIANA'S DESIGNS was tucked away in a small strip mall in Pittsfield, an upscale suburb of Rockford. *Where Alex grew up,* Francey thought as she sat in her truck and stared at her mother's shop. "No time for second thoughts now," she told herself. She'd done it. She'd made a commitment to let their relationship take its course, and she couldn't back out now.

Besides, she didn't want to.

She exited the truck and strode across the parking lot to the storefront. A discreet pink-and-silver sign was staked into a garden of wildflowers and shrubs in front of the store. A soft bell jingled as Francey opened the door and stepped inside. She scanned the interior. More pink and silver—subtly striped wallpaper, the floor tiles. It was so very Diana. Elegant. Sophisticated. Francey reached out and ran her fingers over the cuff of a pink silk blouse.

"May I help you?"

Francey pivoted to find Elise behind her. When her stepsister recognized her, Elise tossed her blond hair and gave her a withering look. "Well, what do we have here? I didn't think you'd wear anything that didn't come from an L.L. Bean catalog, Francey."

Staring at Elise, Francey felt the familiar anger and frustration well inside her. She scanned Elise's coordinated mauve slacks and top and dainty sandals. Maybe it was a mistake to come here. Her eyes narrowed on her stepsister. Then again, maybe it wasn't. Elise would like nothing better than to drive Francey away, as she'd done seventeen years ago. "I've come to see Diana," Francey told her. "Is she here?"

Elise's lips thinned. "What do you want with Mother?"

Mother. "I'd like to see her. If she isn't here, just tell me."

"Elise, do you have the numbers—" Diana stopped abruptly as she came through the doorway and glanced up from the ledger in her hands. Dressed in a short-sleeved knit off-white dress and contrasting peach belt, she was lovely in the bright sunlight pouring through the wall of windows. Her smile was just as dazzling. "Why, Francesca, what a surprise! Did you come to see me?" Her mother's voice caught on the last word.

"Yeah."

Diana crossed to them and hugged Francey. "How wonderful."

Over Diana's shoulder, Francey saw Elise pale. Francey thought about getting even with the other woman for all the grief she'd caused her but realized there was nothing to gain from stooping to Elise's level. She stepped back. "Diana, could we talk somewhere?"

"Of course, I have an office in the back." Diana's face glowed as if she'd been given a gift. "You haven't seen the store, have you?"

"No. I'd like to. Later."

"All right." Diana turned to Elise. "Can you handle the counter for a while?"

Elise stared at Diana. Her face was pinched with jealousy. Amazingly, Francey felt sorry for Elise. "Yes, of course, Mother."

Diana hustled Francey to her office. The room was about twelve feet square, painted a soft peach with rich wood trim. A polished oak desk and filing cabinets took up one wall, a

set of mirrors and a window another. Lights were recessed.
The smell of potpourri delicately scented the air.

"This is a lovely room."

"Here, let me take your jacket." When Francey shrugged
out of it, Diana exclaimed, "Oh, you got your cast off!"

"Finally."

"It makes life easier, I'll bet."

Francey nodded.

"Sit down, dear." When Francey sat, Diana reached out
and squeezed her hand. "It's wonderful to see you." Francey tilted her head. Diana straightened. "I guess I mean it's
wonderful that *you* came to see *me*."

A lump formed in Francey's throat. Such a little thing. "I
haven't gone out of my way to see you much." She swallowed the emotion welling inside her. "I...I'd like that to
change."

"Oh, Francesca."

Francey rolled her eyes. "Besides, I need help."

Diana gave her a watery smile. "All right. With what?"

Feeling her face flush, Francey drew in a deep breath. "I,
um, jeez, I don't even know how to say this."

"Just start." Diana smiled. "I'm your mother—you can
tell me anything."

"I can?"

"Yes, of course." Diana reached out and squeezed her
hand again. "Is this about a man?"

Disgusted, Francey closed her eyes briefly. "God, it's so
lame. I...I have a date tonight. An important one. And I
want to look good." She hesitated, then said, "Oh, damn, I
want to look feminine. You've seen my closet, Diana. It has
one or two dressy things, and the rest are like this." She
flicked a hand down her tan twill pants and light blue tailored blouse. Elise was right about the way she dressed.
Even when she wasn't on duty, her clothes were unisex.

"And the outfits you design, they're so...pretty. I know

they wouldn't look as good on me as they do on you. I'm a lot bigger. But I thought maybe something…'' Francey trailed off. She was a rookie in feminine territory, and she didn't like it any more than she'd liked being a probie in the fire department. But she wanted something special for tonight. For Alex. Remembering the beautiful white roses that had arrived this morning with a card that said, ''I can't wait to see you,'' Francey squared her shoulders. ''Think you can do something with me?''

Diana laughed aloud. ''Francesca, you're gorgeous. How can you not know that?''

Francey smiled at the compliment. ''It's just that I want to be…oh, all right, I want something *sexy.*''

Almost bubbling, Diana stood and clapped her hands. ''I've got several things that would look terrific on you.'' She grasped her daughter's arm. ''Come on.''

Uneasy, Francey glanced out the door. ''Could you bring the clothes in here? I don't want to do this in front of Elise.''

''Oh, of course. I'll be right back.''

Twenty minutes—and four outfits—later, Francey stared at herself in the mirror and sighed. ''This is it.''

''Turn around and let me see.''

Francey pirouetted. The clothes made the gesture seem natural, though she'd never seen herself as a Cinderella type.

''It's breathtaking.'' Diana crossed to her and unbuttoned the top three buttons. The opening revealed a hint of cleavage. ''Now, that's sexy. If you put the little lilac teddy Chelsea got you for your birthday underneath, it will be perfect.''

It was. The deep indigo highlighted Francey's eyes. And the design of the clothing flattered her figure. The top fell in soft folds over her breasts, accenting their fullness. It tucked into the waist of matching pants that slimmed down her hips and nipped in at her ankles. The sleeves narrowed just past her elbow. Around her waist, her mother had braided purple and white sashes. Then she'd brought in delicate slipperlike shoes that fitted Francey perfectly.

Diana rose and stood next to Francey. "Alex will love it."

Francey caught her mother's gaze in the mirror. "How did you know?"

She squeezed Francey's arm. "Just an educated guess."

Giving her mother a weak smile, Francey said, "No warnings? Like from Dad?"

"No, Francesca. None." Briefly Diana's face clouded. "Your father's wrong about this. You aren't like me. You're stronger."

"I'm not so sure." Francey swallowed hard. "I'm afraid of the feelings I have for him."

"Don't be." Diana turned Francey toward her and held her by the shoulders. "Your father made me happier than I've ever been in my whole life."

Francey scowled

"What is it?"

"That's the exact same thing he told me about you."

Diana's jaw dropped. "He did?"

"Yeah. But it didn't stop his objections. He's really against my seeing Alex. It makes me more anxious."

Diana reached out to tuck a strand of Francey's hair behind her ear. "Go for it, honey. It's worth the hard times. If I could do things over, I'd make my marriage work for our family. I know I would."

Francey smiled at her mother. "Thanks, that helps."

Diana smiled, too. "Good." She stepped back. "Now, let's see what jewelry will go with that outfit."

"BEN, DIANA'S HERE."

Ben dropped the heavy black binder he'd been reading, and it clattered to the floor. Eric Scanlon, the captain in charge of training, was standing at the door to his spacious office. "Who?"

"Diana. Your ex."

"Fine. I'll be right out." Scanlon left the door ajar; Ben bent and retrieved the manual from the floor, then crossed to the door, closed it and leaned his head against it. His colleague's words had flashed Ben back almost thirty years.

He'd been a five-year veteran firefighter at Engine Four and he was humping hose onto the truck when one of his co-workers came into the bay.

"Ben," he'd said. "Diana's here."

Ben had looked over to see his wife of three years standing by the door. Dressed in jeans and his Rockford Fire Department sweatshirt, she gracefully crossed the wide cement floor toward him. Just the sight of her made him hard.

"Hi," she said.

He responded with a worried scowl. "You never come here. Is something wrong?"

Her violet eyes shone like purple jewels in her lively face. "No, everything's perfect."

Recognizing the mischief in her expression, he dragged her behind the rig, out of sight of anyone coming into the bay. He couldn't resist touching her. Smoothing his hand down her corn-silk hair, he asked, "What is it?"

"I'm pregnant again."

A lump formed in his throat, and his shoulders sagged. "Oh, Dee, so soon? Tony's only a year and a half, and Nicky's six months."

"It's not too soon. I want a dozen babies."

"I thought we'd agreed to wait."

She circled his waist with her arms. "Mother Nature has other ideas." She seduced him with a grin. "Ma and Pa are taking the boys over to Aunt Jen's about five today."

Ben glanced at his watch. It was three in the afternoon. "How'd you manage that?"

She didn't answer him. Instead, she plastered herself to him, in the firehouse bay, for God's sake, and whispered, "Hurry home."

Then she was gone. And he'd been hard the rest of his shift.

When he got home, they went straight to bed, and he'd kept her there until they heard voices downstairs two hours later. He remembered telling her, "Thank you for my babies. All of them."

She'd looked at him, her eyes brimming with love. "All I want out of life is you and your children."

Swearing vilely, he yanked open the door and stalked to the outer office, which was crammed with cubicles and desks, a table and chairs and a coffee machine. She was reading a bulletin board, her back to him. "Diana?" he said sharply. Anger from the reminiscence surfaced in his voice.

She turned, and as always, just looking at her made him hurt. No wonder men still tripped over themselves watching her. He'd heard that little gem Tuesday night from his mother, and it burned him up. "What do you want?"

"I want to talk to you." She glanced around. Scanlon, along with several others, watched them openly. "In private."

He nodded and turned; she followed, as he'd expected.

Inside his office, he shut the door and waited for her to speak. She squared her shoulders and angled her chin like she was about to face a firing squad. "We need to discuss Francesca."

"What about her?"

"You're making things difficult for her."

Though his heart was pounding harder than it did at a four-alarm fire, he nonchalantly eased a hip onto his desk and folded his arms. "I am? How?"

"She came to see me this morning. She mentioned you were upset about her and Alex."

"They're not just friends, Diana."

"Of course they're not."

"This relationship isn't good for her."

"You may think that, but it's her choice."

He stiffened. "Are you criticizing my parenting?"

"She's thirty years old. She doesn't need parenting now."

"No, she needed it at three, and thirteen." He paused. "When you weren't around."

Diana blanched. "I didn't come here to spar with you. I came here to ask you to let her make her own choices."

"Like your parents let you?"

Stepping close enough to him so that he could smell some light, sweet fragrance on her, she grasped his arm. "She's not me, Ben. He isn't you. They can do this if they try."

"Are you saying we didn't try?"

"No, I'm saying I was at fault. But Francesca's stronger than I was. She can do it."

"I don't want to discuss this with you." He shook her off, pushed away from the desk and gave her his back.

"Well, *she* wanted to talk about it when she came to the shop this morning."

He whirled on Diana and grabbed her by the arms. "Don't you see what's happening here? She's turning to you, instead of me, because she can get your approval. And you're latching on to it because you want to be a part of her life. You're both just using each other."

Huge tears welled in Diana's eyes. "Do you hate me so much that you need to say the most hurtful things you can every time I see you?"

"What do you mean?"

She blinked back the tears. "Today you say Francesca's *using* me when you know I'd give my right arm to have some sort of mother-daughter relationship with her. And Tuesday—" she swallowed hard "—Tuesday you couldn't wait to tell me how much you *didn't* care about me."

"Why should that bother you?" he asked, his grip tightening on her arms.

He expected her to yank out of his grasp. She didn't. Instead, she leaned into him and buried her face in his chest. He was so swamped with emotion he couldn't push her away.

In a voice muffled by his shirt, she said, "You just don't see it, do you?"

"See what?"

"That I've never gotten over you."

Momentarily, he froze. Then, almost against his will, his hand crept to her hair. He buried his fingers in the silky blond mass and let his lips brush over a few strands. It was still as soft as a kitten's fur. And touching it still turned him inside out. "You married someone else," he said raggedly. *And it almost killed me.*

She looked at him with watery eyes. "After I finished at the Fashion Institute in New York, I met Nathan Hathaway. He was kind to me. He needed a wife. I was so lonely for you and the children, I tried to replace all of you." She bit her bottom lip. "It didn't work."

He couldn't do this. He couldn't lose himself in her as he had before. He couldn't live through the pain again. "I don't want to hear this." He stepped back.

Shaking, she straightened and swiped at her face. "Of course you don't. But please, Ben, think about Francesca, not your dislike of me. Think about what she needs now." Diana stared at him for a few seconds, then turned and left.

Ben spun and faced his desk. Bracing his hands on it, he sucked in air like a recruit on his first air pack. But that didn't quell the rage. He swore viciously and swept the contents off the surface of his desk onto the floor.

ALEX'S HEART POUNDED as he rang Francesca's doorbell at eight o'clock Friday night. *You're like a kid on your first date,* he thought, wiping his sweaty palms on his suit pants. Drawing in a breath of fresh spring air, letting the soft breeze calm him, he strove for some of that legendary Templeton cool that had driven the women in college crazy.

When she swung open the door, it fled like leaves in the wind. Stunned, he gulped at the sight before him. He couldn't remember her ever looking so beautiful. So desirable. Her face was radiant, and the knowledge that she'd dressed up for him made his stomach somersault. "Hi," she said softly, almost shyly.

"Hi." He stared at her a moment longer, then picked up his suitcase. "I came right from the airport. I wanted to get here fast.

A Jezebel smile on her lips, she gestured him inside. "You wanted to get here fast?" she asked.

"Yes, very." He scanned her, taking in the stunning purple outfit. "It was worth it."

The color in her cheeks deepened.

He shoved his hands in his pockets. "Not that you weren't always gorgeous, Francesca. But you look...exceptionally beautiful tonight."

In a slow and graceful movement, she pirouetted for him. "You like?"

He had to clear his throat. "I like. Is it new?"

"Yeah." She shook her hair. "I went to Diana's shop this morning. She dressed me up."

"Remind me to send your mother a thank-you note." He studied her. "What did you do to your hair?"

"Chelsea came over today. She played with a curling iron." Francesca seemed unsure suddenly. "Does it look okay?"

Alex's gaze raked her boldly. "Come here, woman, and I'll show you just *how* okay."

Her smile quickened his pulse rate. "Now, don't turn all macho on me, Templeton."

"Then don't tease me with your feminine wiles, Frances-ca." He sobered. "Come here," he repeated more softly. "I can't wait another minute to touch you."

She stepped toward him. When she stood so close he could see the lavender lace peeking from the open buttons of her top, he was hit with a surge of desire so potent he wanted to drag her to the floor and bury himself in her.

I'm scared, Alex.... Could we take it slow?

Remembering his promise, he eased her into his arms and drew her close, the fit as natural as a key slipping into its lock. She stared at him with those fathomless violet eyes made richer by the indigo outfit. He studied every inch of her face, kissed her forehead. "Do you have any idea how much I want to do this?" Her eyelids fluttered closed as his lips grazed them. "What it feels like to have the right to touch you?" His hands slid down to grasp her hips. "To hold you?" Brushing his mouth across each cheek, he felt her sink into him. "How I've *needed* to be close to you?" Struggling for control, he skimmed her jaw with tiny kisses, then moved to her ear. He outlined its delicate ridges with his tongue.

She shivered. "Alex. If you don't kiss me pretty soon, I'm going to embarrass myself and beg."

He laughed and felt an answering chuckle in her chest. Drawing back, he tilted her chin, let himself soak in the sight of her once more, then lowered his head.

Gentleness fled, and he took her mouth hungrily, feasting after weeks of the fast she'd insisted on. He could feel his entire body harden as she aligned herself with him, stood on tiptoe, drew him closer.

Her mouth opened to him, and he needed no more invi-tation to plunge his tongue into her and claim what he craved. She returned the gesture with a throaty moan.

After glorious minutes of tasting her, he was the one to

break the kiss. He knew his body, and if he was to keep his promise to go slow, he'd better ease off now.

She obviously sensed it, too, and drew back from him. But she clasped his hand in hers, brought it to her mouth and kissed it. That small, intimate gesture almost did him in; he closed his eyes, praying for self-discipline. When he opened them, he caught sight of her arm. Encircling her wrist with his fingers, he slid them to her elbow.

"You bewitch me," he said. "I didn't even notice this." Continuing the gentle glide up and down, he asked, "Feel good?"

"Right now it feels wonderful."

"I mean getting the cast off."

"Oh."

He chuckled, and she said, "Yeah, it feels great."

After bestowing a kiss on the petal-soft skin at her wrist, he twisted his hand and linked their fingers. "Let's go sit down. I, ah, need distraction from you."

The seductive smile came back. "I like hearing that."

"Yes, well, you'd better watch it, Ms. Cordaro. I'm barely restraining myself."

Francey led him to the living room and glanced around, hoping she hadn't been too obvious. The lights were dimmed, Harry Connick, Jr., crooned in the background, and she'd fixed a tray of cheese, crackers and fruit. When he saw the scene, he stopped abruptly. She winced. "Too obvious?"

His hand tightened in hers. "No, of course not." He turned to her and tilted her face. "I'm flattered." When she still looked unsure, he said, "Francesca, you can let yourself go with me. Be as romantic as you want." When she smiled he said, "Hey, it's a hell of a position to put me in, but somebody's got to do it."

She smiled. "Thanks."

"For what?"

"For understanding how new this is to me."

"Sweetheart, no man in his right mind would balk at being the recipient of all this." He waved to encompass the setting and her outfit. "How can you think otherwise?"

"When you look at me like that, I don't think otherwise. It's just when I see how…feminine I'm behaving, I panic."

Leaning over, he took her mouth again. Though quick, the kiss was searing. And convincing.

He sat on the couch as she fixed them drinks. Forgoing her usual beer, she poured herself a glass of wine. When she was beside him, he turned to her and held up his drink. "To friendship—" he clinked their glasses "—and much, much more."

They settled into the sofa; Alex edged close, his thigh brushing hers, his arm on the back of the couch hovering near her hair.

"So, how was Boston?" she asked. "Did you get to see your friends?"

He tried to hide his smile behind the glass. "Some of them."

"Which ones?"

His eyes sparkled like rare jade. "Is there something you want to know?"

"Know?"

"Yes. About Boston."

She took a sip of her drink. "Oh, all right. Did you get together with Suzanne?"

Staring at her intently, he let the question hang in the air. "Yes," he finally said. "I had dinner with her Thursday."

"Is that where you were when I called?"

His hand slid to her neck and caressed it. "Francesca, if you're asking if I slept with Suzanne, the answer's no."

"You were going out on her yacht."

"I was." He grinned. "Looks like you called just in time." He brushed her lips with his. "Even if I'd thought about that kind of intimacy with her," he whispered against them, "I wouldn't have pursued it. I wanted *you* the whole time I was in Boston."

"I'm glad."

He sighed and settled his arm around her shoulder. "Except for the warehouse, you were all I thought about."

"The warehouse?"

"Zeleny called the office while I was gone. He wants to meet with me on Monday."

"Oh, good. Maybe the cause of the fire will be cleared up."

"Richard seemed anxious when I spoke with him this morning."

Francey drew back to look at him. "Alex, if you want to talk about Richard and the investigation, I'm a good listener."

"Maybe sometime. I *am* worried about Richard." He pressed a kiss on her nose. "But not now. I don't want to spoil tonight." He fingered the collarless back of her outfit. "So this is one of Diana's designs?"

"Yeah."

"Do you wear a lot of her clothes? I don't think I've ever seen you in them."

"No, this is the first time. I bought it today, and Diana insisted on giving me a few other things, too."

He groaned.

"What?"

"I'm not sure I can handle seeing you in these clingy things very often."

"I'm sure you'll find a way to cope."

He took a sip of his Scotch. "How is it going with Diana?"

Francey remembered her mother's pleasure at seeing her today. "Great. She's made some overtures, and so have I." Francey frowned.

"What's wrong?"

"I'm worried about her, though. My father's being down-right cruel to her. I've never seen him act this way."

"If he's striking out at her, he's probably in pain."

"He is. It's why he's so adamant that we don't..." She hesitated.

"What?"

"Nothing. I didn't want to get into this tonight."

"Your father doesn't want us to see each other, does he?"

She nodded. "He's afraid I'll get hurt."

Alex threaded his hand in her hair. "I won't hurt you, Francesca."

Doubt curled inside her. "You wouldn't intentionally. I know that. But if we let this go further and it doesn't work out between us, we'll both be hurt."

He stilled. "If? You haven't changed your mind, have you?"

"No." She leaned into him, letting her head rest on his chest, breathing in his scent. "I want more from you, Alex. I have from the beginning. I'm willing to risk it."

"But?"

"But if you could see my mother and father together. The pain from them both is almost tangible. Sometimes I don't know how they stand it."

"I'm sorry."

"Me, too."

"They aren't us, though."

"I know, that's what Dylan said."

His hand stopped smoothing her hair. "You talked to Dylan about us?"

She nodded. It took her a minute to note the stiffness that had crept into his body. She drew back. "Alex?"

"I don't think I like hearing that you discussed me with Dylan."

"Why?

He didn't answer.

"Are you jealous of Dylan?" The thought pleased her, given her obvious green-eyed reaction to Suzanne.

"Me? Jealous? Of course not. I don't have a jealous bone in my body. As a matter of fact, I can't remember one time when…" He scowled at her. "I'm jealous as hell of Dylan O'Roarke."

"We're just friends."

"So you said."

She giggled.

"It's not funny."

"It *is* funny. Rockford's most eligible bachelor is behaving like a schoolboy."

He arched a brow. "A schoolboy? Me?" She recognized the error of teasing him a second too late. He snatched the drink out of her hand, set both drinks on the table and had her on her back before she could blink. "You want to see schoolboy—" he covered her upper body with his chest "—well, *this* is schoolboy." His face hovered so close she could detect the faint growth of beard on his jaw. She wanted to run her fingers along it, but he had her arms pinned.

"Now apologize."

"For what?"

"For taunting me with other men."

"What'll you do if I don't?"

"I'll have to exact punishment."

"I'm not into S and M, Alex."

"No? Then you'd better watch your mouth, lady."

"I'd rather watch yours." Her eyes dropped to his lips. "I'd rather *have* yours."

"Not until you make me a promise."

"What?"

"That you won't look at another man while we're together."

"That would be pretty tough. I sleep with five men every night on the late shift."

"Not a good time to tease me, Francesca."

"Sorry."

"You're not."

"You're right, I'm not."

"Don't make me get rough."

She giggled again. "I'm shocked, Alex."

"At what?"

"At this side of you. I didn't expect you to be so... aggressive."

"No? What did you expect?"

"Oh, I don't know. Maybe that you'd be a little stuffy."

"Stuffy?"

"Um, yeah."

"You mean, stuffy, like in bed?"

"Well, I guess I hadn't thought that far."

"You're going to have to pay for this, Francesca."

"I'm sorry. I was wrong."

"Too late."

"Too late?"

"Yeah. I can see I'm going to have to take steps."

"What kind of steps?"

"Steps to drive the point home." He shifted and covered her with his whole body; she could feel him hard against her stomach.

She arched into him. "Oh, dear, if you have to take steps, there's probably nothing I can do about it."

He laughed. So did she. Then he lowered his mouth. Neither of them laughed or spoke for a long time.

CHAPTER NINE

"WHERE THE HELL are you?" Richard asked as he paced Bob Zeleny's office at eight-thirty Monday morning. Slouching in his chair, Alex opened his eyes and studied his brother. Richard looked like hell, despite his meticulous gray pinstripe suit, Italian leather loafers and gold watch, which he checked again. His eyes were so bloodshot it worried Alex.

"I'm right here, waiting for Zeleny to keep his appointment."

It was a lie, of course. All the way over to the Public Safety Building and the time they'd spent in the fire marshal's office waiting, Alex had been back on that couch with Francesca.

He'd kissed her senseless Friday night, and by the time he let her up, she'd been clinging to him. Oh, he'd enjoyed that! And on Saturday night, after dinner at the Rio, when they'd returned to her place, he'd kissed her some more, and she'd melted into him with a glorious lack of restraint.

Alex was surprised at how much he enjoyed this delay in taking their relationship to its natural intimate culmination. Instead of resenting the frustration he felt when he left her, he relished it—the right to touch her more intimately each time; how she clung to him and was just as aroused and excited as he by their contact. And he definitely relished the anticipation of finally having her. It was like waiting for an athletic competition in college—a tennis match or a soccer

game. He'd enjoyed the buildup as much as the contest itself.

"There you go again," Richard said. "You just zoned
out. Is it a woman?"

Alex smiled.

Richard didn't. "It's Francesca Cordaro, isn't it?"

Alex glanced around. "This isn't the place to talk about
her."

"I tried to call you all weekend. Were you with her?"

Nodding, Alex knew he was unsuccessful in keeping the
Cheshire cat grin off his face.

"Did you finally get around to screwing her?"

Alex bolted off the chair with the speed of an angry pan-
ther. Only good sense kept him from lunging for Richard.
"I told you once not to talk about her in those terms. I'm
warning you—"

"Excuse me."

Both men whirled to find Bob Zeleny looming in the
doorway. He stared at them hard, then came into the room.
"Sorry I'm late," he told them, circling his desk. As he
placed his briefcase on the polished mahogany surface, he
added, "There was a pileup on the four-ninety and it took
forever to get around it."

The Templeton men mumbled their understanding and
took seats opposite Zeleny, who drew papers out of his
drawer and eased onto his chair. "I also apologize for the
delay in this investigation, but I've been in the hospital."

"Yes, we heard," Alex said, noting Zeleny's skin had the
pasty color of the seriously ill. "How are you feeling?"

"Better, though I'm exhausted by the end of the day."
He held up papers. "I think we've caught our culprit."

Richard tensed. "Who is it?"

"A homeless man, we think. Name's Ernest Mackey.
There was a fire similar to yours in another warehouse just
last week. We picked up the suspect stumbling around the

perimeter of the building while it burned. Inside we found an electric starter, like the one discovered in your place.'' Zeleny handed Richard a picture. ''You recognize this guy? From that night?''

Richard shook his head. ''I'm not sure.'' He showed the photo to Alex, who'd never seen Mackey before.

''Did he confess?'' Richard asked.

Zeleny drew out glasses, perched them on his nose and perused the documents. ''No, he claims he wasn't anywhere near the Templeton warehouse six weeks ago. But we got a tip that he'd shacked up with a woman a block away for the last six months.''

''Not real proof,'' Alex said.

''We have a few other things. The second fire was put out sooner than the one in the Templeton warehouse, so we found some lighter fluid and wire inside. There were remnants of those two things at your place.''

''I thought you just found a starter,'' Richard said.

''My assistant didn't recognize the rest of the stuff because it was badly burned. He's new. Once I was on my feet and studied the forensic report, I tagged it immediately.''

Alex sank back. ''Is it enough to indict the man?''

Zeleny scowled. ''Maybe—along with something else we found out. We noticed the guy's arms were pinkish—looked like they'd been burned. I had my team check out clinics in the downtown area. Sure enough, the day after your fire, a doc in the Westside Center reported treating Mackey for burn wounds.''

''He reported burn wounds? I don't understand.'' This from Richard.

Zeleny coughed and reached into his drawer. Then he swore. ''Damn, I'm off the butts for six weeks and I still go for them. Anyway, in 1985, New York State instituted a burn-reporting law. It's like the gunshot law. If a person comes into a medical facility with a gunshot wound or burns, the doctor is required to report it to the police. It's really helped arson investigations.''

Richard leaned forward, slipping to the edge of his seat. ''Is this considered arson? If the guy started the fire to keep warm?''

Zeleny frowned. ''Technically, it's still arson. He'll be arraigned on arson four, which is the lowest count. It's a class D felony.'' At Richard and Alex's puzzled looks, Zeleny explained. ''If a person causes a fire intentionally, even if he doesn't mean to burn the building down, and it damages people or property, he's charged with reckless endangerment. Mackey will get that for the last fire, even if we can't prove yours.''

''What's the usual sentence?'' Alex asked.

''Not much, unfortunately.'' Zeleny frowned. ''He'll be charged but probably get six months probation. Community service. The best thing that will come out of this is that he won't start any more fires. It'll scare the crap out of him.''

Alex frowned. ''It's too bad he can't get a job. Will anybody look into that?''

Zeleny shook his head. ''I doubt it. We're not social workers.'' The fire marshal stood; so did the Templetons. Zeleny reached out his hand. Alex shook it first. ''This is probably it. Unless something new turns up, I'll be closing the case.''

After bidding the fire marshal goodbye, Alex and Richard left. On the drive to Templeton Industries, both men were quiet until Richard said, ''Damn, I'm glad this is over with.''

''So am I.'' Alex tried to soften his clipped tone, but he was angry at his brother. He stared ahead, watching the road as he maneuvered the Porsche; it was raining.

''Look, I apologize for the crack about Francesca.''

''That's what you said the last time.''

''I know. I've been stressed out about this fire thing.''

"Me, too, Richard." Alex swerved into his space at Templeton Industries and killed the engine. He faced his brother in the car. "But that's no excuse. And you might as well know. I'm going to be seeing a lot of her from now on."

"You said this thing between you was just friendship."

"That's changed."

"I knew it."

"Richard, I'm crazy about her. I wanted this to happen. I'm...happy."

"It's not a good idea, Alex."

Alex scowled and tapped his fist on the steering wheel.

"She's not from our world."

"Damn it, Richard, do you know how snobbish that sounds?"

"I don't care how it sounds. She's not going to fit in."

"Thank God. I told you, I was bored with society types."

Richard's eyes narrowed on him, then he shook his head. "All right, get her out of your system. Just don't let it get serious."

Before Alex could respond, Richard got out of the car and darted through the rain into the building.

It didn't make sense, Richard's vehement dislike of Francesca. Alex exited the car, too, bothered by Richard's reaction. In the elevator, he decided it might be Richard's bitterness from his recent divorce that had made him so crass and offensive about women. But once in his office, Alex forgot about his brother and reached for the phone to call the woman he couldn't stop thinking about. He concentrated on what the next few days had in store for him and Francesca, what delightful torture they'd inflict on each other until they consummated their relationship.

"I TOLD YOU that you were pushing too hard." Francey made the smug comment as she dug her fingers into Alex's back muscles. "Your neck's all knotted."

Alex groaned and buried his face in the pillow. She grinned at the picture he made, grasping the pillow under his head, his chest on her lap, his naked back big and beautiful with a spattering of freckles. His torso was covered only in gray fleece shorts, and his sinewed legs sprawled out on the couch.

"It's not nice to say I told you so," he mumbled.

As she kneaded his muscles, she drank in the sight of him. "You're trying too hard to catch up with me."

He eased his head toward her and opened one eye. "I did catch up with you. I benched one seventy-five tonight."

"And pulled these muscles in the process. Besides," she grumbled, "I'm not sure I can still bench that much. The doctor won't let me do any weights with this arm for a few more days."

"Smart man." Francey's fingers trailed to the small of his back. "You've got great hands, Francesca. What they can do is sinful."

She leaned over and kissed his spine. "This is only a small display of my talent."

"Don't tease me, woman. Remember what happened the last time."

Francey did. She could picture last weekend like a movie scene she couldn't forget…Alex's weight pressing her into the couch. His mouth taking hers. How his touch felt on her body. It made her want to tease him all the more.

So she slid her hands inside the waistband of his fleece shorts. She kneaded his waist, then dipped lower, kneaded some more. He grumbled into the pillow, "I can't be held responsible for my actions if you keep that up."

She kept it up, but only for a minute longer. Because she didn't want to ruin this delicate balance, didn't want to hurry things along. She just wanted to enjoy the embers of desire she felt when she touched him. Getting to know his body gradually was delicious. It felt so good to explore him, to find out in stages what he liked and didn't like, without worrying about how far it would go, what would happen next. "Alex, is this okay with you?"

"It's wonderful."

She slapped his rump playfully. "No, I mean the whole thing. Taking it slow?"

"Yes, Francesca, it's okay." In a surprisingly quick move, he flipped over and looked at her. "With you?"

"Yeah." She ran her fingers through the whorls of dark blond chest hair accessible to her.

"Why are you smiling?"

"It's like when I was a kid. I wanted this baseball mitt really bad."

"No doll, huh?"

"Of course not."

"Did you get the mitt?"

"Yeah. Dad said we couldn't afford it, but he helped me find ways to make money to buy it. Mowing lawns, washing cars at the gas station. I even baby-sat."

"Girly work. How shocking."

"It was fun walking by the store, staring at the glove, knowing I was going to get it." She toyed with the drawstring on his shorts.

Alex's voice was hoarse when he said, "And when you got it, was it all you expected?"

She smiled at him. "Oh, yeah. It was everything I ever wanted."

A seductive grin suffused Alex's face, and she felt her stomach contract. Slowly he reached to the top button of her yellow cotton blouse. He released it. "Did you go into the store, Francesca, and play with the glove?" His voice hypnotized her.

She swallowed hard. "Once or twice, when the store manager let me."

"Mmm." He released another button. "Did he let you fondle it?"

She nodded, holding his gaze, flushed and feverish, like she was getting the flu. Three buttons, then four were undone.

"Tug your shirt out of your pants." Alex's voice was low and husky. She obeyed, caught in the spell of sexual arousal.

Slowly he drew apart the sides of her blouse. "Oh, God." His eyes turned the color of summer grass when he saw she wore no bra. He took one full breast in his hand. "Fondling is good," he said as he massaged her. When she closed her eyes, he told her, "No, open your eyes. Watch me touch you. Watch me fondle you."

Her breathing quickened. He grasped her nipple between his thumb and forefinger and rolled it back and forth slowly, making her whole body contract. She forgot all about baseball and mitts and steeped herself in the sensation of Alex's touch.

TWO NIGHTS LATER they were in the Jacuzzi, once again draining the tension out of sore muscles. "You hit the ball pretty good for an amateur," she told him.

"Under protest. I still don't think you should play in the fire department softball game next week."

"The doctor said I could. If I'm good enough to go back to work a week from Saturday, I can play in a silly old game."

Alex lay against the edge of the tub and closed his eyes. *Back to work.* Into burning buildings. On runs to tend to guys with knife wounds. Alex pushed the upsetting thoughts out of his mind. "Silly game? I'm dead. How many grounders and pop flies did I hit you?"

She smiled. "About a hundred. Your arm must hurt."

"It does." He scrutinized her. "You're not even tired, are

you?'' Every day, as she worked to gain strength and agility, he was astounded by her fitness.

"Nope. Comes from years of rigorous training."

He shook his head. "Well, you could just dry me off and roll me into bed."

"Now there's a tempting idea."

He chuckled. Somewhere along the line, his tough-as-nails firefighter had become a vamp. "I'm at your disposal anytime, Francesca. Just say the word."

"I'll think about it." They stared at the starless sky in contented silence. After a few moments he felt waves in the water. She stood, and he took the opportunity to observe the stunning curves of her body, outlined in a one-piece black racing suit she kept at his house now; he indulged himself watching those mile-long legs climb out of the tub. "Where are you going?"

"You'll see." She disappeared into the changing room off the deck. She was gone a few minutes. When she returned, she was wrapped in a thick white terry robe. For late May, it was warm, but still, there was a breeze off the lake. She stopped by the bench that abutted the house. He saw she held a pile of towels. "Come out here, Alex."

"Out? What are you offering?"

"To dry you off. Then I'll put you to bed."

"Alone?"

"Yeah, for now."

He gave an exaggerated sigh. "You torture me, woman."

"Come out, and I'll show you what real torture is."

Irresistible, that was what she was, standing there in a simple terry-cloth robe, her hair a little damp, her smile rivaling a harem girl promising her master ecstasy. The fantasy appealed to him, so he imagined her in a gossamer harem outfit. He climbed out of the hot tub and crossed to her. He sat on the bench and she draped his shoulders with a robe that matched hers. She must have stuck it in the dryer; it was warm.

"Ah, that feels good." He leaned against the wall of the house and watched her pick up a towel. She spread his legs and knelt between them. The harem-girl fantasy turned Technicolor with that gesture. She raised her arms, which brought her breasts on par with his face, and dried his hair. He took the opportunity to nose the flap of her robe aside. Damn, she was naked underneath. He planted a kiss on her chest and reached for her waist.

"No touching," she said, plopping his hands on the bench.

He moaned. She took her sweet time drying his chest, then gracefully sat on her haunches and ran the towel over the hem of his swim trunks, which he'd put on in deference to their agreement to take things slow. As she dried his leg, she dipped the towel inside the suit an inch.

"You're playing with fire, Francesca," he said, his voice a harsh whisper.

"I'm a firefighter," she replied as she bent her head and kissed the inside of his thigh. "I love getting close to the flame." Her hair brushed his bare skin, and reflexively, he grabbed her shoulders. Damn her. She knew exactly what she was doing to him. So he forced himself to let her finish drying him, glide the towel up and down his legs, favor each toe with exquisite care. By the time she was done, her breathing was as ragged as his. As he tugged her onto his lap and closed his mouth over hers, he took great pleasure in her reaction.

THE FOLLOWING TUESDAY, she was still taunting him. They'd agreed to meet at his office after her last physical-therapy session. She curled up on the leather couch, perusing a magazine she'd taken from his secretary's desk, while he finished with a contract that had to be express mailed. Without conscious thought, his eyes strayed to her. She wore plain navy walking shorts and a sleeveless white shirt. On her feet were blue canvas sneakers. Simple, unadorned beauty, he thought, basking in the vision of her. Soon all that beauty would be his. He was rocked by the thought. To dilute it, he asked, "What are you reading?"

She didn't answer him. Instead she asked, "Alex, what would you say were the color of your eyes? Green or hazel?"

"You know they're green."

She made a note in the magazine with a pencil. "And you're six-one? Two hundred pounds?"

"I just dropped to one ninety. You were there when I weighed in at Chelsea's last night." In fact, he'd been preening like a peacock at his weight loss and muscle tone since he'd met her.

"And your jacket size is…"

Throwing down his pen, he scowled. "What *kind* of article is that?"

"A quiz." She grinned. "It's called, 'What's your type?'"

He snorted. "You don't need to take that quiz, Francesca. You know I'm the man of your dreams."

"And modest, too."

His shoulders shaking with suppressed laughter, he tried to focus on the contract.

"You are, though, Alex," she said in a sober voice that had his head snapping up. "The man of my dreams, I mean."

He swallowed hard as she tossed the magazine onto the table, rose and crossed to the door. It was seven at night, and his employees were gone, but she turned the lock, anyway. Its snick was loud and meaningful. She pivoted and walked toward him. Her gaze fused with his, and she came around the desk. Swiveling his chair, she removed the pen and contract from his hands and straddled him. Her eyes were slumberous, like they'd be after making love.

He said, "Show me. That I'm the man of your dreams."

With a fiery passion befitting her profession, she did.

THREE DAYS before she was to return to work, Francey was at the refrigerator in her kitchen getting ice for the drink to go with lunch she was fixing for Alex. She was singing a little off-key when she saw, in her peripheral vision, Alex enter the room. He'd shed his suit coat, rolled up the sleeves of his white shirt and loosened his tie. They'd been spending a lot of their time together; he was missing some work, but he told her he'd make up for it when she was back on the job. She was fearful about how that would affect their relationship. Scheduling and time conflicts were a hassle between many firefighters and their significant others.

He felt it, too, she knew. In the past few days, some of the teasing in their relationship had ebbed. And their contact had taken on an intense, heated quality, passion simmering just below the surface.

When she moved to the sink, she sensed him come up behind her. "You were gone too long," he said, his body a mere inch from hers. His nearness made her bones liquefy, as usual.

She leaned into him. "The ice is stuck."

He took the tray and cracked it open. Its contents spilled into the sink. Letting it fall, he circled her waist with his hands. She had on light nylon shorts and a tank top, but she sweltered at his touch. "Mmm, that feels good," she said.

"A lot of things will." There it was again, that just-after-sex timbre in his voice.

"Like what?"

He widened his stance, splayed a hand just below her waist and pressed her into him. She could feel him firm and full against her thin shorts. He whispered, "Later, after the first time we make love, I'm going to take you from behind.''

Francey felt the air back up in her lungs. He palmed her belly in slow circular movements. "Have you ever made love like that, Francesca?"

She couldn't speak. So she shook her head.

"Sometimes, though, that position's not good for a woman. So I'll have to touch you, here." He fisted his hand and slid it an inch lower. His knuckles skimmed between her thighs and up again, singeing her through her clothes.

"Oh…"

"You'll like that, won't you, sweetheart?"

She nodded.

"Answer me."

She couldn't.

"Francesca, answer me."

She shook her head.

"What's wrong? You aren't getting *stuffy* on me, are you?"

His humor didn't break the spell. Probably because he opened his hand and cupped her. Exerted more pressure. And more. Her head fell back, and her arms drooped to her sides. She was completely at his mercy. He kept up the gentle massage, then murmured in her ear, "I can make you fly. Right now. Right here." She shook her head. "Let me."

Not wanting to go alone, she turned to face him. Winding her arms around his neck, she opened her mouth to tell him—

The phone shrilled from its perch on the wall. It jolted her into him. His arms tightened around her. "Shh, let the machine pick it up."

He held her as it did, his magic hands soothing her quivering body.

She willed the machine to hurry. Then she heard, "Francey, it's Dad. Pick up if you're there. Something's happened.''

DIANA STEPPED OFF one elevator and saw Francesca and Alex Templeton exit the car on the opposite wall. Tony held on to her arm, and she bit her lip to keep from crying.

Nicky had been hurt in a fire. Twice now, in six weeks, one of her children had been injured. God was really testing her mettle. And she'd be damned if she'd fail the test the second time.

Wordlessly Diana crossed to Francesca and embraced her. When they stepped apart, Tony squeezed his sister's hand. "They told you he was all right, didn't they?"

Francesca's face was grim. "It's his hands, isn't it?"

"That's what Dad said when he called. He's in the intensive care unit, but he's all right," Tony said again.

Diana realized her oldest child—who always played the Rock of Gibraltar—was trying to convince himself, as well as them. It gave her strength. "If your father said Nicky's all right, he is. Ben wouldn't lie about this.''

Alex stepped forward and clasped Francesca's shoulder. He'd only let go of her when mother and daughter had hugged. "Why don't we try to find them?" Checking the signs, he said, "ICU is this way."

Down a long corridor they found the waiting area for the intensive care unit. Clustered around a table were Ben and four uniformed firefighters, probably men from Nicky's station house. One thing she'd always admired about the fire department was that they were like family. Taking a deep breath, Diana let go of Tony's hand and crossed the room to Ben; Francesca and Tony followed. Up close, Ben looked haggard. His hair was mussed, and worry deepened the grooves around his mouth. He wore his battalion chief uniform with a light tan jacket over it.

"How is he?" Diana asked without greeting. She hadn't

spoken to Ben earlier; he'd called Tony and asked him to go to the store, tell her what had happened and drive her to the hospital.

Ben stared at her. She stuck her hands in the pockets of her mint green linen dress, struggling for calm. He'd always been able to read her emotions with a glance and used to tease her about being a cream puff.

"He's gonna be fine, although he's in a lot of pain now." Studying her a moment, Ben said, "Are you all right?"

"Yes, of course."

He looked at Francesca. "Are you, honey?"

Their daughter nodded. Ben put his hand on Tony's shoulder and gave him a questioning look.

Tony told him, "I'm fine, Dad."

"Can I see Nicky?" Diana asked.

Ben frowned.

"I won't let you keep me from him, Ben."

"It's not that. Actually, he's asked for you."

"For me?"

"Yes, for his mother. I've seen it happen before—burly firefighters calling for their mothers when they're hurt."

Diana was surprised at his sincerity. "Then I'll go to him."

"You can, but not yet. They're still working on him."

"Working on him?"

"Come on." He took her arm. "I'll explain it to you."

For a minute Diana leaned into him. It felt so good. He nodded to Francesca and Tony. "All of you."

Francesca pivoted and looked across the room. Alex had lagged, out of deference to family privacy. He nodded to her, telling her to go ahead.

Ben ignored him.

He sat at one of the tables in the corner and addressed them all. "Nicky has third-degree burns on both his hands and partway up his arms. Right now, he's in the scrub room.

They have to get the burned skin off. They'll rub cream on him and bandage him, mummylike. He'll have a catheter and IV in when you see him.''

''Have *you* seen him?'' Diana asked.

''No, his lieutenant, Jack Carson, called me at work as soon as they knew he was hurt, but the ambulance got here before I did. Jack said he was in pain and in and out of consciousness.''

Francey kneaded her hands. ''Not exactly a blessing in this case. It would be better if he was out for the count.''

Tony gave her a puzzled look.

''It's got to hurt like hell,'' she explained.

Ben said, ''It will. It'll be torture. But the important thing is he's all right. This is not life-threatening.''

Tony reached for Diana's hand, which was shaking. ''Mom, he's all right.''

''I heard that,'' she said. Tony smiled at her, and she smiled the phoniest smile she'd ever given anyone.

''How did it happen?'' Francesca asked.

''There was a fire over on Glide Street,'' Ben told them. ''Nicky's company was first in. Quint Six was right behind them. The blaze wasn't rolling yet, but a victim was trapped inside. One of the probies, Jimmy Arnold, was with his officer doing search and rescue when they found the victim. The lieutenant dragged the old lady out, but Jimmy got lost. The kid called for help on his radio—Nicky heard it. He'd come outside to change his air pack and went back in. A beam came down and knocked Jimmy out. Nicky got hit on the head and was woozy, but he managed to get the rookie out, as well as himself.''

Diana frowned. ''How did he get burned?''

''He had to move a beam blocking their way. The wood was so hot it ate right through his gloves.''

''Oh, my God.'' Diana felt her stomach heave and clasped a hand to her mouth.

Reflexively Ben grasped her other hand. "Dee?"

Praying she wouldn't get ill, wouldn't embarrass herself in front of Ben, she shook her head. "I'm all right."

"Mom, it's okay to be yourself with us. Hell, I feel like bawling like a baby, too." This from Tony.

"No, really, I'm fine."

"Jeez," Tony said. "I wish he hadn't gone back in."

Diana understood the look Francesca and Ben exchanged. "Tony, a firefighter would never let one of his own die without trying to rescue him. It's part of the code."

Ben stiffened. "Are you making fun of us?"

"No," Diana said softly, "it's just an observation. I think it's a brave and heroic thing to do, even if it does endanger the people I love." She reached out and squeezed Francesca's hand.

Her daughter squeezed back, then stood. "I'm going to go tell Alex what's going on."

Tony stood, as well. "I'll get us coffee. And I want to call Erin."

As Francesca went to Alex, Ben frowned. It turned into a glower as he watched Alex hug her tightly, lock a hand around her neck and draw her out of sight. "Damn it."

Diana looked at him. "Could we put our differences aside, at least for today?"

His eyes were full of emotion when he faced her. "Yeah, we should be able to do that."

"Where are Grace and Gus?"

"Went to visit Dad's brother in Corning. I thought I'd call them there after I'd seen Nicky." His voice dropped a notch. "Are you sure you're all right, Dee? You look as green as you used to that second month of pregnancy." He smiled weakly.

Though Diana wanted to throw herself into his arms— much like she'd done at his office that day—she lifted her chin. "I'm fine, Ben. I've changed. I'm stronger now."

He reached for her hand and squeezed. She was surprised by the gesture.

"Chief Cordaro?" Diana tore her eyes away from the warmth in Ben's and looked into the face of a doctor standing by their table. "Nice to see you again, although I'm sorry it's under these circumstances."

"Me, too, Dr. Smith. How's Nick?"

The doctor smiled. "Swore his head off, just like you did that first time they brought you in here burned. What was that, twenty, twenty-five years ago?"

That first time they brought you in here burned. Diana's stomach clenched. Ben had been hurt in the years she'd been away. How many times had she wondered about his safety? Even after she'd left him, she'd driven herself crazy thinking about it. She'd had nightmares for years about his being injured or killed.

Ben laughed. "Close to that."

"Your son's settled in," Dr. Smith told Ben. "He's in pain, and someone will have to play nurse for a few weeks, but he's going to be as good as new. He's doped up and still asking for his mother. Have you been able to reach her?"

"This is his mother." Ben indicated Diana.

Poised, but looking as delicate as a flower in spring, Diana smiled at the burn specialist who'd treated Ben and doubtless many other RFD members for burns.

The doctor's mouth fell open. "Really? I thought this was your daughter."

Ben wasn't all that surprised. Diana was really something. "Thank you," she said, then frowned. "My son's going to be fine?"

"Yes, he is."

"Can I see him?"

"Yes." He glanced at Ben, who frowned, despite his attempt to control his jealousy. "You can go in together this once."

As they stood, Ben put a possessive hand on the small of Diana's back. The way Dr. Smith was eyeing her spiked his blood pressure. Together they went down the hallway and entered the ICU. Nicky was in a private cubicle. He was stretched out flat, and his hands lay palms up next to his body. They were heavily wrapped in gauze. As Ben and Diana got closer, Dr. Smith said, "One tube is a catheter. The other two are IVs."

Ben winced at the tube going into Nicky's groin. God, that had to hurt like hell.

"His arms were too burned to put the IV in the normally used vein," the doctor explained.

Diana shivered. Instinctively Ben put his arm around her and pulled her close. She went to him as naturally as she always had when they were husband and wife.

Dr. Smith gave a polite cough and said, "I'll be in the wing if you need me," then slipped out the door.

Ben rested his chin on Diana's head and held her tight to his chest. "It looks worse than it is," he whispered.

"Don't lie to me. He must be in pain."

"Yes, but he's strong and in top shape. He'll handle the pain, as well as recuperate, faster than the average person."

She looked at him hopefully. "That's good."

Nicky stirred on the bed. "Mom?"

Ben noted tears spring into Diana's eyes. Both Nicky and Francey had stopped calling her mom when they stopped visiting her in New York. *When she got herself a new family.* The thought made him drop his arm. Diana crossed to the bed. "I'm here, Nicky."

He tried to lift his hand and groaned.

"Shh, honey, lie still." She reached out and touched his cheek.

He turned his face into her palm. "Don't go. Please. Don't go away."

Ben watched Diana shudder. It didn't take a psychologist to figure out that Nicky's delirium had sent him back a few decades.

Diana sniffled, then said, "I'm not going anywhere, buddy."

Ben was transported back a few of those decades, too.

Come here, buddy. Mommy loves you best.... It was what she said to Nicky whenever, as the middle child, he acted out, thinking Tony got all the attention as the oldest or Francey because she was a girl.

When Diana leaned over and kissed Nicky, then started to croon "My Pal" to him, Ben slipped out the door. The sight of mother and son and all they'd lost—all he had lost— released too many emotions.

He was just getting a grip when Francey approached him in the hallway. "Dad, is everything okay?"

Ben stared over her shoulder at Alex Templeton, hovering behind his daughter like a wolf waiting to pounce. *Okay? Is everything okay?* No, everything was *not* okay. His whole damned world had turned upside down.

CHAPTER TEN

THE DAY BEFORE Francey was to return to work, Alex followed her through the back door of the house where Dylan O'Roarke's father lived. Alex stayed near the door, as did she, as Dylan held court in the kitchen.

"All right, three easy ones." Dylan said, his grin devilish. "What was the name of the specially designated group of firefighters who traveled around New York City to cut down on arson and stop the torching?"

A tall, dark-haired man, dressed in a loose-fitting linen shirt tucked into well-cut slacks, stood alone by the phone sipping a beer and answered, "The Red Caps."

Next to him, a younger guy swayed on his feet and leaned against the counter as if he needed it for support. He had classic Italian good looks—dark eyes and hair, olive complexion. His jeans and shirt mirrored the dress of most of the others. "I don't think Jake should play." The man whined like a spoiled child.

"Fine. I'll keep my trap shut, Joey." Jake grinned. "It won't help you, anyway. You should have listened to Sister Margaret when she told you to read more."

Joey. As in Joey Santori? The guy Francesca had been engaged to? Great. Just what Alex needed.

"Next is a two-part question," O'Roarke said, barely concealing a superior grin. "What were the first SCBA masks called, and when did we start using the ones we have now?"

"SCBA?" Alex asked Francesca.

"Short for Self-Contained Breathing Apparatus."

Ben Cordaro, who Alex noted had been in deep discussion with an older man across the room, looked up. "We started using the new ones in Boston in 1977. The masks available before that were from the Navy—I can't remember what they were called. But they were bulky sons of bitches, and you couldn't work in them."

"Chemox masks." Dylan supplied the answer cheerfully. "Okay, last one. If you have a heart attack at night and die in bed, and you worked at the firehouse during the day, is it called death in the line of duty?"

"Depends on who you're in bed with." This was from Santori, who'd noticed Francesca had come in and was leering at her as if he'd have her for dinner. Alex's hand crept to the small of her back.

"No, you dumb ass," a guy seated at the table said. "It *is* considered death in the line of duty. Because of the stress on your heart. I know somebody in Chicago that happened to." As the firefighter told his story, Dylan broke away from the group and crossed to Alex and Francesca—where he scooped her into a bear hug. "Francey, baby, it's about time you got to my celebration."

"Congratulations, *Lieutenant*." She pouted prettily as O'Roarke held her close. "But I hate the idea of you going to another station."

"Me, too. I'll miss seein' your legs in the morning."

Alex willed back his irritation. He was beginning to think it was a mistake to accompany Francesca to the party O'Roarke's father was throwing for his son—who had, of course, scored the highest on the recent lieutenant's exam. But Alex had seen little of her since Nick's accident, and she was returning to work tomorrow. Truth be told, though he understood she'd been tied up with her family, he was miffed that she'd wanted to come here instead of spending her last evening alone with him.

Finally O'Roarke let her go. He faced Alex squarely,

holding out his hand. He was a little shorter than Alex, but he had world-class muscles. "You must be Templeton. I've heard a lot about you."

"I've heard a lot about you, too," Alex said dryly, shaking O'Roarke's hand.

"She been singin' my praises again?" O'Roarke reached over and slipped an arm around Francesca's waist. "Jeez, honey, you gotta treat guys better than that or you're gonna end up an old maid."

"At thirty-three, and no prospects of marriage in sight, you should talk, Boy Wonder."

"Yeah, wait till you see my date tonight. A real beauty."

"Another doll, huh?" Francesca had mentioned to Alex that Dylan liked statuesque blondes.

Alex fought the feeling of being excluded. He glanced around the room. There were about twenty men in the large kitchen. Everyone was gabbing except Santori, who threw dagger looks his way, and Ben Cordaro, who sipped a bottle of beer, leaned against the stove and shot Alex equally hostile looks. Tonight was really starting off right.

"Alex, what can I get you to drink?" Dylan asked.

"Beer's fine."

Francesca waited until O'Roarke left and looked at him, her violet eyes sparkling with approval. "You don't drink beer."

"Hey, when in Rome…"

Impulsively Francesca reached up and kissed him on the cheek. Her full breasts brushed his chest. "Thanks."

Well, maybe being here wouldn't be so bad, after all.

Alex was still holding up the wall by the door an hour later, watching Francesca, who'd been dragged over to sit at the table with the men. Occasionally, a couple of women came out of the other room and talked to the guys, got something to drink; a few of the men went into the living room. But there was definite segregation of the sexes at this party—except for Francesca, who was clearly one of the guys. The thought disturbed him, so he pushed it aside. He concentrated on the conversation, trying to ignore the death glances from Santori—who'd drunk three beers and two shots of bourbon since they'd arrived. Instead, Alex stared at Francesca's teal shirt straining across her breasts as she reached to get a second bowl of stew from Sean O'Roarke. The older man had been feeding her all night.

Jake Scarlatta came to stand beside him. Earlier, Francesca had introduced them; she'd told him once Jake was like a third brother. "She's really glad to see everybody."

"Yes, I can see that."

Jake sipped his beer. Alex wondered what was coming next. "She's a special lady, you know."

"I know." Oh, God, Scarlatta was going to ask what his intentions were.

His odd, light gray eyes were sober. "She's tough, really, but more sensitive on the inside than she likes to let on."

"I know that, too."

"Good. It would be hard for her if you didn't get along here tonight."

For some crazy reason, Alex liked the fact that Scarlatta was looking out for her. Of course, it helped that Alex knew he had no call to be jealous of the guy. "I'm having a great time, Jake."

Jake nodded. They watched in silence as Francesca bantered with her buddies. At one point, she got up to get another beer. When she reached the refrigerator, Santori made his way across the kitchen. As Francesca grabbed a beer and closed the door, Santori draped his arm around her shoulders. About her height, he was nose-to-nose with her. Alex stiffened, as did Francesca, when the younger man nuzzled her neck.

Jake laid a hand on Alex's arm. "Don't do anything yet. Let's see if she can handle it."

Alex scowled but stayed where he was.

"Joey's never gotten over her. And he's drinking too much tonight."

Santori's arm snaked around her waist; she tried to step back, but the refrigerator prevented her. When the jerk's hand rose higher, almost touching her breast, Alex straightened. "He's out of line right now."

Setting down his beer, Jake said, "You're right. But let me handle this. A fistfight won't do anybody any good. Joey would like nothing better than to take you apart."

The implication was, of course, that Santori *could* take him apart, and Alex simmered as Jake crossed to Ben, who hadn't been watching Francesca. Jake murmured something to her father, and they both headed to the fridge. In minutes they'd escorted Santori out of the room. Francesca's face was red when she turned toward the table.

"Come here, Cordaro," a big brute of a guy said. "We gotta tell you about Fist." He was clearly trying to break the tension.

Another guy they called Duke pulled out a chair. "You shoulda seen how dirty he got last night."

And so the firefighter family closed ranks around her. No one, not even Francesca, realized or seemed to care that Alex had been left on the sidelines.

On the drive to her house, Alex was silent. It had begun to rain, and he concentrated on driving through the slick streets. The windshield kept fogging up, and he squinted to see the road. He was *not* a happy man. He was worried about Francesca going back to work and trying to block out images of the danger she'd be walking into starting at five o'clock tomorrow night. He was also annoyed at being ignored all evening. And right now, he wasn't even keeping the sexual frustration at bay. He wanted her with a deep and driving desire that was tearing at his insides. Not hard to figure out that one, either, he realized, disgusted with his jealousy and territorial feelings.

Leaning over, she grabbed his hand. "You had a rotten time, didn't you?" she asked as they neared her house.

"No, not rotten." He wasn't lying. Rotten didn't come close to describing his night.

"Sorry, I should have gone alone."

Oh, sure, that's what he wanted to hear. She didn't even consider that she could have spent the last of her free time alone with him. He was starting to get angry.

Oblivious to his mood, she chattered about the guys. How her dad looked tired, but it was probably from dealing with Nicky, who was a grouch being confined to the hospital for a few more days. How good Dylan looked—excited and happy at his progress in the fire department he loved so much. How dumb Joey Santori had acted. All this, and no mention of Alex's feelings or thoughts.

God, Templeton, when did you get to be such a self-centered bastard? Did you think that once she said she felt something for you, her world would revolve around your relationship?

Well, maybe.

He was brooding over that when they darted from the car and sprinted to her porch. He followed her inside to the kitchen while she let the dog out. Finally she gave him her full attention. "Want something? A Scotch?"

"No."

"You were a real trooper at Dylan's, drinking beer and all."

"Such a sacrifice." He tried to joke.

"Are you hungry? We could order out."

He jammed his hands in his jeans pockets. "No, thanks, but if you are…"

"Nah, I ate enough of Sean O'Roarke's stew to feed a

small country." She stared at him for a minute, then closed the distance between him. "How about a kiss?"

He smiled, but didn't feel it in his gut. "I'd never turn down a kiss from you, Francesca."

On tiptoe, she brushed her mouth over his. His hands went to her waist and drew her close. The familiar feel of her settling against him made his heartbeat click into double time. He deepened the kiss, a storm of emotions sweeping through him.

When he pulled back, she stared at him. "Something's wrong."

He shook his head. He wanted her tonight. And he knew why. He wanted to possess her. Like none of the other guys at that party could possess her. The unflattering things that said about him rankled his pride. So he stepped back. "Nothing's wrong."

She held his arms. "I'm sorry you didn't have a good time."

"It was fine."

"Then what is it?" she asked.

"Nothing." Frustrated, he stepped around her and strode to the open kitchen window to stare out. Killer was peering out of his doghouse. A rain-filled, cool breeze drifted over Alex, and he took in several cleansing breaths. "It's my problem, Francesca, not yours. This whole thing is. I'll deal with it."

"This whole thing?"

Still not facing her, he said, "This whole unorthodox relationship."

"*Our* relationship?"

He turned to face her now. "Yes, Francesca, the one I've dragged you into, kicking and screaming all the way."

"Isn't that a slight exaggeration?"

Expelling a heavy breath, he shook his head. "I suppose. I haven't seen anything clearly since I met you."

"Exactly what happened tonight to bring this on?"

He didn't answer. How could she not know?

"Hey, I thought rule number one was we'd always be honest."

Since he wasn't in the mood to joke, he stared at her. Honest? Could he be honest about this? Why not? Silent resentment wasn't getting them anywhere. "You've got something special with them, Francesca. It was so…tangible tonight."

"And you felt left out?"

God, it sounded so immature. He stuck his hands into his pockets again. "No, envious is more like it."

"We've got something special, too."

"Do we?"

She frowned. "Of course we do."

"Yes, well, your caution would indicate otherwise."

"My caution? You mean physically?"

"Not just that."

"Then what?"

"All right, that."

"We *agreed* to take it slow."

Frustrated, he ran a hand through his hair. "I know. It's just that seeing you tonight with all of them made me want…more. Oh, hell, I sound like I'm in high school."

She studied him from across the room. "High school, huh? So, you want me to, ah, like, prove how special you are to me?" She underscored her teenage-girl imitation with a toss of her head and a pout. If she'd been chewing gum, she'd be snapping it. Her hand crawled up her shirt and toyed with the first button of her top.

He watched her, then decided to play along. "Yeah. Like a football player not being sure how the head cheerleader feels about him."

She popped one of the buttons on her shirt…then two…then three. "Hmm, I wonder what the head cheerleader would have to do to get rid of that insecurity." She started toward him, releasing the rest of the buttons as she came closer. When she was halfway between the table and the window, he caught a glimpse of some black lacy thing beneath her shirt. His mouth went dry. "That's a very good start."

Her hands slid to her jeans. With agonizing slowness, she released the snap, then inched her zipper down. From inside peeked matching black lace panties. The sight sent his pulse pounding. She continued to cross the kitchen, her gaze locked on his. "I'm not against proving anything, big guy." When she reached him, she slid her hands up his polo shirt. His heart hammered in his chest, and he began to breathe fast.

"So long as you give me your class ring and letter sweater tomorrow," she whispered.

"I'll give you anything you want, Francesca. Anything at all."

Though she was teasing, *he* wasn't. He *would* give her anything, and the thought scared the hell out of him. Ruthlessly, he pushed it to the back of his mind and crushed her to him.

SO MUCH HEAT. It burst into rolling flames the minute he touched her, dousing all the repartee that had been between them. Every previous touch was a spark, leading to this particular explosion, every kiss fuel to feed their desire. Francey reveled in it. Let the blaze of passion consume her.

He held her so tightly it hurt. "Francesca," he said into her hair, then her neck, as his busy hands scorched her. They roamed like wildfire down her sides to her hips and clutched her bottom. Abruptly he set her away from him, ripped off the shirt she'd unbuttoned and pulled down her bra. His hands closed over her, singeing her skin. "I want to be gentle with you," he said, "but I want you so badly I'm losing control."

"I don't need gentleness," she said huskily. "And I want you weak for me." She tore his shirt out of his jeans and dragged it over his head, made a quick survey of his chest with her fingers before he got in her way. Lifting her with his arms around her bottom, he ducked his head and took one taut nipple into his mouth.

"Alex, oh…" Her senses scattered into a thousand places with the feel of his mouth on her breast, the scent of his aftershave released by his sweat, his groan of appreciation as he suckled vigorously.

"It's not enough," he murmured as he set her down, spun her around, braced her against the wall and reached for her zipper. Pulling it down, he slipped the jeans and panties over her hips, then pressed his palm between her thighs. Pleasure skyrocketed through her, setting off tiny blasts of dynamite in every nerve ending.

"Oh, babe," he murmured, "I've never seen you this needy."

"I've never felt this way," she gasped as he plunged his fingers into her, the heel of his hand grinding against her. She was riding it before she realized what she was doing, what he was telling her. "For me, Francesca. Come for me, just for *me*. Here."

She wanted to say no, that it would be better if it was them both, but she couldn't get the words out before the eruption was upon her, flashes of pleasure so strong they eclipsed awareness. But he didn't stop. Another climax came on the heels of the first, and nothing on earth could have precluded its volcanic force—hotter and more fiery than she'd have believed possible.

Whimpering into his shoulder in the aftermath, she clung to him, vaguely aware that she'd never whimpered in her life. That he could do this to her sent a tremor of fear through her. But she squelched it. "Please, take me upstairs." She wanted more, she wanted to feel him inside her, she wanted to send him off the Richter scale where he'd sent her.

Clumsily, he drew up her jeans and swung her in his arms. "I'm too heavy to carry," she said, her head lolling onto his shoulder. Somehow he made it up the steps; she directed him to her room with almost incoherent phrases.

He set her on the bed. "You're limp as a rag doll." Even in her near-mindless state, she could hear the male satisfaction in his tone. The Templeton cockiness.

She fell back on the mattress, her feet touching the floor, her arms stretched out to the sides. "Your fault." She opened one eye. "You like it, don't you?"

"Oh, yeah." His smug response came out a little breathless. Kneeling, he buried his face in her stomach and bit her gently as he drew off her shoes, socks, jeans and panties. Giving her damp curls one quick nuzzle, he stood and kicked off his shoes, dragged off his jeans and briefs, and then he was on her. "I've got about ten more seconds of sanity left," he said, his weight pressing into her. "Tell me you've got condoms."

"I bought some last week," she confessed, her words slurred by his mouth. "They're in the drawer next to the bed."

He growled again, slid her to the pillows. She heard him fumble in the nightstand while he kissed her, suckled her, delved his fingers into her again. She arched into him hungrily.

But Francey needed to touch him, too. When he moved to his side, struggling to open the condom, she grabbed his wrist. "I want to do it."

He shook his head. "No. I'll never last if you touch me now."

But she took the packet from him and pressed him down

into the mattress. Deliberately she grasped his hard length. His hand went to her hair, and when his fingers clenched in it, she winced. But he was unaware that he'd hurt her. She stroked him. A shudder rippled through his whole body. He let go of her hair and swore, violently writhing on the bed.

"I want to be inside you," he said hoarsely. But now that she was more sane, she wanted him as mindless as he'd made her. She kept up the urgent massage, increasing the pressure. *"Now,"* he said, his voice a harsh bark.

As quickly as she could, she sheathed him. Before she could blink, he had her on her back. He spread her legs and poised above her. "Look at me," he demanded.

She opened her eyes and met his gaze as he plunged into her, filling her completely, becoming more a part of her than anyone ever had before. In some dim recess of her mind, she realized that was his intent—but she didn't care, wanted it. The spirals began just as he stiffened. He thrust once more, and she felt him grow even harder. On the next hot push, she flared out of control. Before consciousness completely eluded her, she heard him cry her name, over and over, as he erupted inside her.

THE SKIES OPENED UP just as Ben Cordaro left Sean O'Roarke's house; the downpour merely worsened his vile mood. His navy windbreaker got soaked as he made his way to the Cherokee, and his head was dripping wet. He spat out every obscenity he'd ever learned, which vented some of his anger.

He started the truck, let it idle and sank back against the seat. What a week. First Nicky got hurt. Then Diana intruded into their lives once again. And tonight Francey brought Templeton to Dylan's party. At least she'd had the good sense to warn him, if not ask his permission. *She's thirty years old. She doesn't need parenting now.*

Damn her. Damn Diana Erickson Cordaro Hathaway. She

was turning him inside out just like she'd done thirty years ago, and he felt as helpless now to stop it as he had then.

Furious with himself, he jammed the car in gear and headed out. It would be rotten driving, but he was only four blocks from home.

Home. God, he didn't want to go to that empty house. His parents were out of town, and he dreaded being alone. Yet he had no inclination to stay at the party, either. Soon after Francey and Templeton left, he'd made the excuse that he'd told Nicky he'd stop by the hospital tonight. Hell, why not? Nothing could cheer him up right now, but seeing his son might help.

The memory popped into his mind, almost coldcocking him. He'd quit smoking and had been a bear. *I'll cheer you up, darling,* Diana had said, prancing into the bedroom from their tiny bathroom, wearing nothing but a black garter belt, stockings and some Chanel Number 5. He'd practically swallowed his tongue and told her he'd stop *breathing* if it meant she'd come to him like that again.

The hospital was quiet as he hurried inside, shaking off the rain. Though visiting hours were over, the staff didn't make a fuss about patients with private rooms circumventing the rules. They were particularly lenient with the police and fire departments.

Nicky's room was on the fourth floor. The door was open. Ben was about to step inside when he heard a sleepy voice mutter, "I'm sorry, I can't help it sometimes." Nicky's words were slurred, as they doped him up pretty good at night.

Intrigued, Ben watched Diana sitting on the side of his son's bed. Nicky's bandaged hand was on her lap, and she was stroking the uninjured part of his arm in a tender maternal caress. "I know you can't, Nicky. You're just like your father. Striking out at me makes you feel better."

"Not really. It's self-protection. So you won't hurt us anymore."

Diana gasped, and Ben held his breath. His son's words hit him like a bucket of cold water. Were they true?

"I won't hurt either of you again, Nicky. I promise."

"You don't know that."

"Give me another chance."

His head moved back and forth on the bed.

"Just think about it."

As his eyes closed, Nicky said, "Okay, I'll think about it."

Diana sat where she was, stroking Nicky's arm for several seconds. Then she stood, leaned over and kissed his forehead. When she straightened and turned, her face was wet.

It poleaxed Ben, just as it had every time she cried. Diana halted when her gaze fell on him. Surprise turned to embarrassment, and she wiped her face. "Ben, I didn't hear you."

"I know."

Turning half away from him, she glanced at the bed, trying to wipe away the rest of the tears surreptitiously. "Nicky's out for the count, I'm afraid."

"Yeah, so I see."

Quickly she gathered her purse and raincoat. "Well, I'll be on my way." She crossed to the door. He stood blocking it. Moisture sparkled in her huge violet eyes. "Excuse me," she said, grappling for emotional equilibrium.

After a minute he stepped aside but followed her out. "I'll ride down with you."

She bit her lip. The bulky purple tunic she wore over white pants accentuated her pallor. "All right."

Keeping her hands clasped in front of her, she rode the elevator with him. As the car hummed, they made small talk about Nicky and Dylan's party until they reached the lobby. He was irked that she treated him like a casual acquaintance. At the front door, Ben saw that the rain hadn't let up.

Diana sighed. "It's raining."

He looked at her. "You always loved the rain."

"Remember how we used to lie in bed and listen to it patter on the roof? From the attic it sounded like a hundred tiny drums. We'd hold hands and plan our future." Her voice, only a silky whisper, caught. "Everything looked so good then."

Because the memory socked him in the gut, he said unkindly, "It was smoke and mirrors, Diana."

Swallowing hard, she averted her gaze. "Good night, Ben."

She'd just stepped outside, under the overhang of the sidewalk, when he grasped her arm. "You're not driving home in this." His tone was a general's commanding troops. He was used to that kind of power. And obedience.

"Why?"

"I heard on the radio the roads were flooding."

"I'm perfectly capable of driving in rain."

He frowned. "You didn't used to be. You hated the roads in bad weather."

She pointed that little chin. "I've changed."

He said gruffly, "Well, I haven't. Wait here."

When she opened her mouth to protest again, he barked, "I mean it, Diana."

In minutes he'd retrieved his car and had her tucked inside, seat belt fastened. She'd fussed about his foolishness, but he didn't listen. When she realized he wouldn't budge, she clammed up for most of the drive, sitting far across from him on the bench seat, staring out the window.

"You need directions," she finally said as they neared her exit off the expressway. He didn't answer her. Instead, he chose the right exit, found her street and pulled up to her house while she was still frowning. "How do you know where I live?"

"Francey told me."

"Oh. Well, thanks." She reached for her door. Tugging her coat over her head, she exited the Cherokee and dashed to her front porch. She didn't seem to realize he'd followed her until she stood under the sloping roof and removed the coat from her head. Covering it had been a useless gesture, for she was soaked through. "Ben, what are you doing?"

"Seeing you inside."

She rolled her eyes. "Were you always this...forceful?"

He felt his pulse speed up at the images her comment engendered. "You used to love it."

Without a word she turned from him, opened the door and stepped into the house. He followed her and closed the door.

"All right. I'm in. You can leave."

Instead of answering her, he surveyed the condo. From the foyer, he could see a huge living room to the right, a hallway off that and another one just ahead. "I don't want to leave yet. I want to wait until it lets up outside."

"What's this all about?"

Her hair was plastered against her head; it reminded him of the long and lazy showers they'd taken together. He reached out and smoothed it. "Invite me for coffee." His voice was husky, the way it got after sex.

She stared at him a minute. "Only if you promise not to yell at me."

"Yell at you?"

"Yes, that's all you do anymore."

He tucked a strand of hair behind her ear and scraped his knuckles over rose-petal soft skin. "We had our best times in bed, after a fight."

She closed her eyes, swallowed hard. "I hated fighting with you." As if the words brought pain, she looked at him and stepped back. "I'm going to change. I'll fix coffee afterward."

Leaving him in the foyer, she disappeared into a hallway,

then returned with a towel. "Here, dry your hair and face and get out of that wet coat."

When she was gone again, he shrugged out of his jacket, hooked it over a doorknob so it would drip on the tile in the foyer and dried off as best he could. He kicked off his shoes and sauntered into the living room. Things were mostly white—walls, carpet, furniture. Scattered around were colorful pillows, afghans, paintings on the wall. There were two white cats, spotted with caramel, lazing by a chair. Ben froze when his gaze landed on a floor-to-ceiling bookshelf. It was full of pictures of his family—Francey, Nicky and Tony at all ages, him, Grace, Gus. Shocked, he moved to it and studied the collection.

"The kitchen's this way." The words came from behind him.

Ben faced her. She'd put on a lilac sweat suit that didn't hide her curves. He noticed them as he followed her silently.

Again there was white—cupboards, appliances, the floor. "Doesn't all this white get on your nerves? I feel like I'm in the hospital."

"It's very chic, Ben."

"It's damn boring."

She smiled. "Probably."

He stood near the phone. "Your answering machine's blinking."

"It wouldn't be the hospital, would it?" she asked.

"I doubt it, but we should check." While she got the coffee on, he pressed the button, then sat at the table. The first message was a long, whiny one from Elise. It reminded Ben of what Diana had done with her life. The second was from Francey, leaving Diana the details about lunch with her and Alex. That one made him mad. But the third message caused his blood to boil.

"Hello, Diana. This is Jeremy Smith. I enjoyed having coffee with you this afternoon. I wondered if you'd like to go to dinner with me this weekend. The Rio is one of my favorite restaurants. I'll call back.''

Ben's reaction to the message startled him. She'd freakin' married another man, slept with Nathan Hathaway for almost twenty years. Why the hell should a date with Nicky's doctor bother him?

But it did. A lot.

He scowled at the pot as it finished dripping.

"Here's your coffee." Diana set a huge mug in front of him.

Roughly he grabbed her wrist, his fingers easily encircling it. "Are you seeing Smith?" His voice was a growl.

"No." She peered at him haughtily. He was embarrassed by his jealousy. But not enough to drop the subject. "Not yet, anyway," she finished.

He yanked her onto his lap.

He noticed she didn't resist. Instead, she curled familiarly into him, her hands flat against his chest, her head on his shoulder, her bottom nestled in his lap.

"The thought of another man touching you almost killed me."

Diana's eyes turned liquid when she looked at him. "No man ever touched me like you, Ben."

He snatched her hand from his chest. "You wore someone else's ring." Rubbing the base of her fourth finger, he brought it to his mouth for a gentle kiss.

"I still have yours," she whispered.

His hands went to her waist and clenched. He bent his head to meet hers. "Don't tell me things like that, Dee."

"I know you don't want to hear them."

"Oh, God," he admitted, "I want to hear them more than I want to take my next breath."

She waited a long time before she said, "I love you, Ben."

"Don't."

''I've always loved you, more than life itself.''

His breath came in heavy pants. Not because of her physical closeness, but because of words he'd wanted to hear again for more than twenty-five years.

Ben struggled to remember that she'd left him. That she'd abandoned their kids. He searched for the gut-sick feeling of loneliness she'd permanently bequeathed him.

But he couldn't summon any of it. Instead, he was swamped by the musical sound of the only words he'd ever needed to hear.

He raised his head; she stared at him with violet eyes that made him want to get on his knees and beg her to be his again.

He said simply, ''Where's the bedroom?''

CHAPTER ELEVEN

"GET THE LEAD out of your ass, Cordaro. You've only been out eight weeks, not eight months."

Her arms soapy up to their elbows, Francey turned to Duke Russo and flipped some of the suds at him. He sputtered and stepped back. "Can it, Duke. You in a hurry to go somewhere?"

Duke smiled. A twenty-year veteran in the department, he was a gruff, dyed-in-the-wool male chauvinist who was as big—and as strong—as a bear. Since he'd been against women entering the fire service, Francey had learned early on she had to prove herself to him. But once she'd showed her stuff, she stopped being afraid of him. Though she still listened to him and paid attention to what he said. She remembered her father saying, "Respect Russo, Francey. He can bench-press a Coke machine."

For a moment Duke eyed her, his bushy salt-and-pepper eyebrows forming a vee. They contrasted to his silver brush cut and gave his face character. "Somethin's different about you."

Striving to keep back the blush, she stared at the sink. "I been outta here for a month and a half. You just aren't used to having a woman around again."

"Nah, it's somethin' else." He picked up a huge metal pan and dried it with hands the size of baseball mitts. "You sure that arm's all right?" His tone told her he wasn't teasing or challenging her fitness.

"Yeah, I'm sure. I'll arm wrestle you later to prove it."

He guffawed. "Just try it, little girl."

Francey smiled, grateful to be healthy enough to work, happy to be sparring with Duke, looking forward to her first run.

"Hey, Duke," Robbie called from the doorway, "can you come in here? Dylan wants you to look at the confined-space plan."

"Go ahead, I'll finish up here," Francey said.

"Well, stop the woolgathering or you'll be here all night."

Francey shot him a rude retort, and Duke laughed all the way to the common area.

Once he was gone, she sighed. God, she *was* daydreaming. About Alex. Who'd left her bed at three o'clock this afternoon with a satisfied smile and a much-too-smug attitude. They'd been in that bed for almost seventeen hours, leaving it only to shower and use the bathroom. They'd even eaten snuggled there. Francey shivered, remembering how Alex fed her chocolate-covered strawberries and champagne at ten in the morning. Though she hadn't exactly *drunk* any champagne, because she had to go on duty. But he had. Well, *drinking* was a stretch—more like sipped. She touched her chest, remembering what the bubbly felt like dribbling down her bare skin as he licked it off. She sighed again.

"Tough getting back?"

Ed Knight had come into the kitchen. "Nah, Cap, it's great."

"Hey, it's all right if it's hard, Francey. Sometimes, being off so long, you lose your concentration."

"A little bit, maybe," she confessed, rinsing the last pan.

Knight crossed to the coffeepot, drew himself a cup and settled into a chair. "I remember when I sprained my ankle and was out for a month. It was tough focusing when I finally got back here." He smiled. "And you've only been on three hours."

She looked at the clock. Seven. She told Alex she'd call him around ten.

Francey chatted with Ed as she sponged off the counters and stored the leftovers. When he went to check on the confined-space plan, she let her mind drift to Alex again—to just after the first time they'd made love. Both of them had been a little awed.

"You pack quite a punch, Francesca," he'd said, looking at her, his complexion still flushed from the vigor of his response.

"So do you." She stared at him. "I practically lost consciousness."

He looked smug. "I know." He was still inside her, and he flexed his hips, sending aftershocks through her.

She closed her eyes and moaned.

He chuckled. "I do hope this puts all notion of that nasty S-word out of your mind."

"S-word?"

"You know, as in stuffy?"

She giggled. "I think this pretty well proved me wrong."

"You were wrong about a lot of things," he said soberly.

She reached up and brushed her fingers down his cheek. "I know I was." Choking back emotion, she'd said, "And I'm so glad."

Easing to his side, he took her with him. And frowned.

"What is it?" she asked.

"I lost it with you. I couldn't even have told you my name."

"Mmm."

"I'm not sure I like that."

"Alex?" she said, nuzzling into him.

"What?"

"I did, too. I lost it, too."

He'd drawn her close. "We're in this together, I guess."

"Yep. We are."

The overhead speaker clicked on; Francey had forgotten how full of static it was. "An automobile accident on the ramp off four-ninety and Child Street. One car involved. Quint/Midi Twelve and Engine Seventeen go in-service."

For a moment Francey was disoriented. Then years of training kicked in. Dylan and Robbie had reached the bay by the time she got to it. Both had their bunker boots on and pants half on before she'd flung off her shoes. Duke and Adam were right behind her. Ed Knight stopped to grab the computer printout of the call and was the last one into the Quint; Duke and Adam took the Midi. After donning all their goods, they exited the bay; Robbie jumped out to close the doors. Quint and Midi Twelve were rolling within three minutes of the call.

The evening was warm and dry, so maneuvering the roads was easy. As Dylan drove, Captain Knight addressed Robbie. "What do we do, probie, if a victim is trapped?"

Snapping his turnout coat, Robbie answered, "Try the doors and windows first before compromising the body of the vehicle."

Dylan glanced at Francey, who sat behind the officer. She said, "Before you touch the car, what do you do?"

"Damn. You check for utilities that pose a hazard."

"Then?"

"You stabilize the vehicle."

Above the blaring siren, Knight told him, "Right, kid. And do exactly what I say."

As they pulled up to the accident, streetlights illuminated the dusk-shrouded scene; cars whizzed by on the expressway behind them, and horns broke the monotony. Captain Knight reported in to the dispatcher. "Quint/Midi Twelve is on the scene. Only one car involved. No fire or hazards evident."

And then they were out of the truck.

As with most collisions, the vehicle remained upright. It had slid off the ramp and crashed into a concrete abutment.

The front end looked like an accordion. Ed Knight raced to the car; Dylan and Francey began to remove the chocking from the bed of the truck while Robbie and Adam dragged out the Hurst tools, generator and manifold from the side of the Midi. As Francey and Dylan approached the car, the other two men hooked up the manifold so the three rescue tools could be used on generator power if necessary. When Francey and Dylan reached the captain, he was talking to the woman inside. "You okay, ma'am?"

The driver's side window was smashed, providing an opening, but glass had cut the victim's face. Blood trickled down her cheek. She was conscious. "I hurt," she said.

Sirens from Engine Seventeen and the ambulance sounded faintly in the background. Out of the corner of her eye, Francey saw the battalion chief's car pull up.

"Chock the wheels." The captain issued the standard operating procedure to stabilize the vehicle before any rescue work was attempted. As they followed orders, Francey could hear Ed talk to the chief before the blare of the sirens reached fever pitch as the rest of the emergency vehicles pulled into the scene. She was dimly aware of the actions of the other firemen, police and paramedics as she and Dylan placed steplike rubber supports under each side of the car. By the time the vehicle was secure, the captain had ascertained the situation. Into the radio he said, "Confirming that a victim is trapped. We'll proceed with extrication. Engine Seventeen is on the scene. Ambulance and police just arrived."

He turned to Francey and Dylan and directed the action. Doors were jammed too badly to spring them with the spreaderlike Hurst tool, commonly known as the Jaws of Life; Knight made the decision to cut open the top of the car with the hydraulic shears, removing the car from around the victim, rather than vice versa. "Dylan, get inside with her."

Through the broken window, the captain, who'd donned rubber gloves, spread a blanket over the woman to cover her. Francey taped the passenger-side window before she popped it with a small cylindrical metal tool. Glass shattered outward, and they removed the pieces. Dylan crawled in through the opening wearing protective plastic gloves and face mask. Once inside, as he began his assessment, Francey heard him say, "Hi, Mrs. DeVeigh. My name's Dylan. If you'd keep talkin' to me, it would help me figure out what's going on here."

"About what?"

"Got grandchildren?"

"Yes. I was coming from their house."

"I miss my grandma. She was my best sweetheart."

The victim smiled weakly at Dylan.

"Mrs. DeVeigh, we're going to cut you out of here," the captain said from outside. "Can you handle that?"

"I think so." Her frail hand gripped Dylan's big one; he held on tightly.

Francey watched Captain Knight tape the front windshield; it required a separate removal procedure as it was made with material that would shatter in a different way from the side glass. Within minutes, with a specially designed handsaw from the Midi toolbox, Francey cut vertically along each side, then across the top, watching the metal slice the glass like butter. The front windshield folded down.

Duke, wearing goggles and leather gloves, came up behind her with the heavy Hurst shears dangling from one hand. Back at the Midi, Adam started the generator; a lawn-mowerlike roar split the air. Duke lifted the shears and popped the A, B and C posts of the body of the car. They came apart like toy building blocks. The captain checked the car. Dylan had treated the woman's superficial wounds, taken vitals and told Ed Knight she was fine.

"Okay, Mrs. DeVeigh, we're gonna spring you now," Dylan told her. "You all right, darlin'?"

The older woman said, "Don't get fresh, young man."

Outside, Duke began cutting the roof with the shears; the metallic grating made Francey's teeth hurt. The tool ate away at one side, then another, cutting a vee in the rear of the car. Francey hopped on one side, Duke on the other; grunting, they folded back the hood.

Dylan stood and reached for the neck gear the paramedic handed him. The entire scene was controlled by the fire department; when the extrication was complete, the ambulance personnel would take over. "You still with us, sweetheart?"

"Yes," Mrs. DeVeigh answered groggily.

"Good. You know, your calm's keepin' me from panicking."

She smiled. "You're a charmer, young man."

"We're gonna stabilize you with this ugly-lookin' neck brace," he said, fitting the cervical collar around her. He winked. "Though it's not my idea of high fashion."

In another minute, the woman was secured. One of the medics handed Dylan a backboard, which he slid into position behind Mrs. DeVeigh. As they'd done countless times before, Francey, Dylan and the captain hefted the victim out of the vehicle and onto the backboard. A stretcher was ready for her. As Francey and the others exited the car, the medical crew strapped Mrs. DeVeigh down. In a few minutes, she was in the ambulance and speeding away.

Their adrenaline rush subsiding, Dylan and Francey leaned against the car. The captain spoke into the radio; Duke took the tools to the Midi. As Robbie approached them, Francey felt a sting in her shoulder. When they were lifting the woman out, she must have caught her turnout coat on the jagged edge of the hood.

Dylan looked over and gave her a tired salute. "Welcome back, Cordaro."

DIANA RAISED her glass of Chardonnay and clinked it with Jeremy Smith's Manhattan. The subdued lighting of the Rio cast his longish gray hair and kind brown eyes in a flattering glow. His well-cut suit was the perfect complement to his good looks. "Cheers!"

"Cheers." She smiled at him. She was holding it together pretty well, considering.

"How long have you been back in Rockford?" he asked her.

Long enough to make a mess of things. No, she wouldn't think that way. She'd made a conscious decision this morning and she'd stick to it, no matter how many demons hovered in the wings waiting to get their claws into her.

"About eight months." Again she flashed him a smile full of bravado. "Tell me about your practice," she said, adjusting the light beaded jacket she wore over a one-piece black silk jumpsuit. She was determined to enjoy this date. She'd decided to go out with the handsome doctor tonight and have a good time.

But as Jeremy Smith filled her in on the daily life of a burn specialist, she only half listened.

Her thoughts were on her ex-husband. Ben had acted exactly as she'd expected he would this morning. Like the young man she'd married, he'd swept her upstairs last night and made sweet love to her—twice. The reality of having him inside her again brought tears to her eyes; when he'd linked his hands with hers and told her it had never been as good, as meaningful, with another woman, the tears had slipped onto her cheeks. But he'd shut down when sanity returned, which happened to be late morning.

Only this time Diana had been ready for him. She'd awakened to find him staring at the dressing table in the corner of her bedroom. He'd been up for a while, she guessed; he looked youthfully sexy, dressed in his slacks and white undershirt, with a dark growth of beard stubbling his face. He'd made coffee and was sipping from a mug. When she spoke his name, he'd turned and said only, "How did you get it?"

"Grace. She made Gus pull it out of the trash pile and hide it in your basement." Diana had angled her chin. "She knew how much it meant to me."

He ran his hand over the smooth surface of the wood, which looked as good as it had more than thirty years ago. Their first year of marriage, Ben had spent hours honing it, since it was the only Christmas present he could afford for his young bride. "It lasted," he said hoarsely, then swung his gaze to her. "Unlike us."

She struggled to sit up and tucked the sheet around her breasts—poor protection against the thunderclouds on his face.

His eyes narrowed on her coldly. "You're still as good in the sack as you always were, Diana."

His words were in stark contrast to the endearments he'd murmured as they'd made love. *I never forgot how you smelled... You're so, so sweet.... Oh, God, Dee.*

She'd shaken her hair back. "You can try to demean what happened between us, Ben. But I was here in this bed with you last night. I know how you really feel now." She'd straightened her shoulders. "Still."

He'd watched her.

"And you may as well know something else. I'm through letting you tromp all over me. I've paid long enough for my weakness years ago. If you want to see me again, you're going to have to get over my leaving you."

His brows had practically skyrocketed off his face. "Who says I want to see you again?"

"You did. With every touch last night."

That had gotten him mad. Probably because he knew it was true. "Good sex always made you spunky."

"Some things haven't changed."

Diana could read him so easily. He was petrified, confronted with that idea. He'd jammed his hands in his pockets. "Yeah, that's right. There's still chemistry between us, like there always was. We're matches and tinder when we get near each other. If you want to screw occasionally, it's fine with me. But don't expect any more."

Angry, she'd whipped off the covers and stood naked before him. She took satisfaction in watching his jaw drop. "No, thanks, I'm not into casual sex. Not with you, anyway," she'd told him as she crossed to her closet and pulled out a robe. She donned it but left the top scandalously gaping. "I love you, Ben, but I'm not going to let you treat me badly anymore. I deserve better than that." She'd headed for the bathroom, glancing over her shoulder. "Be sure to lock the door on your way out...."

"Shall we order?"

Jeremy Smith's words drew Diana to the present. He smiled at her.

"Yes, the lobster thermidor looks good to me. How about you?"

He reached out and squeezed her hand. "My choice exactly. We have a lot in common."

She nodded. "Yes, we do. I'm glad you called me to go out, Jeremy."

And you can go to hell, Ben Cordaro, she thought as the waiter approached them. *Just go straight to hell.*

ALEX WAS WORRIED when he awoke at eight Sunday morning. He threw the covers off the bed, yanked on sweatpants and hurried downstairs to check the answering machine. He didn't really expect a message, though; he'd have heard the phone if she'd tried to reach him. He hadn't dozed off until two, and even when he'd slept, he'd dreamed of leaping flames and falling timbers—with Francesca trapped in the middle of them. Just like the mural in the Philadelphia museum.

There was no blinking light on the phone.

Damn.

Zombielike, he assembled the coffee and paced while he waited for it to drip. All right, he told himself, she didn't call him at ten last night as they'd planned. In all fairness, she'd said if they got a run, she wouldn't. But surely they'd been back to the firehouse at some point, and she could have phoned. He knew better than to call the station to see if she was all right. She'd told him once that it was an unwritten rule that a significant other didn't call—especially late at night. He glanced at the clock. She was off at seven this morning, so he'd try her at home. He dialed her number, his hand clutching the receiver when the answering machine turned on. "This is Francey. Leave a message."

"Francesca, it's Alex. I'm…ah, worried. Call me as soon as you get in. Oh, and don't forget the brunch at Mother's. We're supposed to be there at ten."

After he hung up and got coffee, he sat at the table facing the lake. The wind whipped the boat moorings, and the waves crashed onto the shore this morning, matching his tumultuous mood. So different from yesterday, when he'd awakened with her and they'd made love with sleepy passion once again. He could still feel the sensation of being deep inside her, still hear those tiny little gasps she made when she came, still remember how she'd looked at him as if he was all she wanted in the world.

How could his sense of well-being change so fast?

He was still anxious and angry that she hadn't called as he pulled up to his parents' home at ten o'clock. He'd phoned her twice more and left the Templeton number. He tried to quell his panic that something had happened to her. Instead, he concentrated on his disappointment that she was missing this chance to meet his parents.

His mother met him at the door. She looked good today, her face having lost some of the tension Alex's being injured in the warehouse fire had caused. Dressed casually in a yellow skirt and matching top, she smiled. "Hello, darling." She glanced behind him. "Where's Francesca?"

"I don't exactly know," he told her, kissing her cheek.

"Well, come in. Your father and Richard are in the back." Alex followed her to the screened-in porch that jutted off the kitchen.

"Hello, son," Jared Templeton said warmly.

"Hi, Dad. You look great." He had a tan, probably from golfing these past few weeks.

"Well, *you* don't," Richard observed from across the room. "You look like you've been up all night." He frowned. "Do we dare ask why?"

Alex scowled. "It's nice to see you, too, Richard."

Richard ignored his remark. "Where is she?"

Sticking his hands into the pockets of his dress khakis, Alex prayed for patience. He didn't appreciate Richard's needling when he was already feeling raw.

"You said you didn't know, dear?" Maureen asked.

"No, Mother. She worked last night and she didn't call this morning." He shifted his stance, angry at being put in this position. "It probably wasn't a wise idea to plan to have her join us. If the station had runs during the night, she'd be too tired to come, anyway. More than likely she's home in bed."

Richard gave him an I-told-you-so look.

"Can we discuss something else?" he asked, crossing to the table. "We'll set up another time for you to meet her."

"Of course." His father had always been the diplomat. "Hand me the paper, and we'll see how Templeton stock is doing today."

Alex's mother reached for the *Rockford Sentinel*. Flipping through it to find the business section, she stopped abruptly. "Oh, look at this!" Maureen raised surprised eyes to her son. "Alex, I think you should see it first."

As she handed him the Living section, Alex was bemused. But not for long. He looked at the paper. There she was, Francesca Cordaro, smiling at him. It was a picture that had been published when she'd rescued him six weeks ago.

Obviously this had been a planned article. It was entitled A Family of Heroes and had shots of her, her brother Nick and her father in single photos, then one of the three of them together.

He scanned the story. It focused on how Francesca had saved Alex and how Nick had dragged the rookie out of a burning building; both had been hurt in the process. The article also detailed two of her father's rather startling rescues when he was on the line. Once he'd rappelled into a basement full of flames to save the lives of two firefighters; another time he'd dragged a child out of a blaze, sustaining second-degree burns in the process. It was an emotional piece.

But what really shoved a fist in Alex's stomach was a side bar—under Late Breaking News. It read, "The saga continues… The Jaws of Life…or Death" and described the "daring rescue" made last night by firefighters from Quint/Midi Twelve. There was a picture of a demolished car on a ramp. The text told how the city firefighters had extricated a sixty-five-year-old victim from the disabled automobile. The woman just happened to be the mayor's sister. It played up the firefighters' heroism— "…they pulled her from possible death…" —and the danger— "…the probability of the gas tank exploding…"

Alex took one more quick glance at the article, then looked up. His mother wore a puzzled expression; his father's eyes held questions. Richard, of course, was gloating.

"Well," Alex said dryly, "at least I know she's all right."

ANXIOUS TO SEE Alex, Francey threw open the front door as soon as the bell chimed. He stood on her porch dressed in crisp beige cotton trousers and a green-striped golf shirt. "Hi."

His hands in his pockets, he said, "Hi." After scanning her outfit, he locked his eyes on hers. "Another of Diana's designs?"

She nodded. Diana had put together cream-colored shorts and a matching sleeveless top, accented with a peach belt and a lightweight peach jacket to throw over her shoulders. It was more a debutante's outfit, or perhaps one Chelsea would wear.

Without a word, Francey stood aside and Alex stepped into the foyer. As soon as she shut the door, he pulled her into his arms. His kiss was drugging. And a little bit desperate. Francey knew why. Things were strained between them.

"Never again," he mumbled against her lips, "are we going this long without a kiss." They hadn't managed time together since Saturday morning—and it was Tuesday night.

Francey kept herself from stiffening. She didn't want to get into a discussion, but it was likely that kind of separation would continue. And she knew from the guys at work that firefighters' schedules wreaked havoc with their partners. She hugged Alex and said diplomatically, "I missed you."

He drew back, and his face took on a lazy grin. "We could stay here tonight. Lock the door. Not answer the phone."

"I couldn't do that to Tony and Erin." Francey was expected at her nine-year-old nephew's birthday party in half an hour.

Alex's face went blank, but not before she saw annoyance in his eyes. "And tomorrow night's the department softball game."

"Yeah."

After a moment he let her go and eased away from her. "Well, can I make an appointment for Thursday night?"

Francey sighed. "You're still angry about the weekend, aren't you?"

"Angry isn't the right word. More like disappointed." He took a long, hard look at her. "It would help if I thought not seeing me for three days—after lovemaking that should go into the *Guinness Book of Records*—bothered you as much as it does me."

"Wow, Guinness?"

He didn't smile.

She sobered. "It does bother me that I haven't seen you, Alex. It's just that I've lived my entire adult life like this— missing out on dates and special events because of my schedule."

"And which am I—a date or a special event?" He turned away in disgust and glanced at a huge package wrapped in Buffalo Bills paper on the floor. He said flatly, "Is this the present? I'll carry it to the car. We should get going."

As he bent, Francey grasped his arm. "Wait a minute. If you've got something to say, say it now."

Straightening, he faced her. "I said everything I had to say on the phone Sunday—when you finally got around to calling me."

Inside, she felt bad for letting him down, but his tone put her on the defensive. "I apologized about brunch. I didn't know I had to wear sackcloth for a week to atone for it."

Anger turned his eyes into green flame. "A simple note of apology to my mother will do it."

"Fine, I'll write her." Francey glared at him. "What do I have to do to appease *you?*"

"I'm not sure I like the way you phrased that."

"Well, I don't like your whole long-suffering-husband attitude about this." She ran a hand through her hair. "I explained that we'd gotten another run as soon as we returned from the accident.''

''The accident I had to read about in the paper.''

She cringed inwardly. ''I'm sorry. There just wasn't time to call you. And in the morning, I was waiting until seven to phone so I wouldn't wake you up. Before I could do that, the chief summoned us to the hospital for the mayor's sister to thank us properly.'' Actually, though Francey had been punchy from lack of sleep Sunday morning, she'd loved the recognition. It was as rare as February sunshine in Rockford. ''I take responsibility for all of it. I should have known not to make plans when I'm on nights. I'm not used to being accountable to anyone. But this is how my life works.''

''You were home in plenty of time to make the brunch.''

''Yes, I was.''

''I left my parents' number.''

She threw up her hands. ''I was still running on adrenaline when I got home and got the message. I just closed my eyes for a few minutes….'' A few minutes to marshal her strength before she called and fought this out with him. ''I was exhausted. I fell asleep.'' She stared at him beseechingly. ''I told you all this on the phone.''

''I know, in between your hectic work schedule.''

Again, the comment triggered defensive sparks in her. ''And yours. I was off yesterday, and you flew to Toronto.''

''Sorry I wasn't here when you could fit me in.''

''What do you want me to say? A firefighter's life is crazy.''

He stared at her.

''I told you there would be problems.'' It was a low blow, to remind him of her hesitancy to get involved with him. She'd chosen freely to start seeing him. But he'd backed her into a corner, so she struck out at him.

Closing his eyes, he leaned against the wall and crossed his arms over his chest. ''I know. I'm behaving badly. Just like you're not used to being accountable to anyone, I'm not used to being shoved into the background of a woman's life.''

"You're not in the background, Alex.''

He sighed. "It's going to take some time to work this out, isn't it?''

She nodded.

"Come here and kiss me again. That will help.''

Francey crossed the room. Alex grasped her shoulders and slid an arm around her back.

She winced.

"What the hell?''

"It's nothing. I got cut Saturday night, and it's still sore.''

"You got cut?''

"On my shoulder. It's no big deal. I didn't need stitches or anything.''

"You just cringed in pain.''

"You grabbed my shoulder blade.'' At his thunderous look, she snapped, "I'm okay.'' She pulled away and picked up her jacket and the present. "Come on, we're going to be late to the party.''

The drive to her brother's house, which was only minutes from Diana's, was made in tense discomfort; they traveled most of it in silence. They'd reached Tony's front porch before she realized she'd never kissed Alex.

Her nephew swung open the door just after they rang the bell. "Aunt Francey.'' His eyes widened as he spied the gift. "Is that for me?''

"You bet, sport. But I gotta have a hug first.''

Kevin hugged her, then grasped her hand and dragged her inside. She glanced over her shoulder. "Are you coming?''

"Yes,'' Alex said from the doorway, clearly unhappy. Hell, so was she. She had no idea a relationship was a series of tests you had to pass. She'd obviously failed this one big-time.

The Cordaro family had congregated in the back of Tony's house, which sprawled into a spacious family room off an equally spacious kitchen—filled with the smell of marinara sauce and oregano. Her brother Tony, her father, grandfather and Jake Scarlatta hovered around the stove.

"It's done," Ben said, wiping his hands on the red-checked apron tied around the waist. "Al dente."

"It's not done," Gus told him, his apron fancier than his son's. It was a the type bakers wore and read, Firefighters Feel The Heat. "Thirty more seconds."

"What good will seconds do, Grandpa?" Nicky asked from the table. He'd left the hospital yesterday and was staying at his grandparents' house. He could barely pick up the beer he sipped.

"Just like fire fighting, seconds are important in cooking spaghetti."

"Hi, everybody," Francey said. Five men looked at her and Alex. Gus, Jake and Tony smiled.

"Well, it's about time you got here," Ben grumbled.

Jake waved.

"Hi, kid." Tony approached them and hugged Francey. Spaghetti sauce dotted his short-sleeved yellow shirt, and there was a trace of it on his arm. "Nice to see you again, Alex."

Francey's grandfather came over. He kissed his grand-daughter, then held out his hand to Alex. "I'm Gus," he said cheerfully. "Heard a lot about you, boy."

Alex smiled genuinely. "Is that good or bad?"

Grandpa encircled his arm around her, carefully avoiding her injury like an experienced smoke eater. "Good."

Erin, Tony's wife, entered the kitchen holding Francey's eight-month-old nephew. Introductions were made. Alex nodded congenially through them all, then Francey led him into the family room, where the others sat.

Alex smiled—even if it was somewhat forced—at her grandmother's comment. "So, this is Alex." He kissed Diana on the cheek and shook hands with Sue, Nicky's ex-wife. Sue and her ten-year-old son were still invited to all the family gatherings, though she and Nicky barely spoke to each other. Francey hugged Jake's daughter, Jessica, who whispered to her, "He looks like Matthew McConaughey." When they reached Diana, Francey stopped cold. Next to her on one of the sofas perched Elise, blond hair skimming bare shoulders, which a sleek white dress revealed. Her blue eyes were full of a prom queen's confidence.

The surprise on Francey's face must have shown. "Erin invited Elise, dear. Wasn't that considerate of her?"

Francey said, "Remind me to thank Erin."

Unaware of the vibes, Erin said from behind her, "No thanks necessary. She's family, too."

God forbid, Francey thought.

Elise stood up, took Alex's hand and kissed him on the cheek. "Hello again."

Francey had the unkind urge to shove the younger woman into the leather couch cushions.

"Speaking of family, you've met my father, haven't you, Francey?" Erin's voice broke into Francey's satisfying fantasy.

"Yes, a couple of times." Elise, Francey noticed, had yet to let go of Alex's hand.

"Dad," Erin said, "you remember Tony's sister, Francey. And this is Alex Templeton. Alex, my father, Cameron Lester."

Erin's widowed father stood. He was tall, with classic blond good looks, dressed in chic golf-on-Sunday clothes. "Francey, how nice to see you again. After meeting your mother, I can see where you get your beauty from."

A loud metallic sound reverberated from the kitchen. Ben Cordaro had carried a huge pot to the table that faced the family room and would be used to set up a buffet. The pan's metal top had fallen onto the ceramic tile floor when he'd placed the spaghetti on a hot pad. Francey noted that her father was staring at her mother—and at Cameron Lester.

She turned. "Nice to meet you." Cameron and Alex shook hands.

"Going to join me in here, son?" Cameron asked Alex. "It seems the other men are cooks, and I'm hopeless in the kitchen."

Diana laughed. "This is an equal-opportunity family. Firefighters learn early to do their share. *We'll* have to clean up, though," she said, touching his arm.

Intending to go to the kitchen to get drinks for her and Alex, Francey turned away. She saw her father scowling at her mother's hand on Cameron's arm.

This was gonna be a hell of a dinner.

It was. Amidst the baked ziti, spaghetti and meatballs and Chianti, daggers were zinging around the room.

Nicky couldn't take his eyes off Sue, but when she looked at him, he glowered.

Ben glared at Cameron Lester every time he addressed a comment—which was often—to Diana.

Elise, who had maneuvered a seat next to Alex, found numerous reasons to gaze at him with her big doe eyes, frequently brushing his arm with hers. God only knows what she was doing under the table.

And though he was friendly to everyone else, Alex gave *her* the silent treatment. Francey was so uncomfortable she was glad when it was time to tackle the dishes.

All the cooks headed to the living room, and the women grabbed aprons and picked up dish towels. They insisted Alex and Cameron join the men for the start of a Yankees game.

Erin held her squirming son in her arms. "I'd like to help,

but Ian's fussing." She smiled at Diana. "Want to rock him, Grandma?"

"And miss out on dishes? I'd love to."

Diana reached out. "Come to Grandma, baby," she crooned. Ian gurgled and snuggled into her breasts. "Let's go up to your room for some peace and quiet." She asked Erin, "Shall I get him ready for bed and put him down?"

"Yeah, he's overdue. And he won't know he's missing birthday cake later." She handed Diana a bottle. "Give him this, too."

Diana trekked upstairs with the baby, clasping the tiny bundle to her, singing softly to him.

Ben found her there, ten minutes later, rocking Ian as she fed him his bottle. He stood in the doorway, staring at her; as he sipped strong coffee, he remembered how watching her nurse his babies had been one of his favorite pastimes. She looked even more beautiful tonight than she had then, dressed in rose-colored pants and top, accented by gold jewelry. Her blond hair fell softly around her face. She was focused on Ian, and she hadn't seen Ben yet. Unobserved, his defenses lowered by a few glasses of wine, he drank in the sight of her.

"You've got your grandpa's eyes, sweetie," Diana told the baby as he suckled noisily. "So brown they're almost black. What a lady-killer you're going to be. Just like him."

"He's got your nose, though." Ben's comment startled Diana. She jumped. Ian lost the bottle's nipple and started to cry. Diana yanked her gaze from Ben and soothed Ian. Soon the baby settled down.

"You haven't lost your touch," he remarked grudgingly from the doorway. He drank coffee for something to do, his heart lurching at the memories elicited by the homey scene.

"Mmm. This was my favorite age. I loved how cuddly they were."

"I liked them when I could get a good grip on them."

Diana smiled at him, the emotion in her face staggering him. "You did your share of walking them in the middle of the night when they were infants."

"You were exhausted from breast-feeding." He came into the room and stood over the rocker. Gently he smoothed Ian's tuft of dark hair. "I tried to talk you out of nursing Francey, remember? It wasn't in vogue back then. You got so tired out, feeding the other two."

"I know. It took Grace telling you that all the old Italian women did it for eight or nine kids to convince you."

Ben lifted his hand to her cheek and brushed his knuckles down it. She was lovely, sitting there with the baby, a soft smile on her face. And he wanted her so badly he hurt.

God, he'd behaved like an ass Saturday morning. She'd been right—he was running scared. He was still afraid, so he stepped back. Slowly he crossed to the window and stared at the trees in the backyard. "The woods are pretty this time of year."

"Tony's done well for himself," Diana said.

Ben was looking for something to irritate him. "They all have. Just because Tony makes six figures and the other two are firefighters doesn't mean they aren't as successful."

When Diana didn't answer, he turned to find she'd put the bottle down and was cradling Ian on her shoulder. As she rubbed the baby's back, she said quietly, "Fire fighting is one of the most heroic jobs a person can do. You know I've always felt that way about it."

Ben's whole body went taut. "You left me because I was a firefighter."

Her eyes clouded. Even in the dim light, he could see the sadness in them. She rose gracefully and crossed to the crib. Soothing little Ian one last time, she laid him down. Then she circled her waist with her arms. Ben recognized the self-protective gesture; she used it whenever she was upset. "Just to set the record straight, I left because of the danger, not the prestige or the money. You know that." She frowned. "Hate me for what I did, Ben, not for what I didn't do."

He set his mug down and was in front of her before he could stop himself. He grasped her arms, but not roughly. It was more of a caress. "What you *didn't* do was stay with us." One hand slipped up to lock around her neck. "I loved you so much," he admitted hoarsely.

Tears pooled in her eyes. "I know you did." She ran feather-soft fingers down his cheek. "You still do, or you wouldn't be this angry with me." Her voice dropped a notch. "You wouldn't have made love to me the way you did last weekend."

He shook his head and stepped away. "I won't be seduced into this."

She stood still.

"Like you seduce everybody else," he added.

Looking puzzled, she frowned.

"Erin's father can't take his eyes off you—he kept finding excuses to touch you all evening. And Nicky told us you went out with his doctor Saturday night to the Rio."

Still, she remained maddeningly silent.

"Saturday, after you'd been in bed with me till ten in the morning."

Diana shook her head. "I love you, Ben—I told you that. But I'm not waiting around until you come to your senses." Her voice caught. "For ten years before I married Nathan I waited for you to come and get me, to tell me we could work it out somehow. It was the worst time of my life. I'm not going to do it again."

He never knew she'd wanted him to come to her. He was leveled by the knowledge. By the indescribable sense of loss.

Hesitating, she moved in on him, stood on tiptoe and kissed his cheek. Then she padded softly out of the room.

The baby started to fuss as soon as she left.

Ben leaned over, picked up his grandson and sat on the rocker. The seat was still warm from his ex-wife's body. He could detect the faint smell of her perfume in the air. As he rocked Ian, he was unable to banish the vision of Diana standing proudly before him, telling him she loved him. Overcome with emotion, he buried his face in the baby's neck, having no idea how to contain the feelings that swirled inside him.

ALEX WHIPPED the Porsche into Francesca's driveway and cut the engine. Neither of them had turned the radio on and silence had reigned all the way there.

He turned toward her at the same time she faced him. Bathed in the dim light from the street lamps, she was so lovely he was silenced. But it was the sadness in her eyes—the discouragement—that made his heart clench.

"I watched your parents all night," he finally said.

She didn't look surprised. "Me, too."

"It was hard to see."

"I wonder if they knew how transparent they were."

"I doubt it. No one wants witnesses to that kind of longing." He reached over, slid his hand around to her nape and threaded his fingers in her hair. "It's so sad. They obviously never got over each other."

Francesca expelled a heavy breath. "I don't want that to be us, Alex."

"I know. I don't want that, either."

Her voice turned soft. "We could stop this now, between us, without being hurt."

Her words were a quick uppercut to his heart. Stunned by the punch of her statement, he was speechless. After a moment, he managed to say hoarsely, "Is that what you want?

Wordlessly she stared at him.

He made a split-second decision, damned if he'd come

this far to let her go without finishing the fight. "Because I don't."

Still she said nothing.

"And to set the record straight, it's too late for me to get out of this, even now, without being hurt." He couldn't watch her tell him she didn't feel the same, so he let go of her, turned in his seat, closed his eyes, laid his head against the headrest.

And waited for the final blow of her rejection.

After a torturously long time, he felt her hand creep into his. She linked their fingers intimately. "For me, too. It's too late for me, too."

The air whooshed from his lungs. After a few seconds he tilted the steering wheel and pushed the seat back. Francesca climbed awkwardly over the gearshift onto his lap. Wrapping her arms around his neck, she breathed him in. "I don't want to be fifty, Alex, and wonder if I could have changed things and wished I'd done something different."

He gripped her waist, burying his face in her hair. "You won't be. We'll make this work."

"I'm sorry I've been so stupid about everything. I'll be better, I promise. I'll call when I say I will. I know I worried you. I didn't mean to."

"And I'll try not to worry. I'll swallow my pride and call the station if I do. I'll keep better control of my temper."

Hugging him tighter, she seemed to sink into him. After a very long time, she whispered, without teasing, without wit, "Take me inside, make love to me. Stay with me."

"Always," he promised. "Always."

CHAPTER TWELVE

FURNACE-HOT AIR blasted Francey when she reached the front door of the duplex. A charged hose line, carried by Engine Sixteen firefighters, led the way; with Dylan ahead of her and Captain Knight behind her, they halted momentarily. Though they were covered with turnout gear, the extreme temperature assaulted them. Francey's head perspired beneath the hood and helmet, and her face beaded with sweat under the breathing mask and eye shield.

The fire hid, playing cat and mouse. Had it crept over from the other side of the house? Was it waiting to ambush them? Peering into the front room was like looking through dark sheer curtains; they could see, but smoke made things hazy and indistinct. They crouched because of the heat; it was cooler down here. Francey followed Dylan, who was moving as fast as possible, to search for the trapped victims. A neighbor had told the incident commander that two children were inside; the bedrooms were in back, behind the kitchen. Since it was two in the morning, the kids were most likely there. Nevertheless, another group scoured the front of the house, and Quint/Midi Twelve headed for the rear.

Francey knocked her knee on something and swore. They crept a few feet farther and her shoulder bumped what looked like the leg of a table; when a heavy metallic object hit her back, she yelped and was knocked forward into Dylan. He swung around. "You okay?" he asked, his voice tinny from the SCBA. She nodded, shaking off the ache. What the hell had fallen on her?

Static blasted from Captain Knight's radio as they inched to the next room behind the hose. Two doors were visible on the far wall of the kitchen. She and Dylan sprang up; Dylan darted to one doorway, she to the other. It was blacker inside the bedroom, hotter. Her breathing accelerated. Her uniform stuck to her like a second skin. Again she dropped to her knees. Banging the floor in front of her with a halligan, she headed straight in—at least she thought it was straight—until she came up against an object. *Please let it be the bed.* It was. She stood, placed two hands on the mattress and pushed down hard. It bounced, indicating someone was there. She felt around, then grasped a limb—a leg, she thought. Little. Francey slid her hand up. It was a body—and it was moving. *Thank God.* She grabbed the kid and hefted him up when he whimpered. "It's all right, sweetie, I gotcha," she said, probably scaring the poor thing with her Darth Vader voice. Hugging the child to her chest, she faced the doorway. Oh, God, *was* it the doorway? She'd lost her bearings.

Don't panic. Think. And move.

She couldn't crouch, so she sidled to a wall. She'd pick a direction and follow it out. Before she moved, she held her breath and listened hard. It was then that she heard her captain's static-filled radio barking. Relieved, she turned toward the sound and in seconds found the door. Visibility was better in the kitchen; Knight said something she couldn't hear and motioned to her. She took two steps toward him—and the exit—when a cloud of flame burst in front of her. It drove her to her knees. Ed fell, too. Francey toppled with the child's weight. Righting herself, she pried little arms from her face mask and clasped him to her chest again.

The hose had opened on the blaze as soon as she fell; its water closed the fire's jaws, and Francey and the captain raced through. She could see the front door, and staggered toward it. One, two, three steps. Her heart slammed against her ribs. Finally she was outside. She stumbled several yards before she sank to her knees, closing her eyes. A firefighter lifted the child from her arms. Francey yanked off her helmet and mask, hung her head, braced her arms on her legs and breathed deeply.

When she looked up, she saw Dylan handing a second child to two people who motioned frantically toward the duplex. Then Dylan exploded in movement. He flew to the truck, grabbed another air pack, threw it on and headed to the house. She glanced behind her to see that the building had become fully involved and the other firefighters had mounted an exterior attack. She prayed they'd all gotten out. Dylan strode by her; she grasped his arm. "What are you doing?" she yelled at him.

"The grandma's in there. I'm going back in."

Francey gripped him tighter. "You can't."

He shook off her hold and took a few steps before Captain Knight tackled him from behind. Another firefighter joined the fray to restrain Dylan.

Beyond them, hungry flames feasted busily, gobbling up the roof, digesting the lifeblood of some poor family.

Francey sank back and stared at the house.

They'd lost someone.

ALEX SIPPED his morning coffee as he studied the glassy surface of the lake. He'd worked out, showered and called his office for his voice mail. Not bad for only seven o'clock. His energy level was high these days—because he was happy. Last Friday night had been a turning point for him and Francesca. He smiled, thinking about the sweetness of their lovemaking after their fight, her murmuring, "I'm sorry. I care so much about you."

He cared about her, too.

Too much.

No, he wouldn't think that way.

The doorbell rang, startling him. It was rare to get company at this hour. His parents were visiting relatives in Syracuse, Richard was on vacation for two weeks, and Francesca wouldn't be off the night shift yet. He tightened the belt of his robe and crossed the kitchen to the foyer barefoot.

Whipping open the door, he found Francesca leaning against a white post, staring at him with an unreadable expression on her face.

"Well, I must have been a good boy to deserve this surprise."

She smiled, but it appeared forced. "Hi."

"What are you doing here?"

Wrapping her arms around her ribs, nicely encased in a yellow T-shirt tucked into denim cutoffs, she said, "I wanted to see you before you went to work."

He angled his head. "Something wrong?"

"No, no."

He glanced at his watch. "It's only seven. You don't usually get off this early."

"No, I don't. We had a fire at two this morning. My relief heard it on the radio and came in early."

A fire. He noticed the red blotch on her neck. *Sometimes embers get under the hood,* she'd once told him.

No, he wouldn't comment. She needed something from him, and he'd give her whatever it was. He seized her hand and kissed her quickly. "Come in."

She followed him through the foyer. "Nice rags," she said with humor that seemed feigned.

"Oh, white terry turns you on, does it?"

"Anything you wear turns me on."

That earned her another kiss, deeper than the last, when they reached the kitchen. He poured her a cup of coffee, diluted it with cream and sugar while she plunked down in a chair. He sat next to her and observed her.

For the first time since he'd known her, Francesca did not look good. Her beautiful porcelain complexion was colorless. Her hair was damp and mussed. Her eyes were bloodshot and clouded with fatigue, heavily smudged underneath. The skin around them had a pinched look. He'd learned firefighters were plagued by carbon monoxide headaches for hours—even days—after a fire.

"Did you take something for the headache?" he asked.

Surprise flickered on her face. "Yes."

He waited a moment. "Want to talk about it?"

She shook her head. "No." She drummed her fingers on the tabletop. "I just wanted to see you." She sipped her coffee. "I, um, didn't want to go home."

Alone. She didn't say the word, but he heard it.

"How about some breakfast? I've got the makings for French toast, scrambled eggs and ham."

"No, thanks." She looked away from him, around the kitchen. Her eyes met his again.

He held her gaze as she drew in a deep breath.

"We lost someone," she said. "An old woman." Her voice was gravelly.

"Oh, honey, I'm sorry." He scraped his chair back and reached for her. She hesitated, then let him tug her onto his lap.

Still she remained taut. Brave warrior that she was, she resisted his comforting. But after a moment, she curled into him. Smoothing a hand down her hair, he said, "You can let it out with me, you know."

She shook her head fiercely.

"You *can*. You don't have to, but you can."

She fisted her hands in the lapels of his robe. "It's just that every time I close my eyes, I see her. Burn victims are…"

He waited for her to go on. When she didn't, he said, "Tell me."

In halting words she related the grisly details. "Their skin is so tight, like burned leather. It pulls back from the bone structure. This woman…her mouth was open, like she was screaming." Francesca dug her face into his chest. "I can almost hear her scream for us to get her out."

Alex promised himself he'd never let her know how much her words terrified him. Francesca had been in that building, too. That charred body could have been hers.

She drew back. "We missed the victim. Dylan and me. She was in one of the other rooms."

"What happened?"

"We each found a kid and brought them out." She gave him a wobbly smile. "Mine was a four-year-old boy. A runt. Scared as hell. I thought he was gonna pull my face mask off."

"You and Dylan saved two children, Francesca."

"I know."

"I'm sorry about the woman."

"She was their grandmother." Her eyes took on a faraway look, and Alex wondered for a moment how firefighters lived with the horrors they saw. "Dylan's beside himself. Just after we got them out, the building became fully involved. He tried to go back in, but the cap tackled him before he got to the porch."

"Oh, my God."

"Captain Knight will have his ass for that."

"How was Dylan afterward?"

"I don't know. He tore out of the firehouse as soon as his relief arrived. The other guys were going to have breakfast together. We do that when something bad happens."

But Francesca had come here. To him.

Did she have any idea what a gift she'd given him? As she sank into his chest, he picked up the cordless phone that sat on the table and punched out his work number.

After two rings he heard a voice say, "Templeton Industries."

"Sally, it's Alex. I'm surprised you're there already. I was going to leave a message."

"I'm quitting early, remember? What's up?"

"I'm not coming in today. I'll be, um, working at home."

Francey tried to draw back, but he held her to him with his other hand. "Shh," he whispered in her ear. Into the receiver, he said, "Cancel all my appointments."

Pulling away, Francey bumped her head on the phone. "Ouch." She rubbed her scalp. "Alex," she said in a harsh whisper, "you don't have to do that."

"Can't Richard fill in for meetings?" his secretary asked.

"Richard's on vacation."

"Oh, I forgot."

Francesca watched him. "Alex…"

He pressed the phone to his chest. "Francesca, shut up." Back on the line, he said, "I'll need some things here."

He felt Francesca cuddle into him.

"Get a courier to bring over—"

It was then that he became aware of it. A change in her body. Soft shudders. Shaking shoulders. Unsuppressible sobs. "Sally, I'll call you back."

He clicked off the phone and banded his arms around her. After a moment she laid her head on his chest and looked at him. Tears filled those gorgeous violet eyes, making them sparkle like marbles caught by the sun. "You'd do this? For me? Not go to work because I need you?"

Gently he wiped the moisture on her cheeks with his fingertips. "You'd be surprised how much I'd do for you, love."

She wept again at the endearment. He held her close, murmuring softly, "Let it out, you'll feel better," and glided his hand in circles on her back.

When at last she'd cried enough, she stared at him. "Oh, God, I never do this. The guys would die."

Alex kissed her nose. "I won't tell."

She gave him a watery grin, then tangled her fingers in his collar. "So, um, you're gonna stay here all day?"

"Yes. Even while you sleep." He smoothed her hair off her face. "You're exhausted."

"I'm wired. I probably won't sleep."

"Mmm."

"Not unless you help me."

His brows arched. "Is that what you want?"

"It's what I *need,* Alex."

He nodded. He knew the psychology of affirming life in the midst of death. "I think I can handle that," he said, reaching for the hem of her T-shirt. He drew it over her head and slid his hands to her back. When he inched them into the waistband of her cutoffs, she gasped. "What is it?" he asked.

"I…I'm probably a little black-and-blue."

He drew in a breath. *Cool it, Templeton, she's at her worst.* "Well, let's take a look." He set her away from him; she stood, unzipped her shorts and turned. "Oh, Lord."

Her entire waistline was bruised. Uneven patches of purple and blue marred her body. Alex swallowed hard. "Did a doctor see this?"

"No, they're just bruises. Part of a ceiling fan fell on me."

"You've got other marks on your legs and arms." In truth, she was a patchwork of bruises.

She stiffened almost imperceptibly. "Fire fighting's nasty business."

Fire fighting's crazy, he thought. But he didn't say it. Instead, he stood and grasped her hand. "Come on."

"Where?"

"To the hot tub."

"Oh, God, it sounds like heaven."

He led her outdoors, uncovered the hot tub and took great pleasure, despite the bruises, in watching her strip and get in. He also took great pleasure in joining her.

Twenty minutes later he held her arm as she climbed out. Handling her like rare and precious crystal, he wrapped her in a warm robe and led her to the bedroom off the deck.

Inside his huge, admittedly sybaritic bedroom, he laid her on the cashmere bedspread, closed the blinds, sat down beside her and kissed her. She clung to him. Slowly he unfolded her from the robe. He started at her ear, knowing how she reacted to the slide of his tongue there. He licked between her breasts, then suckled her nipples. When she moved restlessly, he slid his hand below her taut abdomen and nestled it in the soft curls there. He kissed his way down her body, avoiding bruises, ignoring the terror they instilled in him, until later, when he could address it alone.

This was for her.

As his tongue circled her navel, she tugged on his hair. "Alex."

"Shh. Let me."

"Both of us."

"No, let me take care of you. Just you." When she started to protest, he grinned against her belly. "You can take care of me later."

"Promise?"

"I promise."

Surprisingly, she lay back on the pillows.

His mouth closed over her gently. And with the greatest of love....

She slept for four hours before the nightmare came. Alex was reading a contract in his den, off the bedroom, when he heard her moans. By the time he reached her, she was writhing on the mattress in the clutches of the dream's demons.

"No, she's there. On the next bed. Turn left, not right. Please...please..."

He covered her body with his to get her to stop flailing. She was bathed in sweat, her hair a tangled mess. When she opened those eyes he loved, they were haunted. "Where am I?"

"You're with me. It's all right, sweetheart."

"I had a dream." She stared at him hard, then sank into the bed, gulping for air. "It was real, wasn't it? We lost her."

"Yes, you did."

She swore. Colorfully.

He was glad to see some of her grit surface.

"I'm so tired."

"Go back to sleep."

"Stay with me until I do."

"You can count on it."

Midafternoon, Alex was on the deck at an umbrella table finishing the last of the work he'd gotten from the courier. Late June had brought high temperatures; he basked in them, wearing gym shorts and no shirt. Francesca joined him fresh from sleep and dressed only in the terry robe. Her color was restored, her eyes clear. She took a chair opposite him. "Busy?"

"Nope." He stuffed papers into his briefcase. "Perfect timing. I'm all done."

She smiled. Then she leaned over, grasped his hand, kissed it and brought it to rest on her heart. "How can I thank you for being here today?"

Pressing his hand into her, he gave her a tender smile. He wanted to tell her no thanks were necessary, that he'd do anything for her. But he knew it wasn't the time for declarations. So he gave her a suggestive look. "I can think of several ways."

An uncharacteristic Lolita smile spread across her face as

her eyes dropped to his bare chest. "I'll bet you can, big guy."

"Well, I did promise you could take care of me later."

She glanced at his lap, which made him instantly hard. "Like for like," she said, licking her lips.

Oh, God, Alex thought. Could life get any better?

"STRIKE TWO!"

Francey spun to her grandfather and said, "What? Do you need new glasses? It was a mile high."

Gus gave her a long-suffering look. "Watch it, girl. You'll be out of the game."

"He means it," her father said, punching his glove and squatting behind the plate like Yogi Berra. "Come on, Chelsea, baby. Let's get this pudding out."

"Pudding? *Pudding?* Not on your life, old man." Except, of course, where Alex Templeton—who sat distractingly in the stands next to her mother—was concerned. Then she was Jell-O, pudding and complete and utter mush. Wiping her hands on her red T-shirt, which along with cutoffs formed their station's uniform, she faced the pitcher, determined.

Chelsea wound up on the pitcher's mound and windmilled the ball, her incredible arm hurling it at seventy miles an hour. It was high.

"Ball."

"Good call, Gramps."

Both men chuckled. Chelsea pitched again. This time, it was low and inside, but Francey swung anyway. Wood cracked on leather. The ball popped into the air. Flinging aside the bat, Francey took off for first base.

Jake, coaching there, circled his arm. "Keep going, slugger."

The left fielder backed up, and up, but the ball sailed over his head and hit the ground behind him with a thunk.

At second base, Billy Milligan, the guy Chelsea dated, scoffed. "You'll never make it, hotshot."

Francey stuck her tongue out at him and darted for third. From the sideline, Dylan yelled, "Go for it, doll."

Adrenaline pumping through her, Francey rounded the base and sprinted for home. The crowd's reaction told her that the ball was traveling toward her father at the plate. She put on an extra burst of speed. Her dad was standing up, blocking the plate as much as the rules allowed. Francey ran faster. She was almost there when Ben leaped into the air, his arm stretched above his head. Then her body collided with rock-hard muscle and two hundred pounds of man, but her foot connected with white rubber. Ben fell on top of her—and dropped the ball.

"Safe!" she heard her grandpa yell.

Francey giggled from under her father, who sprawled unforgivingly over her. *This* was gonna be a great day.

Fifteen minutes later, she was sipping a beer in a pavilion at Highland Park. She dissected the game with her teammates and several guests at the annual Rockford Fire Department's Fourth of July picnic—which had begun with a league softball game.

"You could have taken it easy on Francey," Grace chided her son. "I'd hate to see another broken arm."

Ben slid an arm around his daughter, his orange academy jersey clashing with her red shirt. "She wouldn't have wanted that, would you, kid?"

"Not a chance."

Briefly she felt Alex stiffen beside her, but his smile seemed genuine. "Well, my heart only stopped for a little while."

Duke said, "Get used to it, Templeton. You should have seen her race through those flames last week."

This time Alex's smile disappeared. Francey was thankful

when her father said, "Speaking of fires, Dylan's brooding by the tree. Wanna come talk to him with me, France?"

Discreetly she looked to Alex, who nodded. "I'll stay here," he said, "and let your grandparents tell me how you managed to survive childhood."

She kissed his cheek, warmed by how he seemed to be fitting in; even her father had been civil to him. And Alex was dressed more casually than usual, in a plain white T-shirt and khaki shorts. Another effort to be a part of the group.

On the way across the field, Ben said to Francey, "Why did you ask your mother to come today?"

"I didn't. Captain Scanlon did."

"Eric Scanlon from the academy?"

"Yeah. Did Diana come and see you a few weeks ago?"

"Uh, yeah."

"Why?"

"Different stuff."

"Apparently she met Scanlon at the academy, then saw him at Bright Oaks Country Club the next weekend. He's a member there."

"Where does Scanlon get that kind of money?"

"Beats me," Francey told him as they approached Dylan.

Her buddy looked up from *Firehouse* magazine. Dylan brought printed matter everywhere he went and often disappeared in the midst of things to read. "Hi," he said. "Did you know that in the space of one year, the U.S. fire service responded to a fire every sixteen seconds?"

The Cordaros exchanged a look. "Nope." Francey dropped to the ground next to him. "Read us some more."

"A structure fire occurred every fifty-five seconds, a vehicle fire every seventy-six seconds." His faced darkened. "And nationwide, someone died in a fire every hundred and five minutes."

Bracing both hands on a low overhead tree limb, her father knitted his brow. "What happened to you two last week wasn't unusual."

Dylan's eyes blazed like blue crystals. But he said casually, "Nah, of course not. Death is a part of the job."

"It is," Ben told him. Though Francey had seen Dylan several times since the fire and tried to talk to him about what had happened, he'd kept to himself like a hermit for days.

Ben stared hard at Dylan. "You did a foolish thing, boy."

"So I was told. By the captain and Chief Talbot."

"It needed to be reported."

Dylan nodded. "I've got to meet with the department psychologist." He furrowed his brow in imitation of the chief. "'Something's eatin' at you, O'Roarke. Find out what it is.'"

"Reed Macauley's a good man and a fine psychologist," Ben said. "He used to be a firefighter. He's housed at the academy."

Dylan stared at Ben silently.

Francey asked, "Do you *know* what it is, Dyl, that's eating you?"

His usually roguish eyes turned so bleak Francey hurt for him. "Yeah, I know. But let's not get into it now." He glanced at the group by the pavilion. "Damn, Francey, who got Lizzie Borden to come to the picnic? She's never at these things."

Francey glanced to where Beth sat at a table with Chelsea and Billy. They were chatting and laughing with animation. "Chelsea did. She practically had to drag Beth here."

"Well, that ruins my day."

"Come on, I'll buy you a beer." Ben ignored the well-known feud between Dylan and Beth. "No more mopin' around."

"Yes, sir," Dylan said, saluting.

Ben said, "Screw you, O'Roarke."

Francey found Alex ten minutes later, frowning as he eavesdropped on a conversation between two battalion chiefs. "Then the deputy told Talbot that Quint/Midi Twelve should have waited until Seventeen ventilated. Knight's group could have bought it."

Damn, Francey thought, *that's all Alex needs to hear.* His face went ashen. "Come on, big guy. Let's go talk to Beth."

Alex gave her a strained smile. "Should they have?" he asked, as they crossed the lawn to Beth and Chelsea. "Waited to ventilate the roof? You told me the engine group did the right thing."

Francey stopped and peered at him. "*I* don't think they made a mistake. And it's easy to Monday morning quarterback."

Alex sighed and ran a hand through his hair.

"It scares you, doesn't it?"

He nodded.

"Then I appreciate even more how good you were about it on Tuesday."

His smile was tinged with sadness "I wanted to be there for you."

"You were."

"Besides," he said, the devil dancing in his eyes, "I got my reward."

Francey's whole body shivered as she remembered. She grinned and said, "Hey, you take care of me, I take care of you."

"You're on, babe." Despite his chuckle, Francey knew that buried just beneath the surface was worry.

BEN WATCHED his daughter practically melt when Alex Templeton touched her. Just like Diana used to melt when Ben touched *her.* Like she *still* melted. He swung his gaze to his ex-wife, who sat at a picnic table with a group from the academy. Looking lovely in a wide-brimmed straw hat and a scoop-necked yellow sundress of some gauzy material, she took his breath away.

He hadn't seen her since Tony's party. But he'd been haunted by her words. *I love you, Ben, but I won't wait....*

Well, she sure as hell hadn't. What was she trying to do—notch all the over-fifty men in Rockford into her bedpost her first year back in town?

Unfair. He doubted she'd slept with Smith. Certainly not with Erin's father. But Scanlon was a good-looking son of a bitch, like some Norse god dressed in modern designer clothes.

I'm not into casual sex, Ben. At least not with you.

Ben watched her sidle out from under Scanlon's arm with finesse. It made him smile smugly. She'd never pulled away from *him*. Hell, she tried to get inside his skin, most of the time.

I waited for ten years for you to come and get me....

Of all the things he'd found out since Diana returned to Rockford, that was the hardest to take. It had caused him to snap at secretaries and tear the covers off the bed at night. Could he have gotten her back years ago? Could they have worked it out? He glanced at his daughter, who visited with her two friends while Templeton stood behind her, massaging her shoulders.

In his peripheral vision, he saw Diana heading for the john, which was up a hill, out of view. He took a swig of beer, then tossed the can into a receptacle and followed her.

He was standing by the drinking fountain, a wet handkerchief in his hand, pretending to cool off his face and neck, when she emerged from the women's bathroom.

She gave a start when she saw him. "Ben, hello."

Framed by the July sun, she was stunning—and he told her so.

Her eyes widened. "Well, thank you."

"Yellow always was your color."

She smiled. "Remember how you always bought me yellow underwear? My drawer looked like a field of daisies."

"*You* look like a daisy right now."

"If so, a wilting one. It's got to be in the nineties."

"Eighty-nine." He scanned her bodice. "You're sweaty."

She swallowed hard; even *he* could hear the come-to-bed tone in his voice.

With exaggerated nonchalance, he reached over and ran his handkerchief under the cold water of the drinking fountain, then wrung it out. When he took two steps toward her, she backed up the same distance. But her back collided with the rough-hewn green shingles of the shed. He trapped her with his body, one arm braced next to her head, the other, holding the cloth, raised to her cheek. "Here, let me cool you off."

Her eyes sizzled. "I...Ben, I...oh..."

Slowly he ran the cloth over her face. First her brow, then each cheek, then her chin and jaw. "You're sunburned here." He kissed her nose.

She held his gaze; her eyes darkened.

He went lower, bathing her throat. Tiny rivulets of water dripped down her chest. He captured a droplet with his tongue.

"You're getting me wet," she whispered.

He chuckled as he lifted his head. "I could always get you wet, Dee. With just a touch."

She closed her eyes. "I never denied that. Why are you doing this, Ben?"

"Ditch Scanlon. Let me take you home." He dipped the cloth inside the neckline of her dress. She moaned.

"No."

He frowned.

"No," she repeated. "I came with Eric, so I'm leaving with him."

Ben could be generous about this. "All right. He can take you home. But get rid of him fast. I'll come over when he's gone."

She shook her head.

He nuzzled her ear.

Again a refusal.

"Why not? You want me."

Her laugh surprised him, considering *he* was about to combust. "I've wanted you since I was seventeen. That's nothing new."

"Then what's the matter, baby? What do I have to do?"

"I told you my conditions."

His hand went to her waist and squeezed. "I won't yell at you."

"That's a switch."

He kissed her hair. "I want to be with you."

"Then call and ask me. Properly."

He drew back. "What?"

"If you want to see me, call and ask me."

"Court you, you mean?"

She smiled as if she liked the thought. "Yes, I guess I do."

Thoughtful, he cocked his head. "I never did that, did I?"

Her eyes clouded with sadness. "I never gave you a chance."

A lump formed in his throat. He wondered what else he'd never done for her as they'd rushed headlong into marriage.

She squared her shoulders. "But don't expect me to behave the way I did when we were young." Her tone turned feisty. "Or the way I did two weeks ago. I won't sleep with you again until I hear what I need to hear from you."

He stepped back and shoved his hands into his cutoffs. "And what's that?"

Straightening her dress, she said saucily, "You'll have to

figure it out on your own, love.'' She flattened the top of her hat with her hand. "Now I have to get back to Eric."

Ben watched her until she was out of sight. Curiously, he felt better than he had in years.

CHAPTER THIRTEEN

A FEW WEEKS LATER Alex flipped a couple of dozen hamburgers on the large stone grill in Ellison Park as if he'd been cooking for a hundred people all his life. He hadn't, of course, but today he was the designated chef for the Templeton Employee Barbecue, as the writing on his dark green T-shirt proclaimed. He checked his watch. Another thing he wasn't accustomed to—getting stood up. Francesca was supposed to meet him here, and she'd pulled a no-show.

"I think they're done, son," Jared Templeton pointed out. Though retired, he still attended the annual parties.

"Oh."

Several factory workers lined up, and the Templeton men doled out the food with humor and goodwill. Around them, the lush greenery of Ellison Park on a mid-July day celebrated summer. Sun sparkled off the leaves, and rich thick grass grew beneath their feet. Alex couldn't have ordered a nicer day. He just wished he'd picked a different one.

"Francesca, where are you?" he'd asked when he'd finally called the station house because she was an hour late.

"Linehan, my relief, didn't show. He called in and said his father had been rushed to the hospital. He asked me to stay a couple of hours."

Without thinking, Alex had responded, "Why didn't you tell him you had plans?"

There'd been a pause on her end. "His father's in the hospital."

Alex had felt like a slug. "I'm sorry. That was a thoughtless comment. I'm just disappointed. I wanted you here with me. It seemed important for us to share this.''

"It *is* important. Linehan's calling back in soon. If he isn't going to make his shift, I'll ask the chief to get somebody to work overtime.''

"You don't have to do that.''

"I want to. And it's okay. The guys like the extra money. I'll be there, I promise,'' she'd said.

"Alex, who's the man with the shaggy beard and long hair alone by the pond?''

Drawn from his thoughts by his father's question, Alex grimaced. "Oh, well, I've been meaning to tell you about him.''

His father's blue eyes twinkled. "You look like you did that night I caught you and Suzy Henderson in the boathouse at our cottage.''

Laughing, Alex recalled his amorous teenage escapades.

"Tell me about the guy.''

Alex sobered.

"It's a long story, Dad.''

"I've got time. Tell me,'' Jared said.

"I was driving by Jay Street three weeks ago and passed this homeless man on the corner. He had a sign that said, 'Vietnam vet—will work for food.'''

"That's sad.''

"Yeah, I drove by him, but I couldn't get him out of my mind. So I went back and asked him if he really meant it. That he'd work for food. When he said yes, I gave him the company address and told him to come by the next day, ask for me and I'd give him a job.''

Jared stared at his son. "And he did.''

Alex nodded.

"I'll bet Davidson in personnel loved that.''

Alex reddened. "Everybody's been ribbing me about Ernest.''

"I'm proud of you, son. You always did have a generous heart."

Drawing in a deep breath, Alex, said, "There's more to it than that. I...I recognized him."

"You did?"

"He's the homeless person who was suspected of starting the fire in our warehouse."

"Why would you hire him, then?"

"Because he started the fire to keep warm, Dad. And no one was going to help him get a job. It bothered me at the time. When I had the opportunity to do something for him, I took it."

Jared smiled wisely. "Like I said, I'm proud of you, Alex."

"Well, Richard wasn't. He threw a fit. It's one of the reasons I'm glad he took a vacation."

"We need to talk about that—"

"Hey, Alex. It's time for the egg toss," one of the workers who organized the games yelled across the lawn.

Alex groaned. "I'll be right there, Denise." He angled his head to the employees. "Wouldn't want to pinch-hit for me, would you, Dad?"

Jared chuckled. "No, you're on your own in this. One of the many benefits of retirement."

Afternoon drifted into evening as workers and management participated in an egg toss, a water balloon contest and bingo. They even managed a few games of volleyball, which Francesca would have loved, had she been able to get there. Around seven the picnic began to wind down.

Jared left, and some of the staff social committee were loading the gear onto their trucks; Alex was checking the barbecue area in case they'd left something behind. He looked up to see Ernest Mackey hovering by a tree. "Did you have a good time, Ernest?"

The man stepped out of the shadows and stared hard at

Alex, the wisdom of the streets in his old eyes. "Yeah, Mr. Templeton, I did. It's, ah, why I wanna talk to you. If you got time."

"Sure."

Ernest smoothed his fingers over his mustache. "I wanna thank you for hirin' me."

Alex smiled. "Your supervisor said you're doing a good job."

"I ain't been late or nothin'," he said proudly.

"Good. What did you want to talk to me about?"

Ernest straightened his shoulders. "I wanted you to know somethin'." The man looked down for a moment and kicked some dirt with his foot. "I, ah, I didn't start your warehouse fire."

Alex stilled.

"I know you think I did and you hired me anyway. Nobody's ever done that for me. Given me a second chance. Only it ain't a second chance, and I wanted you to know that. I didn't do it."

Alex said, "The case is closed. You got community service, didn't you?"

"Yes, sir, and I did the service. For the other fire. I *did* start that one. It was rainy and cold, and I was lookin' for heat." He tilted his chin. "But I didn't do yours. I swear."

Alex glanced at the man's arms. "You had burn wounds right after our fire."

"I was cookin' some hamburger meat in a garbage can and it blew up. Hell of a fire I had to put out."

Alex shrugged. "All right. Thanks for telling me that."

"You don't believe me."

"In all honesty, I'll have to think about it."

"Fair enough." Ernest straightened and shifted his feet. "You know the wire and lighter fluid they found?" Alex nodded. "I been on the streets since I got back from Nam.

I seen that stuff before, plenty of times. It ain't always for keepin' warm.''

Alex cocked his head.

"Druggies use it to cook their stuff. Maybe somebody was gettin' high there, freebasin' coke or somethin'.''

"Could be,'' Alex said carefully.

"Them investigators, they see what they think they're gonna see. Soon as they seen I started one fire to keep warm, they think yours was the same thing.'' Ernest turned away from Alex but glanced over his shoulder and said, "Just wanted to tell you to this, 'cause you been so good to me.''

And then he was gone.

Alex thought about Ernest Mackey as he bade good-night to the last of the employees and walked to his car. The man's comments bothered him. He inserted the key into the lock just as the Red Devil pulled up behind his Porsche.

Francesca flew out of the cab and headed toward him.

Her eyes were full of concern when she reached him. "It's over,'' she said simply.

"Yes,'' he said, gazing at her. "It is.''

DIANA TUCKED IN her short-sleeved mauve top, wiped her sweaty palms on her jeans and scolded herself for her nervousness. It was just a date, for God's sake. She pulled open the door.

Ben leaned on the doorjamb, his hair tousled, his navy blue T-shirt straining across his chest, his worn jeans hugging him indecently for a fifty-three-year old man.

"Hello,'' she said, her voice throaty.

Silently he perused her. "Jeans look even better on you than thirty years ago,'' he told her. His smile was thousand-watt. "And they were dynamite then.''

Her heart thumped in her chest. "Is that why you told me to wear them?''

"One of the reasons." He winked. "I was hoping to stick my hands in the back pockets when we danced."

"Are we going dancing?"

"Yep."

"Do you want to come in first?"

His sexy stare could have melted ice. "Not if you want to go out."

She grinned girlishly. "I'll get my purse."

Inside the Cherokee, Ben stuck the key in the ignition but didn't turn it. Instead, he leaned over, wrapped a hand around her neck and drew her close. Diana didn't even think about protesting. He kissed her long and lusciously. "God, you taste good."

"So do you."

Staring into her eyes, he said, "I missed you, Dee. Every single day you were gone."

Her bones turned to mush. "I missed you, too."

He let her go, started the car and took to the road. It was early evening, on a Tuesday; twilight bathed the near-empty streets. When they got to an intersection, Ben pulled the car to the shoulder. Diana willed back the tears when she saw why. A flower vendor had set up shop, hawking an assortment of blooms out of the back of his van. She watched Ben exit the car, purchase a bunch of daisies and get back in, just as he'd done so many times when they were first married.

A sheepish grin accompanied the flowers when he gave them to her. "You always loved these from the roadside guy," he said huskily.

She inhaled them deeply, then sighed. "I'm not sure why. It was just so romantic."

"Hathaway probably bought you hothouse orchids."

Diana gripped his arm. "These are special, Ben. Don't demean them."

"Old habits die hard."

"We'll work on them one at a time."

She was still sniffing the flowers when they pulled up to the GT—the Green Tavern, a bar in Fairfield where he'd taken her on their first date. "Oh, Ben," she said.

He looked at the new sign above the door. "I thought, maybe, if we started over…"

"It's a lovely idea," she said. "I'm impressed."

He gave her a youthful grin. "You were then, too."

"I doubt they'll have Mel Carter, though." She smiled as she referred to the artist who sang the song they'd danced to until the bar closed. It became *their* song.

Inside, the room was dim. Since it was only seven o'clock and early in the week, they practically had the place to themselves. They ordered beer and munched popcorn. Diana felt eighteen again.

She stared at Ben when he got up and crossed to the jukebox. She loved him even more than she had when they were married. Maybe because she knew now what it was like to lose him. Her morbid reflection was interrupted by the familiar strains of "Hold Me, Thrill Me, Kiss Me."

Tears pooled in her eyes. It was the one song she could never listen to after they'd spilt.

Ben sauntered to her, as cocky and confident as the twenty-year-old firefighter he'd been then. He didn't ask her to dance, just reached down and spun her out of the chair as if she belonged to him.

She guessed she always had.

Burying her face in his chest, it took a minute before she said, "This isn't Mel Carter."

"No, Gloria Estefan remade the song about five years ago. This is her CD."

"Amazing they had it here."

He didn't say anything.

"They didn't, did they?"

"No, I bought it and brought it over. Cost me an arm and a leg to get them to put it in the damn thing for tonight."

"Oh, Ben."

"Well, honey, you said you wanted to be courted." He rubbed his hand in a slow, sexy circle on her back and whispered, "How does it feel?"

"It feels great."

ON SUNDAY NIGHT, Alex was restless and out of sorts over his relationship with Francesca. They'd talked about her missing the picnic, and she'd apologized again. Though he'd been glad she was disappointed, he knew down deep it wasn't her fault. The situation, *her* situation, her being a firefighter, was the problem.

She'd stayed with him last night, and their lovemaking had been bittersweet.

I'm sorry, she said between kisses.

I know. So am I, for making such a fuss about things.

They'd spent most of the next day together on the lake and had a quick supper at Schaller's. At about seven, she'd gone home because Richard had called in the morning and asked if he could see Alex tonight. His brother had sounded strained, almost urgent, and Alex had agreed, though he hated missing any of Francesca's off time. He hadn't told her, but he was hoping to sneak over to her house after Richard left. He'd showered and dressed in jeans and a light cotton shirt she'd told him turned his eyes the color of the forest, so he could leave when Richard did.

The bell rang. When Alex opened the door, Richard was standing there, dressed in a black polo shirt and jeans. He was grim-faced. Alex invited him in, then led the way to the deck, where they seated themselves in lawn chairs.

"You don't look good, Richard," Alex said. "Two weeks in Acapulco should have made you more rested."

Richard clasped his hands in his lap. "I didn't go to Acapulco."

"Excuse me?"

"I didn't take a vacation."

Alex felt panic flutter in his stomach. "Something's wrong, isn't it? Very wrong."

Richard swallowed hard. "Actually, it's better now." He looked at Alex. "God, I hate disappointing you. I've lived my whole life worrying about disappointing you. Did you know that?"

Alex sat back. "No, I didn't."

"It's true."

"I...I'm sorry."

"Yes, so am I. For everything I've done."

"What have you done?"

"I didn't go on vacation. I checked myself into a detox clinic in Pennsylvania."

"Oh, Richard."

"I...I got back on the dope. It's a long story."

"I've got time."

"There's more, Alex."

"All right, tell me."

"The warehouse fire?"

Ernest's words came back like a bad dream. *Druggies use it to cook their stuff....* "Oh, my God."

"I see you've put it together."

Alex said, "Why don't you tell me, anyway?"

"I was freebasing in the basement. You weren't at the warehouse when I arrived." He stood, jammed his hands in his pockets and began to pace. "I didn't know you'd come in. I was high. The fire got out of control. It just... happened."

"Thank God you weren't hurt."

Richard turned abruptly to face him. "How can you say that?"

"I mean it. Nothing else really matters, Richard."

Tears formed in his brother's eyes. "I can't believe you're real sometimes."

Alex shook his head. Deep inside, he *was* angry with Richard. "I'm all too real, Richard. And I'm concerned about you."

"I wanted to confess right away. But I couldn't. When I saw what it was doing to our relationship, I knew I had to take steps to get clean—then come clean with you."

"To our relationship? The case was closed."

"Yes. But I...I couldn't forget about it." Richard sat again and linked his hands between his knees. "And it was Francesca Cordaro who kept reminding me."

"I don't understand."

"In detox counseling, I learned a lot of things. Francesca was a constant reminder of the fire. And the fire happened because I'm a drug addict. It's the reason I've harped on your relationship with her. Every time you mentioned her, it underscored my weakness."

Alex blew out a heavy breath. "I see."

"She seems like a nice person. And I can tell you're crazy about her. I hope I haven't ruined things for you."

"That's not important now."

Richard stared at him bleakly.

"What do you want to do?"

"The counselors said if I was going to stay straight, I had to get all this out. Deal with it emotionally and legally. You're the first step. And the hardest."

"What can I do?"

"I'd like you to go with me to tell Mother and Dad."

"Fine."

He cleared his throat. "Then we'll go to Zeleny."

"Or maybe a lawyer first."

"Maybe. I'm worried about all that."

Richard rose; Alex stood, too, and crossed the deck. He

reached out and embraced his brother. "I'll help, Richard. So will Mother and Dad. We'll get you through this, I promise."

It was eleven o'clock when Alex got home. He was drained. But what he needed right now was Francesca. Though it was late, he strode to the phone and dialed her number.

"This is Francey. Leave a message."

She wasn't home? Where could she be?

"Francesca, it's Alex. Pick up if you're there."

Nothing.

Swearing, Alex hung up.

On impulse, he dialed the fire station. After two rings, he heard, "Quint/Midi Twelve. Firefighter Cordaro speaking."

"Francesca?"

"Alex?"

"You aren't on tonight. What are you doing there?"

She hesitated, then said, "They asked me to sub."

"Oh."

"You were tied up with Richard."

He was quiet.

"I'm glad you called, though."

"I need to talk to you," he said.

"Well, I'm on watch. I got a lot of time."

"Good. Something awful has—"

He heard the PA in the background.

"Oh, God, Alex, we've got a run. I have to go."

Disoriented, he said, "Go?"

"Yes. I'll call you when we get back, okay?"

He said simply, "Don't bother."

BEN AND DIANA sat on a blanket on the old familiar Lake Ontario beach, watching the waves crash on the shore. It had been a typically hot July Saturday, right up until now, at six o'clock. Ben reached into a bag and pulled out a fire-department sweatshirt. Gently he tugged it over his ex-wife's head. Poking through it, she surfaced with her hair in her eyes. He brushed it away, taking the opportunity to lean over and kiss her soundly.

"Still cold?"

"A little."

He looked at her legs, garbed in modest white shorts. Tenderly he pulled up the second blanket that lay at their feet. Then he cuddled her close and leaned against the picnic table.

"Nicky's hands looked good last night," she said.

Absently he smoothed her hair. "He only asked about you ten times before you got there."

"He's at loose ends."

Ben kissed the top of her head. "He's missed his mama."

Diana stiffened.

"I didn't mean offense."

"I know. It's just hard."

"You've made more progress with him than I ever thought possible." His hand stroked her arm idly.

"He still doesn't trust me." She paused. "And neither do you."

"Trust doesn't come easy to Cordaro men. I'm doing the best I can."

She kissed his chest through his lightweight cotton shirt. "I know you are. And I appreciate all the gestures this week."

Ben thought back to what a sap he'd been. Bringing her Fanny Farmer candy—her favorite—in the middle of the day. Making dinner for her, Nicky, Gus and Grace last evening. Calling her late at night just to tell her he was thinking about her.

He looked at her. "Do you? Appreciate them?"

"Yes."

"Then I want something in return."

She gave him an affected glare. "Sex, right?"

He smirked. "Nah. I could talk you into that in a second."

"Modest in your old age, aren't you?"

"Right now, baby, I feel about sixteen, so I'd watch it if I were you."

She chuckled.

He said, "This is more important."

She waited.

"I don't want you to see other men, Dee. I don't want you to go out with anybody else."

Her hesitation annoyed him, and he felt the stirrings of his old nemesis, jealousy. Finally she said, "All right, I can do that, though for the record, I haven't exactly been out with other men painting the town red."

He didn't smile. "It's important to me."

"Okay, but I want something, too."

"What?"

"It's about our daughter. Francesca's having a tough time. I'm not sure what's going on, but it has to do with Alex."

"I don't want to discuss them."

"Why not?"

"We'll fight."

She gripped his shirt. "Ben, don't you see? Your attitude toward them—it says a lot about us. If you're against them, do you really think we'll make it this time?" He drew away from her, but she yanked him back. "No, don't shut yourself off from me."

His shoulders sagged. "Don't spoil this, please. It's been so good between us."

"Just promise me you won't undermine Alex and Francesca's relationship. And you'll think about my point."

Torn, he stared at the only woman who ever meant anything to him. Could he trust her again? Did he dare risk it? "Fine, I won't interfere. And I'll think about…us."

She snuggled into him, and they sat under the blanket in silence like high school sweethearts.

As darkness closed around them, Ben refused to admit he was scared to death.

CHAPTER FOURTEEN

RICHARD POKED his head into Alex's office at noon on Thursday of the following week. His face was as white as his pristine shirt. "God, Alex, have you heard?"

Alex's first thought was that Richard had gotten news on his part in the warehouse fire. A week ago, when they'd gone to their lawyer, steps for Richard to confess to the authorities had been set in motion; the lawyer believed Richard would get off with probation and some community service. They were waiting for a hearing date. "Heard what?"

"University Avenue and Main Street are cordoned off. Davidson went out to the bank and couldn't get through."

"What happened?"

Quickly Richard strode to Alex's big-screen TV. Switching it on, he said, "It's all over the news. A ChemLabs storage facility caught fire."

Alex's heart thumped wildly in his chest. "That building's only a few blocks from Quint/Midi Twelve."

As he found channel thirteen, Richard said, "I was afraid of that."

Slowly Alex rose from his chair and rounded his desk. Perching on the edge, he folded his arms and watched the TV. *Stay calm,* he told himself.

A well-groomed anchorwoman and her male partner appeared on the screen. "Chemical fires can be complicated," she was saying.

The other reporter nodded to her gravely, then faced the camera. "If you've just tuned in, this is Channel Thirteen

News with coverage of the explosion at a storage facility of ChemLabs Incorporated on Main and University. All on-duty fire and police personnel are at the site.''

"Is she working today?" Richard asked.

"Yes."

"We now switch you to live coverage at the scene."

An on-site reporter appeared on screen. His cheeks were red and his eyes blazed with excitement. "John Evans here at University Avenue, where firefighters are battling one of the worst blazes to hit Rockford in years.''

Alex's eyes focused behind the reporter. He could see the red of a fire engine. From the background echoed screeching sirens and voices barking orders.

"The danger is another explosion and keeping the fire contained so it doesn't spread to neighboring buildings," the reporter continued. "Firefighters are working on contain-ment now.''

The camera shifted to an aerial ladder, impossibly angled, a hundred feet in the air. A thick stream of water gushed from the stick, as Francesca had called the pipeline. The two firefighters in the bucket at the top of the ladder were dan-gerously close to the building. *The building that could ex-plode at any time.*

Was Francesca in that bucket?

Alex's hands began to tremble, and he dug them into his armpits. But he couldn't control his hammering heart.

The camera zoomed to the reporter. "Over on the next block, residents are being evacuated because of chemical vapors drifting downward. School is in session, so most of the homes are empty. Unfortunately a senior citizens com-plex, Dutch Towers, is in dangerous proximity. Mike Deer-field is on-site there.''

Dutch Towers came into view. Alex watched as a frail woman with white hair was assisted out of the building by a firefighter. He recognized Jake Scarlatta. Somehow seeing one of Francesca's friends made the scenario even more of a nightmare. Then the camera panned the complex. Other older people were being evacuated.

Richard asked, "Is there anyone you can call to see if she's all right?"

"I..." Alex cleared his throat. "I'm not sure."

As if on cue, Alex's phone rang. Immobilized, he stared at it. Richard finally picked it up. "Yes, Sally, put her through."

"Francesca?" Alex asked.

"No, it's her mother."

Alex grabbed the phone. "Diana?"

Diana's voice was strong. "You know?"

"Yes, I have the news on."

"Ben just called me. Francesca's on the scene with her crew. She was safe as of ten minutes ago. Ben's there, assisting. He said he'd stay in constant touch on his cell phone."

"Oh, good."

"Are you all right?" Diana asked.

"Uh, yes, sure."

"Alex, she's good at her job. She'll be fine."

"Aren't you worried?"

"I'm scared to death. But I'm handling it." Diana hesitated, then said, "You have to handle it, too."

Stupidly he nodded at the phone.

"I'll call you each time I hear from Ben."

"Thank you." Alex drew in an unsteady breath. "Where is she, Diana? On the scene?"

"Right now she's in the bucket."

She hung up, and Alex fumbled the phone trying to cradle the receiver. He jammed his hands in his pockets to still them.

"Is she all right?" Richard asked.

"For now." He related what Ben had told Diana.

Alex glanced at the TV. "That concludes our special report. Channel Thirteen will keep you informed of the latest development in the ChemLabs fire." Looking grave, the male adjusted his tie nervously.

The female anchor matched his expression. Her pink summer suit seemed a mockery, given the grim circumstances. "In the meantime, keep those brave Rockford firefighters in your prayers."

Suddenly the screen transformed into a passionate kiss between two soap-opera stars. The image immobilized Alex. His mind replayed the last time he'd kissed Francesca.

Richard picked up the remote.

"No, don't turn it off."

"I'll mute it," his brother told him. Then Richard said, "What would you like me to do?"

"Do?"

"Yes. Stay here with you?"

Shaking himself from his torpor, Alex said, "No, that's not necessary. You can go back to your office. I'll let you know what's happening."

"You're sure? You look devastated."

"I'm fine. I'm just worried about her."

"All right."

Once Richard left, Alex sank onto his taupe leather sofa, staring blindly at the TV. The couple on-screen had made it to the bedroom. The woman lay on the bed, staring at the man.

Vividly Alex remembered tucking Francesca into his bed the morning after the last fire. Would she come to him after this one? Would she be able to? Or would something happen to her today?

The thought sickened him. His stomach heaved. He closed his eyes to quell the nausea.

Exactly thirty-five minutes passed before Diana called again to report that Francesca was still safe. Half an hour later, Alex caught the lightning bolt across the TV, indicating a special bulletin. He'd just read the same paragraph in a contract eight times. Hurriedly he picked up the remote, pressed the sound button and leaned forward, bracing his forearms on the desk.

"Channel Thirteen reporting on the ChemLabs fire in downtown Rockford. We're told all of the endangered buildings have been evacuated. The Red Cross has set up emergency housing for residents of Dutch Towers and other displaced people at the Disciples Church on Ford Avenue. The community is safe, folks."

But what about the firefighters?

As if the commentators heard him, the female reporter said, "Meanwhile, the blaze rages. Chief Jeffrey Misner tells us that every available firefighter is on the scene. Here's John Evans with Chief Misner."

Again the camera switched to ChemLabs. Evans stood in the foreground of the building. Alex could see the hungry flames behind him. Next to the reporter was a tall man of about forty dressed in turnout gear. "Chief Misner, can you update us on the fire attack strategy?"

The chief frowned. "Entry into the building has been delayed because of the danger of chemical explosions. We've mounted an exterior attack and will stick with that until it's safe to go inside."

Inside? Into a building full of chemicals. Oh, God!

The reporter asked, "Was…is anyone inside?"

The chief scowled. "We have no way of knowing that."

"What are the chances of someone inside surviving this?"

The scathing look the chief gave the reporter said it all.

Chagrined, the reporter asked, "How endangered are the firefighters?"

"All fire fighting is dangerous," Misner said soberly. "But our personnel is well-trained in chemical fires. They've had recent refresher courses. And they're good men and women.''

A reporter's gleam came into the newsman's eye. "How many women are here today?"

No, please, don't focus on the women.

"Three."

Alex wondered if Chelsea was there, too.

"Chief, can we—"

Suddenly there was a low rumbling, like the sound of distant thunder. The chief dashed away.

"On the scene here, it sounds like some sort of—"

The screen went blank. There were long seconds of dead time.

Then the two anchors came on. "It appears we've lost contact with our reporter in the field. We're trying to reestablish it."

The anchors' eyes darted off camera. They glanced nervously at each other.

One said, "It looks like we'll return to our regularly scheduled programming until we can—"

"No!" Alex shouted at the TV. "No, don't...." He raced to the phone.

After a split-second ring, Diana answered. "Ben?"

"No, it's Alex."

"Oh, God, Alex, were you watching?"

"Yes."

"Get off this line. Ben will call."

Fourteen minutes later—Alex tracked the time on the Tiffany clock that sat on his desk—Diana called. "She's all right. There was another explosion. Two firefighters were hurt. One was Dylan O'Roarke."

"Oh, no." Francesca would be devastated if something happened to her friend.

Diana said, "He's on his way to the hospital, but he'll be fine. No burns. He has a concussion."

Why couldn't it be Francesca? At least she'd be safe.

"Alex, are you there?"

He swallowed. "Yes."

"Would you like to come over here? Wait with me?"

Alex felt his stomach clench. Could he share this fear that ate away inside him like acid? "No, thanks. I'll stay put."

She hesitated. "All right. If you change your mind, just come over." She gave him brief directions.

"Call me, Diana, when you hear anything."

As the afternoon progressed, Alex tried to work. A few times, employees brought something to him to sign or review, but they left quickly, understanding his distraction. Richard stopped by every half hour, the strain evident in his face, too.

Diana continued to call with updates. *She's on the ground now.... She and Ed Knight relieved the firefighters on the west side of the building.... She's filling in for the roof crew.*

Alex passed the hours like a sleepwalker. With each special bulletin, his mind cleared enough to listen, but the rest of the time, he kept seeing Francesca's face, laughing as she told him stupid firefighter jokes; he kept recalling the silken texture of her hair as it threaded through his fingers; he kept remembering her moans when he was inside her.

Abruptly he stood and threw down the folder he held. He grabbed his sports coat, left his office, stopped by Richard's office to tell him where he was going and was at Diana's doorstep twenty minutes later.

She answered the bell immediately. "Alex, hi."

"Anything new?"

"No. Ben just called."

In the living room, Alex sank wearily onto a tufted sofa. Diana sat next to him. She asked, "How are you holding up?"

"I'm a wreck."

She reached out and squeezed his hand.

"How did you do it, Diana? Endure this…waiting? It's agony."

Her eyes turned bleak. "I didn't do it, remember? I left them because of this."

"I can understand why."

Diana frowned. "Don't make any decision now, Alex. And think very hard before you take any action. I—"

A special bulletin flashed on the screen. Diana's hand clutched his arm. Again the faces of the anchors. "Fire officials report the blaze is under control enough to go inside. Crews have been organized to enter the building…."

Alex buried his face in his hands.

An hour later, Ben called. "Oh, wonderful," Alex heard Diana say. She looked at him. "It's under control. New crews are coming in for salvage and overhaul. Francesca's finished." She turned to the phone. "What? Oh, yes, yes, please."

Diana glanced at Alex, covering the mouthpiece. "Do you want to speak to her first?"

Alex stared at Diana. His knees were weaker than when he'd been sick with a virulent flu. His stomach cramped spasmodically. He shook his head and walked out of the condo.

MORE EXHAUSTED than she'd ever been in her life, Francesca unlocked the door to her house and stepped into the foyer. Every muscle in her body ached. Though she'd taken some analgesic, she had a dull throb in her temples. As she closed the door, she wondered where Killer was. He usually greeted her as soon as she got home, nipping a welcome at her feet.

And why had she left the light on in the living room?

Before she had time to panic, she spotted Alex on the couch, an arm crooked over the back, sipping a drink. He was encased in shadows, but she could see his suit coat was off, his tie askew. His hair was rumpled.

"Alex, hi."

"Hello."

Francey crossed to the living room, her sagging spirit lightened by his presence. She needed him more than she wanted to admit. "How long have you been here?"

"I came about seven. I got in with the key you gave me."

"I wish I'd known. I tried to reach you at the office and at home. I've been at the hospital."

"I figured."

"What have you been doing all this time?"

"Thinking."

Francey hesitated. After the fire, she'd thought about him all night long, had been unnerved when she couldn't reach him. "I'm glad you're here."

Without a word, Alex stood, set down his drink and approached her. She recognized the look in his eyes a moment before he grasped her shoulders. "Tell me now, if you're too tired or too sore for this."

Raising her chin, she felt a resurgence of the adrenaline that had pumped through her all day. "I'm not too tired or too sore."

He yanked her to him. The kiss was long and drugging and tinged with blazing savagery. He tore off her T-shirt, her shorts, then her undergarments.

His frenzy was contagious, passion exploding between them like an inferno. Francey clawed at his clothes, too. She wanted Alex with equally fierce intensity.

Within moments he had her pushed against the wall. His only moment of sanity was when he reached into the pocket of his slacks for a condom.

The two of them climaxed in seconds, his grip on her bottom so strong she winced with it.

FRANCEY AWOKE to darkness. The red numbers on the clock by her bed winked 3:00 a.m. She reached out for Alex, but he was gone. Somehow they'd gotten upstairs. He'd made love to her as tenderly as the first time was violent. She shivered with the memory.

Easing out of bed, she groaned. The stiffness in her muscles had doubled. God, she wished they were at Alex's so she could slip into the hot tub. Donning a satiny summer robe, she left the bedroom. Wending her way downstairs, she found him staring at the firefighter print Beth had given her months ago. He was fully dressed—right down to his wing tips.

"Alex?"

He didn't turn.

She crossed the room to him and slid her arms around his waist. "Why are you dressed?"

Slowly he pivoted. When he looked at her, she was stunned by what she saw. Sadness so deep it hurt to look at him. And hopelessness.

"Do you love me, Francesca?"

"What?"

"I asked if you love me."

When she hesitated, he said, "If you don't want to say it first, I will. I love you. Like I've never loved anyone in my entire life."

Her breath hitched. "This is unexpected."

"Do you love me?" he repeated tightly.

And suddenly it hit her. The truthful answer to his question. The depth of her feelings for him. "Yes."

He swallowed hard.

"Alex, what brought this on?"

"How can you possibly not know?"

"The fire."

"Yes."

"You were worried."

He drew in a shaky breath. "Worried doesn't begin to describe how I felt all afternoon."

"I'm sorry the attack took so long. I've never been involved in anything that lasted so many hours."

"Did you know it was televised?"

"I heard. That must have been awful for you."

He stared at her.

"Talk to me, Alex."

If possible, his face got even bleaker. He raised his hand and brushed his knuckles down her cheek. They were rough, as if he'd scraped them on something. "I want you to marry me."

Her jaw dropped. "M-marry you?"

He nodded.

Something inside Francey clicked into place. A piece of the puzzle of her life, so long absent that she was surprised by its arrival. She turned her face into his hand. "Oh, Alex. Yes."

"There's a condition."

She stared at him. "I won't intentionally let you out-bench-press me."

He didn't smile. "You have to give up your line position in the fire department. If you have to stay on—which I'd prefer you didn't—then get a staff job."

Francey froze. Everything around her became accented. The ticking of the clock, the crickets outside the window. After a long time, she said,

"Alex, giving up my job isn't an option. It's also not fair to ask me to do it."

"Why?"

"If I asked you to give up Templeton Industries, would you?"

He didn't even hesitate. "Absolutely."

"What?"

"I'd give up anything to have you. I love you that much."

Again Francesca stared at him openmouthed. "It's because of today, isn't it."

He nodded.

"Look, this was the fire of a lifetime. It's highly unlikely one of this duration and severity will happen again."

"All fires are dangerous. Do you have any idea what it was like to sit in my office and watch you walk into that building?"

She shook her head.

"I can't live my life like that."

Francey felt chilled despite the summer heat that seeped through the open windows. "Like my mother," she said raggedly. "Just like my mother."

He stared at her.

"I don't know what to say."

"It's simple. Say you'll quit the fire department."

"No, Alex, I can't. There's another way." She stepped back. "There's *got* to be another way."

"There isn't."

"How can you be so sure?"

"You weren't the one listening for special bulletins and waiting for phone calls that would decide the rest of your life, Francesca. I can't do it for a lifetime," he repeated.

She stared at him unblinkingly.

"What's more, I wouldn't subject our children to it."

"What do you mean?"

"I could barely keep it together today myself. I can't fathom holding my little girl on my lap and trying to assure her that her mother's going to be all right." He held Francey's gaze. "Trying to explain to her *why* her mother risks her life every day."

Francey's throat clogged. The image he drew sent jagged pain through her. Tears burned behind her eyes, but she willed them back. "You promised me this wouldn't happen.

You promised me, if I let myself fall in love with you, you could handle it.''

"I was wrong."

"I can't give up my job, Alex. I'd do anything for you but that.''

"Nothing else is enough.''

She stared at him.

He stared back.

After a moment, he leaned over and picked up his sports coat. Shrugging into it, he walked silently to the door without looking at her.

Francey heard the click of the latch as it closed. Stunned, she sank into a chair.

She knew he wasn't coming back.

CHAPTER FIFTEEN

ALEX HIT the ball so hard it shot toward the front wall like a bullet, ricocheted off the low left corner, fired back and struck his brother in the shoulder.

Richard tossed his racquet down and rubbed his injury. "Damn it, Alex, I'm through."

Wearily Alex leaned against the wall and slid down it. Sweat poured from him, soaking his shirt. His limbs were shaky. His eyes closed, his knees up, he dangled the racquet between his legs. "I'm sorry."

After a moment, Richard dropped down beside him. "This has to stop. For two weeks you've been playing and working like a maniac. You've lost weight and you look like hell."

Head down, Alex didn't respond.

"You can't go on like this."

"What do you suggest I do?" Alex finally asked.

Richard hesitated before he said, "Call her. Work this out."

Alex banged his racquet on the wooden floor; its crack echoed through the enclosed court. "Absolutely not."

"Is this any better?"

"No, but I'm banking it will be." He looked at his brother. "Pain now for peace of mind later."

And Alex believed it. A surgeon's quick, precise slice, which would heal cleanly, was preferable to opening an old wound over and over.

"If you get through it."

"I'm going away," he told Richard.

"Where?"

"To Saint Lucia."

"The Caribbean at the end of summer's hot."

"I like hot weather."

Richard stared at him. "You stayed around for me, didn't you?"

Alex nodded. Richard's hearing had been last week. The combination of a good lawyer, documents from the detox clinic and Richard's coming forward of his own will had gotten him probation and community service for six months. He also attended drug-addiction meetings twice a week. Richard was back on track.

It was Alex's life that had derailed big-time. He was barely functioning at work. He'd refused to go to the gym or run, since it conjured up too many associations with Francesca, but he'd kept his fitness up with rabid games of racquetball with Richard.

It hadn't helped. He still thought about her every single day. Still dreamed about her at night—some dreams graphically erotic, some sweet and tender. Both woke him in a cold sweat.

"Maybe the trip will help," Richard said.

"Maybe." But Alex doubted it. He simply didn't know what else to do.

AS SOON AS FRANCESCA entered Diana's Designs, she was swamped with memories of the last time she'd been here. To buy something for her first date with Alex. She'd been so excited, so optimistic. She'd been a fool.

"May I... Oh, Francey."

Great, just what she needed. Miss America. "Elise. Is my mother here?"

Elise stared at her for a minute. Something odd flickered in her stepsister's eyes. "No, she went to lunch with your father."

Francey shook her head. Her mother and father were dating. How ironic. "Fine. Tell her I stopped by." She turned to go.

"Francey?"

She pivoted. Elise had come around the desk, the soft knit of a beige summer dress shimmering around her. For the first time, a hint of uncertainty shadowed the younger woman's face. "I wanted to tell you something." She clasped her hands in front of her. "I watched the television coverage of the fire the other week."

Do you have any idea what it was like to sit in my office and watch you walk into a burning building?

Elise gave her a tentative smile. "I was so impressed seeing you fight that fire. You're so brave. I would have fainted on the spot."

Oddly, Francey felt tears sting her eyelids.

"I, um, just wanted you to know that." Elise took a deep breath. "And also to tell you that nothing ever happened between me and Alex, if it matters."

"It doesn't matter anymore," Francey said dejectedly.

"Yes, I heard." Elise stepped closer. "If I had a chance with him—which I don't—I'd do anything to keep him."

Francey swallowed hard. "He wants too much."

"Does he?" After a moment's hesitation, Elise went on, "Your mother...she always had this pervasive sadness about her." Elise gave her a meaningful look. "Until recently."

Francey thought of her father's long-standing restlessness, until he started seeing Diana again. Still, she said, "There's nothing I can do."

Elise shrugged. "I just thought I'd tell you."

"Thanks." Francey turned away. Needy and confused, she stopped when she reached the door; after a moment she faced her stepsister again. "Anybody else working here today?"

"Yes, another employee is in the back. Why?"

"I thought you might want to go to lunch with me. You know, and talk about girl stuff."

A smile beamed from Elise's face. "I'd love that." She

crossed her arms and studied Francey. "Somewhere inside me, I think I always wanted that. Let me get my purse."

THE SANDALS RESORT in Saint Lucia was ten sprawling acres of lush greenery. Tropical shrubbery and palm trees dotted the golf course and encircled it. The smell of salt water permeated the air. Alex lifted his club and swung it for a drive worthy of the PGA. The ball sailed more than two hundred yards. Thirty-six holes a day had honed his game. He played the rest of the course with intensity—and a gloom he'd brought with him to the Caribbean. Even this place reminded him of her.

Someday, I'm going to take you to the Caribbean, he'd told her the afternoon she'd lost the elderly woman in the fire. He remembered thinking, *Maybe on our honeymoon. Maybe we'll even get married down there.* He swore vilely at the memory.

After leaving his clubs with his caddy, he stopped at an outdoor bar for a drink. Gazebos shielded the area from the hot sun; huge whirling fans hung from the wooden rafters. A semicool breeze off the water made the temperature comfortable. From the bleached wood bar, patrons could look out over the Caribbean Sea, so blue it resembled a child's Play-Doh. When he wasn't golfing, Alex had spent his time in that sea, scuba diving, snorkeling and kayaking.

"How'd ya do today, handsome?" The blond, deeply tanned bartender had been sending out signals for the four days he'd been vacationing. So far, he'd ignored them

"I hit under eighty finally."

Uninvited, she tested his biceps. "You're in great shape."

A flash of Francesca, watching him at Chelsea's gym, came to him. She'd reached out and tweaked his arm. *Hey, you'll get there.*

"Want the usual?"

He nodded.

As the bartender—Millie, he thought her name was—

fixed him a gin and tonic, he studied her. She had a center-fold's body. Blond curls rippled down her back.

And she did nothing for him whatsoever. He swore again under his breath. He stared at a grainy sand dune a hundred yards away, where seagulls fluttered and cooed.

"Hey, why the scowl?" Millie placed a tall, cool drink in front of him. "Nobody scowls in Saint Lucia."

Alex pasted on a fake smile.

It was all the encouragement she needed. She leaned over the bar and scraped long, vampire-red nails on his bare arm. "I'm off in two hours. I could make you smile the rest of the night."

He cocked his head. She was the opposite of Francesca in every way. Maybe she was what he needed. After all, that's why he'd come to Saint Lucia—to forget the woman he loved.

At midnight, in his room, as he unbuttoned his shirt and she started to pull the slinky silk top over her head, he stilled her movements. "I'm sorry, Millie. I can't. It was a nice dinner, and you were terrific company. But I can't do this."

Not now, he thought as he closed the door behind the bartender. *But someday.*

"I'M NOT GOING!" Francesca plunked down on a plush chair to underscore her objection.

"Yes," Chelsea said implacably, "you are."

"Alex will be there."

"Why? He wasn't there in past years."

"Because of the warehouse fire. Templeton Industries is contributing megabucks to the firemen's ball."

"If you don't go, I'm not going." Beth held up a shiny green dress that highlighted her hazel eyes and auburn hair. The women shared a huge dressing room—with wall-to-wall mirrors—in one of Rockford's snazziest boutiques.

Chelsea spun, soft folds of black crepe swirling at her ankles. "You guys, we promised."

"That pact years ago was stupid," Francey told Chelsea.

Smugly, Beth arched a brow at her in the mirror. "*I've been telling you that all along.*"

Francey stared at her friends. When she and Chelsea had graduated from the academy, the three of them had promised each other—after one too many drinks—that they'd go to the annual firemen's ball dressed to the nines. If she remembered correctly, it had something to do with asserting their femininity.

"Oh, all right." Francey gave in grudgingly.

Chelsea and Beth exchanged looks.

"I know this is a conspiracy to get me to go out," she said, flinging off her jeans and sweatshirt. She took the gold silk dress, accented with Cleopatra-inspired beads—whatever the hell they were—from Chelsea and whipped it over her head. It slithered down her hips to the floor. The front scooped low, with a gold band across the bodice that circled to become straps; the side slit was indecent. She turned in front of the mirror. It was backless.

Beth's eyes widened. "Oh, my God, you'll be beating them off with a stick."

That outfit ought to be illegal. I'd better go get a stick or something. I'll be beating off the guys at L'Auberge.

Francey choked back a sob.

"France? You okay?" Beth asked.

"Yeah, sure," she managed to say.

Quietly Chelsea came up behind Francey and put her hands on her shoulders. "No, you're not. You've lost weight, and it's obvious you haven't been sleeping. If you aren't going to fight for him, you've got to move on, kiddo."

Torn, Francey's eyes pleaded with Chelsea's in the mirror. "The only concession he wants I can't give him."

Beth looked up from fastening the strappy sandals she'd slipped into. "Then find somebody else. He has no right asking you to give up your job."

Chelsea said, "Men in love do stupid things."

"Men, *period,* do stupid things," Beth said absently.

Francey smiled. The familiar repartee was comforting. "All right! I'll buy the dress."

"Great." Chelsea smiled impishly. "Now we have to get you a date."

A WEEK after he returned from Saint Lucia, at eleven o'clock at night, Alex stood at his office window overlooking the Rockford skyline. The city lights twinkled, and a few lonely cars meandered along the streets. Suddenly a siren spilt the air, and he tensed. It whined mercilessly as a fire truck came into sight. From where he stood, Alex couldn't tell if it was a Quint, an engine or a ladder truck. Six months ago he wouldn't have known—or cared about—the difference.

He swallowed hard. Was she on tonight?

Of all that he'd endured the past three weeks, wondering if she was safe had been the worst torture. He didn't watch the news or read the paper because he didn't want to know what she'd been involved in. He wondered if, years from now, he'd think of her and still worry.

No, she'll belong to another man then.

Alex pounded his fist on the window frame, sending pain splintering up his arm. Fine, let some other jerk worry about her. Coddle her when she comes home exhausted and sore. Put her to sleep when she's so wired she can't settle down.

The images of how he'd taken care of her socked him in the gut. He'd given it all up because he couldn't stand the stress.

He stepped back, saw his face reflected in the window. And for the first time he asked himself, *When did you become such a coward?*

NIGHT WATCH was the loneliest time in the shift. At one, the station was quiet. Francey sat in the glass-enclosed booth staring at the trucks in the bay with only the hum of the computer to keep her company. It was almost impossible not to think about Alex here. She recalled vividly the nights she'd talked to him while on watch.

Remember in Backdraft *how William Baldwin made love to the girl in the bed of the truck? Wouldn't that be fun? Close your eyes, sweetheart, and imagine I'm touching you.*

Juxtaposed with those seductive words was the last time he'd phoned the station. Richard had confessed that he'd started the warehouse fire—though Francey hadn't known why Alex needed to talk to her. But it wouldn't have mattered. She was a firefighter; she would have had to leave under any circumstances.

It was her *being* a firefighter that he couldn't accept. Francey sighed heavily.

A movement to her left caught her attention. Ed Knight stood in the doorway, sipping from a coffee mug. "You okay, kid?"

Francey nodded, battling tears. God, every time someone showed concern these days, she felt like bawling. Combined with the fact that she could barely swallow food, she knew she was on the skids. "Sure. I'm fine."

"Want some company?"

"I'd love some."

Casually he took a chair across from her. They made small talk about the station for a while. Then Francey asked, "Ed, how'd you do it? Keep a marriage going all these years?"

"It was tough sometimes. It still is."

"Did...does Cindy worry?"

The captain sat back and propped his feet on the desk. "Yeah, she does. She says she handles it, but I can see in her eyes when she's terrified." He stared into space. "And I've caught her crying."

"But she tolerates it. For you."

He nodded. "Sometimes it makes me wish I'd chosen some other line of work, though. I can never take the fear away."

"Is it hard to live with? Knowing you cause her to worry?"

He cocked his head. "Not compared to the alternative. I can't imagine life without Cindy. And she feels the same way. Marriage is full of compromises, but this firefighter thing is the worst. And the burden is mostly on her." He looked at Francey. "Which is hard for me, knowing I hurt her just by being who I am."

After Ed left, Francey told herself it was better this way. Why get herself in that position? It hurt too many people. Her mother and father—who were dating like freakin' teenagers. Ed and Cindy Knight—who had the best marriage she'd ever seen and two beautiful sons. It *did* hurt too much, didn't it?

She caught a glimpse of herself in the windowpane. Impatiently, she swiped the tears from her cheeks, then buried her face in her hands.

BEN CORDARO swore silently as he rang Francey's doorbell. He shook his head, thinking about her mother, who still had the power to wrap him around her little finger.

You know what you have to do, darling. Not just for us. But for our daughter.

Despite his chagrin, he smiled. God, it was good to be with Diana—to hear her laugh, to see her eyes go dark with desire when he kissed her. He felt whole for the first time in years.

He leaned on the bell.

Francey finally opened the door. She looked like hell. Hair limp and lusterless. Purple smudges under her eyes. Thin. Too thin.

"Where's the fire, Dad?"

"I gotta talk to you. Now."

Brushing past her, he strode into the living room. It was a mess. Stacks of magazines covered the floor. Empty glasses left rings on the table; a cup tilted over on the rug. Articles of clothing were strewn everywhere.

His daughter was a wreck. He was right to come here.

"Honey, we have to talk."

"Sure." She perched on the edge of a chair.

He paced, wondering how to begin. Aw, hell, he'd just jump right in. "I'm going to ask your mother to remarry me."

Stunned, she stared at him. "What?"

"I think she'll say yes." *After this, anyway.*

"Oh, Dad, that's great." Francey bit her lip. "I'm happy for you."

Jamming his hands into his pockets, Ben studied the child of his heart. His little girl. He'd bandaged her scraped knees, soothed her bruised ankles from soccer games and held her hand when she was burned in a fire. Now he'd do some emotional emergency service. "Don't be happy for me, France. Learn from me. From my mistakes."

"I don't understand."

"I…" God, it was hard to admit. So much wasted time. "I was wrong to let your mother go all those years ago."

Francey gaped at him.

"I should have fought harder to keep her. I should have gone after her when she went to New York to school."

"Why didn't you?"

He shrugged. "Pride. Youth. Foolishness."

His daughter shook her head. "No, Dad, she should have been able to handle it. She even admits that now."

"I've never loved anyone else, Francey. Twenty-seven years, and there was no one else. I was twenty-six when she left. Younger than you are now."

She threw up her hands; they landed with a slap on her ragged cutoffs. "I know you're trying to help, but it's not the same. Alex and I aren't married. We don't have kids. We'll get over each other."

He surveyed the living room, then scanned her from head to toe. "You're not doing a very good job of it."

"It's only been a month."

"My guess is it'll be the same in a year. In a decade. It was for me."

She shook her head, her eyes suddenly wide and frightened.

He forged ahead. "If I had to do it all over again—knowing what I know now—I'd give up the fire department."

Francey bolted upright. *"What?"*

He nodded.

"But you loved your job. It was your life."

"I loved her more. *She* was my life." He swallowed hard. "I just didn't know it when she left."

"Are you saying I should quit fire fighting for Alex?"

Ben crossed to her and grasped her shoulders. His touch was gentle, for he'd never seen her so fragile. "No. I'm saying you can work this out. Go with Alex to see Reed Macauley. Talk to a marriage counselor. And we're going to start a support group at the academy for spouses." He smiled at the girl he loved with all his heart. "Just don't set yourself up for the kind of pain I've had. Nothing in the world is worth it."

ACROSS TOWN, Diana found Alex skimming stones on the lake. It was early evening, and a balmy end-of-August breeze rustled around them.

"Alex."

When he turned and saw her, his face drained of color and he clenched his fists. Finally he said, "Something's happened to her."

"No, no. I'm sorry to frighten you."

"Oh." Alex shifted away, to compose himself, she guessed.

After a moment Diana asked, "Are you going to live your whole life like this—waiting and wondering if she's safe?"

He rounded on her. His eyes blazed, matching the setting sun behind him. "That's precisely why I left her, Diana. So I *don't* live my life like this."

Diana moved closer to him. "And you think it will stop because you left her?"

"In time."

"Then take some advice from me. I thought that, too. When I was twenty-four and left Ben. When I was thirty-four and remarried. Then again when I was forty-four."

"You don't mean…"

"Yes, I do. I never stopped worrying. And you know what? I lost him anyway. I still worried, but I didn't have the good times together with him, with all of them, to make it worthwhile."

"It's not the same."

Diana gave him a sympathetic smile. "It is, Alex. And I'm here to tell you that you're making a horrible mistake."

When he didn't answer, she went on. "You'll live the rest of your life wondering and waiting—without her love in return." Diana squeezed his arm, then turned and walked up the hill toward the road, feeling his gaze on her.

THE ANNUAL firemen's ball took place every Labor Day to benefit the families of Rockford firefighters who'd been injured or killed in the line of duty. Put on jointly by the Rockford Firefighters Benevolent Association and local businesses, it was held at Bright Oaks Country Club—which was decorated in the rich reds and deep oranges of autumn. But Ben Cordaro only had eyes for the sequined beauty in his arms.

"You outdid yourself tonight, Dee," he said as he held her against him on the dance floor. The band played oldies, and the lead singer bellowed out the Righteous Brothers' "Soul and Inspiration." "Did you design the dress?" The white silk floor-length gown hugged her every curve and dipped low at the neckline. Its silver sequins glittered when she moved.

"No, I don't make anything this fancy."

"Oh, you bought it to wreak havoc with my blood pressure?"

Diana's musical laugh was muffled as he tugged her close to his heart. She smelled of some alluring female scent. He shook his head, wondering why he ever thought he could live without her.

"You look like dynamite in that tux, too, Chief Cordaro."

Grinning, he bent and whispered, "Come on, I want to go outside for some air."

She followed him to the terrace and up a small path that led to a bench. They were totally out of sight of the ballroom—which fit perfectly into his plans.

Without warning, he sat and pulled her onto his lap.

"Ben, what are you doing?"

He nuzzled her breasts. "You can't sit on the bench. You'll get your dress dirty."

After a moment, she wound her arms around his neck. Music from inside floated around them.

He looked up. "Do you remember when I proposed?"

"Yes. We were out in the garden at my parents, sitting on a bench...." She stilled. He saw her swallow hard, and he kissed the pulse in her neck. "Ben?"

"I want you to marry me again, Dee. As soon as possible. With my ring that you saved. In that same justice of the peace's living room in Warsaw. I called. He's still in business."

She stared at him. When tears pooled in her violet eyes, his heart began to hammer. "I talked to Francey this week. I told her—" Diana brought a finger to his lips and pressed.

"Shh." She gave him a wobbly smile. "Yes."

"Just like that? No questions?"

"Just like that," she whispered. "Just like the last time."

"I want you to know what I told our daughter."

"All right." She kissed his cheek. "But I know you did the right thing for her."

Holding her gaze, he prepared to make the biggest confession of his life. "I told her," he began hoarsely, "that if I had to do it over again, knowing what I know now, I'd quit fire fighting before I'd let you leave me over it."

At first Diana froze. Then her whole body trembled. The moisture in her eyes spilled onto her cheeks. "I never expected you to do that, Ben."

"I know." He trapped the tears with his fingertips. "But I love you more than fire fighting. I just didn't know it then."

Diana lowered her head to his shoulder and wept.

Ben held her and felt his eyes mist. So many years wasted. So much pain. It was why they couldn't let their daughter make the same mistake. Beneath the canopy of twinkling stars, Ben vowed he'd help Francey and Alex any way he could.

WHEN FRANCEY ENTERED the Bright Oaks ballroom, the first thing she saw was her mother and father coming in from outside holding hands. They looked happy and…settled. The underlying restlessness in her father was gone. So was Diana's pervasive sadness.

"Want some champagne, France?" Jake, her date, asked. As usual he was dressed to kill in a funky black collarless tux with a pleated shirt. He smiled warmly at her.

"Yeah, sure."

"Better come with me to get it." He gripped her hand. "I don't dare leave you alone in that dress. It's lethal, kiddo. I shouldn't have let you out of the house in it."

"Spare me, Jakey."

But she went anyway, needing the security of his presence, which was why she'd asked him to accompany her to the ball. When they reached the champagne bar, she scanned the room.

And saw him.

Alex was leaning against a pillar by the double French doors, sipping a glass of champagne and staring at her. She faced him fully—so he could get a good look at the dress—and stared back. He lifted his glass to her in a subtle salute. Her confidence wavered. Oh, God, what if she couldn't pull this off?

Jake handed her some champagne. As he drank his, he

glanced around. ''Templeton's here. Boring a hole through your dress with his eyes.''

''Good,'' she said, pivoting to give Alex a view of her back. Francey was suddenly very grateful for Chelsea's insistence that she buy the slinky gold dress.

As she socialized with her friends, Francey was aware of Alex's eyes on her. Chelsea and Beth stopped by to chat, looking sensational in their new outfits—the ice green sheath for Beth and the black chiffon for Chelsea. Her mother outshone all the women, and her father was devastating in a black tux. The guys in her crew who'd attended looked handsome—and different—in their suits, too.

Dylan pulled her out on the dance floor when the strains of ''Yesterday'' filled the air. His classic tuxedo was accented by a whimsical red cummerbund and pocket handkerchief. ''You clean up real good, France.''

''So do you.''

His eyes sparkled their blue magic. ''I got news today. I wanted you to be the first to know.''

She looked at him questioningly.

''I'm going to the academy in a few weeks. As a lieutenant, to help train the next recruit class.''

''Wow! This is a surprise.''

''No, it isn't. I asked for it. There aren't any officers' positions coming up, and I'm itching to do something else.''

''But the academy? Nobody wants to go there.'' She studied him. ''You were always different, Dyl.''

''Well, I've got my teaching degree from Cortland State, remember?''

''That's right.''

''Anyway, I'm looking forward to all of it,'' he said, shooting daggers across the room at Beth, who was dancing with Eric Scanlon, ''except working with Lizzie Borden. I—'' A hand clapped Dylan's shoulder as the song ended.

Francey was so surprised by Dylan's news that she hadn't seen Alex come up behind them. ''I think this next dance is mine, O'Roarke.''

Francey's heart skidded to a halt. After a full month without seeing him, she couldn't wrest her gaze from his face.

Dylan turned to Alex. "It's about time, Templeton. How could you wait this long after seeing her in that dress?"

"I gave her exactly one half hour to socialize with her friends," he said, insinuating himself between her and Dylan. His touch was firm on her waist, and his hand clasped hers.

Nodding, Dylan patted Alex on the back and kissed Francey's cheek.

Francey stared at Alex as they moved to some soulful Motown. He looked heartbreakingly handsome in his raven tux and snowy shirt. His face was drawn, though, as if he'd lost weight. She searched for something to say. "A half hour, huh?"

He pulled her to him. "Yep. It's all you get."

"Pretty autocratic, Templeton."

"You ain't seen nothin' yet, babe. Now be quiet and let me hold you." Possessively, he drew her close. His hand stroked her bare back. After a moment he whispered hoarsely in her ear, "I've missed you so much."

She tightened her grip on his neck. "I've missed you, too."

When the song ended, Alex stared at her. He cleared his throat, almost unable to bear how beautiful she looked tonight. "Come outside with me for a bit."

Her eyes smiled at him, and she nodded.

Securing her hand in his, he led her through the throng to the patio. He didn't stop until they reached a small bench down a deserted path. Stars twinkled approvingly at them from an inky sky. When they faced each other, they spoke simultaneously.

"Your mother came to see me—"

"My father came to see me—"

They smiled.

"Me first." Alex smoothed her hair. She'd arranged it so

it curled soft and fluffy around her face. "I've been miserable."

"Me, too. I can't eat."

"That bad?"

She nodded. "Alex…"

He slid his hand into his pocket and pulled out a long, thin box. Handing it to her, he said, "Open it."

She cocked her head as she lifted the lid of the burgundy jeweler's box. Inside nestled a delicate gold chain. Attached to it was a finely etched medal.

Saint Florian. The protector of firefighters.

Francesca gripped the box. He hoped she understood what this meant. In case she didn't, he said quickly, "I'll pray every day of our lives for God to keep you safe. I'll go to counseling indefinitely. I'll do anything, love, but we've got to find a way to work this out."

When she lifted her gaze, there were tears in her eyes. "Oh, Alex. Me, too. I'll go to counseling, too. My dad says they're starting a support group for spouses out at the academy. I'll be careful and I won't take any unnecessary risks." She drew in a deep breath. "And when we decide to have kids, I'll rethink all of this. I'll be in a staff position, anyway, for a while when I'm pregnant and after—"

He pressed his fingers to her mouth. "We'll cross that bridge when we come to it."

"I love you, Alex."

"I love you, too. Marry me soon. This month."

"Yes, as soon as possible."

His arms went around her, and he held her tightly. Then he drew back, removed the medal from the box and slipped it over her head. He kissed the icon, then tucked it into the neckline of her dress. "Be safe, love."

"I will. For you."

Briefly he closed his eyes and sighed. Then he ran his hands down to her hips. "And enjoy wearing this dress tonight."

She'd caught his mood. "Oh, why?"

''Because I'm burning it afterward, sweetheart.''

''Well then, make sure I'm around to put out the fire.''

He threw back his head and laughed. ''From now on, Francesca, you can put out all my fires.''

She smiled demurely and batted her lashes at him. ''Whatever you say, Alex.''

''Like hell.'' He laughed.

Then he lowered his head and kissed her.

* * *

Dylan O'Roarke—The Man Who Loved Christmas—loves women.
With one exception—Beth Winters!

Follow Dylan and Beth's story in
The Man Who Loved Christmas,
the second instalment in Kathryn Shay's exciting series CITY HEAT.

Available from Silhouette Superromance in December 2003.

SILHOUETTE®
SUPERROMANCE™

AVAILABLE FROM 21ST NOVEMBER 2003

MAN WITH A MIRACLE Muriel Jensen

Men of Maple Hill

Evan Braga has moved to quiet Maple Hill to escape his past as a big-city cop. He's not looking for all the trouble that runaway witness Beazie Deadham drops on his doorstep. But when the killers at Beazie's heels track her down, Evan finds he would give his life to protect her!

THE MAN WHO LOVED CHRISTMAS
Kathryn Shay

City Heat

Fireman Dylan O'Roarke loves Christmas. Every year he organises events for disadvantaged kids. But Dylan is a risk-taker and fights fires by confronting danger head-on. So when he meets cautious Beth Winters the clash is inevitable. But so is the attraction between them…

THE HEART OF CHRISTMAS
Tara Taylor Quinn

With her business sold and her family out of reach, Abby Hayden is at a loose end. Then Abby starts helping out at a home for pregnant teens. Here, Abby finds her gift—she knows how to make the girls feel loved and valued—and she's found a special gift for herself…Dr Nick McIntyre!

WE SAW MUMMY KISSING SANTA CLAUS
Brenda Novak

Running into 'bad boy' Cole Perrini again is not what single mum Jaclyn Wentworth wants. Cole brings out desires that Jaclyn thought she'd buried. But will Jaclyn be able to break down Cole's defences and get the husband and father that she and her children deserve?

AVAILABLE FROM 21ST NOVEMBER 2003

SILHOUETTE®

Sensation™

Passionate, dramatic, thrilling romances

PROTECTING HIS OWN Lindsay McKenna
THE PRINCE'S WEDDING Justine Davis
ONCE A FATHER Marie Ferrarella
UNDER SIEGE Catherine Mann
BACHELOR IN BLUE JEANS Lauren Nichols
A YOUNGER WOMAN Wendy Rosnau

Special Edition™

Vivid, satisfying romances full of family, life and love

RYAN'S PLACE Sherryl Woods
SCROOGE AND THE SINGLE GIRL Christine Rimmer
THEIR INSTANT BABY Cathy Gillen Thacker
THE COWBOY'S CHRISTMAS MIRACLE Anne McAllister
RACE TO THE ALTAR Patricia Hagan
HER SECRET AFFAIR Arlene James

Intrigue™

Danger, deception and suspense

ROYAL PURSUIT Susan Kearney
HER HIDDEN TRUTH Debra Webb
MEMORIES OF MEGAN Rita Herron
OFFICIAL ESCORT Jean Barrett

Desire™ 2-in-1

Two intense, sensual love stories in one volume

AMBER BY NIGHT Sharon Sala
PRINCESS IN HIS BED Leanne Banks

EXPECTING...AND IN DANGER Eileen Wilks
CHEROKEE MARRIAGE DARE Sheri WhiteFeather

SKY FULL OF PROMISE Teresa Southwick
THE WOLF'S SURRENDER Sandra Steffen

1103/38b

*Celebrate the joys of Christmas
with three wonderful romances
from favourite Silhouette authors*

Midnight
Clear

Debbie Macomber

Lindsay McKenna

Stella Bagwell

On sale 21st November 2003

*Available at most branches of WHSmith,
Tesco, Martins, Borders, Eason, Sainsbury's
and all good paperback bookshops.*

1203/55/SH63

FREE!

2 Books
and a surprise gift!

We would like to take this opportunity to thank you for reading this Silhouette® book by offering you the chance to take TWO more specially selected titles from the Superromance™ series absolutely FREE! We're also making this offer to introduce you to the benefits of the Reader Service™—

- ★ FREE home delivery
- ★ FREE gifts and competitions
- ★ FREE monthly Newsletter
- ★ Books available before they're in the shops
- ★ Exclusive Reader Service discount

Accepting these FREE books and gift places you under no obligation to buy; you may cancel at any time, even after receiving your free shipment. Simply complete your details below and return the entire page to the address below. *You don't even need a stamp!*

YES! Please send me 2 free Superromance books and a surprise gift. I understand that unless you hear from me, I will receive 4 superb new titles every month for just £3.49 each, postage and packing free. I am under no obligation to purchase any books and may cancel my subscription at any time. The free books and gift will be mine to keep in any case.

U3ZEB

Ms/Mrs/Miss/Mr ....Initials.................................

BLOCK CAPITALS PLEASE

Surname...

Address..

....

....Postcode ....

Send this whole page to:
UK: The Reader Service, FREEPOST CN81, Croydon, CR9 3WZ
EIRE: The Reader Service, PO Box 4546, Kilcock, County Kildare (stamp required)

Offer not valid to current Reader Service subscribers to this series. We reserve the right to refuse an application and applicants must be aged 18 years or over. Only one application per household. Terms and prices subject to change without notice. Offer expires 27th February 2004. As a result of this application, you may receive offers from Harlequin Mills & Boon and other carefully selected companies. If you would prefer not to share in this opportunity please write to The Data Manager at the address above.

Silhouette® is a registered trademark used under licence.
Superromance™ is being used as a trademark.